Under the Mask

A SUPERPOWERED HEARTS NOVEL

LISABEL CHRETIEN

THREE DRAGONS PRESS

For Jon,
the Tony Stark to my Pepper Potts
and the Pepper Potts to my Tony Stark.

Prologue

Claire Green didn't see the Superhero fall from the sky.

A mere fifteen minutes earlier, Claire had been having a fairly predictable first day as a New York City EMT. She'd spent the morning running around with her trainer/partner, Freeman, helping heart-attack and car-crash victims. In between calls, Freeman—who was in his fifties, had been doing this job for three decades, and had the dark sense of humor and endless anecdotes to go along with it—told her stories of heroin addicts who had OD'ed and bloody gunshot wounds. Not exactly the sort of stories Claire wanted to hear on her first day of work, but it did have the effect of letting her know what she was actually in for, not just what her teachers had suggested.

But then, the call came in about a Supervillain attack.

"Listen to me," Freeman said, all humor drained from his voice as he switched on their ambulance's siren and made a sharp right turn. "Take orders from me and no one but me. Stay focused at all times. Do not do anything stupid. This is one of the most dangerous situations you will ever encounter in this job. I've known guys with forty years under their belts who let themselves get caught up in the fray between Supers and paid the ultimate price. Do you understand, Green?"

Claire was struck by a lightheaded giddiness, part anticipation, part fear. Even after four years in New York City, the Super capital of the world, she had only seen Supervillains or Superheroes on the news or social media. Her rejected applications to the International Association of Superheroes Training Program had all been handled online. Those disappointing boilerplate emails were the closest she had ever gotten to a real, live Superhero. But now, that was about to change. She swallowed down the lump that had formed in her throat. "Affirmative." She was impressed that her voice had come out sounding relatively normal.

"Good. Keep your head on your shoulders, and you just might come out of this with the best first-day-on-the-job story ever!"

When they arrived on the scene, Claire followed Freeman's lead and hopped out of the ambulance, her reflective EMT jacket keeping her warm despite the chill in the November air. She was glad that she had already taken the time to roll up the slightly-too-long sleeves and secure them tight with Velcro bands around her wrists. At just under five feet tall and a hundred pounds soaking wet, she knew that the last thing she needed in this kind of situation was to flounder in her jacket. She and Freeman gathered their medic bags and headed in the opposite direction of the fleeing civilians, right toward the conflict.

They were parked in front of the police perimeter about two blocks from the site of the Supervillain attack on the tight intersection of Broadway and Wall Streets. Civilians were stampeding away, but being unsure of where to go, they ended up in a churning crash of confusion. The police already on the scene were trying to direct people to safety even as several other EMT crews and other emergency personnel were also pulling up.

At first, Claire could see nothing other than a sea of hunched shoulders and terrified, ashen faces, but the shrill screams of frightened civilians and the *whoosh* of a body hitting the concrete helped her imagination fill in the missing details. The harsh shriek of brakes echoed and bounced off the surrounding stone, brick, and concrete buildings, but she couldn't tell where the sound was coming from. The acrid scent of burning gasoline and oil made her wrinkle her nose. Her heart pounded in her chest, and the rush of adrenaline left her feeling slightly light-headed, but she focused on her training and calmed her breathing as best she could while racing forward to keep up with Freeman. If she could just pretend this was a major building fire or auto accident, she might be able to quell the bubbling excitement she felt about the possibility of not just seeing, but also working alongside a Superhero to protect the people of this city.

A harsh cackle echoed through the intersection as if it were being amplified, drawing Claire's gaze up and away from Freeman's back. She looked up just in time to see a purple-robed man with long white hair and a white beard slowly float down to the ground from above, his hands glowing electric-blue as bolts of lightning leapt between his claw-like fingers. He laughed maniacally, his head tipped back, and his eyes closed in mirth.

She recognized this Supervillain: Vengeance, a magic-user who had been actively taking on—and taking down—Superheroes for years. He was obsessed with them, rather than with committing crime, and most of the Superhero bloggers she followed assumed he had some kind of axe to grind against them, though no one knew why. Claire had even written a post about him and his motives on her own Superhero blog a few months back.

"Green, with me!" Freeman shouted, yanking Claire out of her momentary trance.

The sight of the floating Supervillain had turned the frightened crowd into a terrified stampede. The two EMTs pushed forward as the sounds of screams and explosions and laughter melded into one roaring cacophony of fear and pain. This was nothing like the Superhero battles on the news. Claire wasn't even sure if any Superheroes were on the scene yet. It was all confusion and burning fumes and frightened people crying for help as bolts of magical energy blasted into the buildings above, causing debris to rain down.

Claire's feet felt heavy, but she continued into the fray, one boot landing in front of another. The screams around her slowly faded to nothingness in her awareness, and all she could hear was her heartbeat pounding in her ears and her own heavy breathing. Her vision narrowed until all she could see was Freeman's back, the reflective lettering that read "EMT" silvery-bright.

Claire was used to watching encounters between Superheroes and Supervillains on TV. Both the news cameras and cell phone cameras followed the literally Superhuman movements of the scene's central players as both flew through the air, bounced off buildings and vehicles, shot laser beams at each other that could slice a normal personal in half, and generally made a mess of things. What these cameras failed to capture was the chaos of the regular humans caught up in the action. And the reality inside that churning mass was one of terror.

Before she was aware of it, Claire found herself kneeling beside a young woman with bright-blue hair who couldn't have been much older than Claire herself, her hands pressing down on a gushing wound in the woman's thigh. Freeman was beside her, moving in perfect concert to bandage the gaping laceration. It must have been deep because the bandage was soaked through with a brilliant crimson almost instantly.

"Green, compression bandage!" Freeman shouted.

The woman's face was becoming ashen, and she moaned in pain. Her dark jeans hid the fact that they were probably completely soaked with her blood.

Claire dug in her medic bag. Someone—she didn't see who—barreled right into her, toppling over her and knocking her down. They were up and running again before she could right herself. Her medic bag had been kicked away, and as she crawled on her hands and knees to retrieve it, she almost collided with an elderly man who had fallen in the crush of bodies. His cane lay out of reach and was being kicked around by the stampede.

That's when the Superhero fell out of the sky.

He landed face-down with a *thud* just a few feet away, a silver-and-blue mass of spandex and muscle. The Superhero grunted, probably due to the wind being knocked out of him by the fall, but then, he slowly climbed to his feet, his back to her. He was apparently unharmed and dusted himself off, stepping out of Claire's childhood daydreams and into the chaotic, dust-covered reality of a Manhattan Superhero battle. For just a moment, the weak November afternoon light hit him in such a way that he seemed to shimmer. His perfect physique was set off to advantage by his full-body silver-and-blue spandex unitard, the silver crisscrossing his body in seemingly random angles and planes. All she could tell about him personally was that he was very tall and lithe, yet incredibly strongly built, like a swimmer or a gymnast.

Time slowed down, and Claire watched as he slowly straightened and rolled his shoulders back, even as his chest heaved with exertion. That was what Claire admired so much about Superheroes: the way they got up again and again despite the odds, never backing down, never giving up. While many of her girlfriends had giggled about their crushes on various Superheroes, Claire emulated them. She wanted to *be* a Superhero, not date one.

Claire didn't recognize this Superhero's costume, and she was familiar with every single Hero operating in the Tri-State area. He was probably a new Superhero, maybe even making his official debut. She should have felt thrilled at the chance to see such a thing firsthand, but the adrenaline racing through her had left her feeling somewhat numb.

The soft roar of small engines sounded overheard, and Claire looked up to see The Electric Defender, the armored Super-suit-wearing hero, hovering just overhead. Silver-and-Blue pressed his hand to his ear and muttered something Claire couldn't hear, likely a response to his fellow Superhero through his earpiece. Then, he was up and moving toward Vengeance again, his movements noticeably faster than the average human's would be.

Assuming that was the beginning and end of her Superhero encounter for the day, Claire turned away from the Superhero battle raging behind her. They had their duty, and so did she. She hadn't been able to become a Superhero, but she was working alongside them, doing her part to save the city and help people. She was being a superhero—with a lowercase 'S'—in the only way she knew how.

She grabbed the elderly man's cane and extended her hand to help him up. At that moment, a small explosion rocked the street, and a fresh round of screams echoed around the intersection. Someone's elbow connected with her head and sent her sprawling back down onto the icy slush right beside the old man. The cold and wet immediately permeated her coat, as did the unpleasant scent of the New York City street—a mixture of urine and exhaust fumes. A panicked civilian tripped over her, kicking her in the ribs and knocking the breath out of her as someone else stepped on her outstretched hand, causing her to gasp. Another person tripped over the old man and flew forward into the pavement beyond the pair.

The old man rolled to his side and pulled Claire toward him, trying to protect her from being trampled. She was touched by the gesture. He smelled of peppermint and tobacco. "Are you okay?" he asked, and Claire nodded as she cradled her crushed left hand to her chest. *Just my luck: I got to see a real Superhero on my first day of work, and now, I'm going to be stampeded to death.*

From her prone position, Claire could actually get a good look at the Super fight going on in the air above. The Electric Defender and Vengeance leapt back and forth across the street several stories above the road. They bounced off of brick walls and windows and each other, trying to attack the other in an impressive display of strength and speed. Vengeance appeared and disappeared at random—the online consensus being that he could actually fold space—and they were both moving too quickly for Claire to get a clear glimpse of either of them. It seemed like The Electric Defender was trying to lure Vengeance toward the ground, where Silver-and-Blue swung unnaturally powerful fists at the Supervillain, who shot bolts of blue lightning from his fingers. He cackled with each bolt he threw. The intersection echoed with the eerie laughter and the resounding *pow*s and *boom*s of the Supers' impact on the buildings around them.

As the crowd around them started to thin, Claire climbed to her feet and helped up the elderly gentleman who had saved her. Her medic bag was just a few steps away, but the crowd had kicked it around enough to spill its contents all over the street.

Luckily, she spotted the compression bandage easily, grabbed it, and rushed over to Freeman, who was applying almost his entire body weight to the young woman's leg.

"You okay, kid?" he asked as she dropped to her knees beside him and handed him the bandage.

Claire was shocked to see that her hands were shaking. She wasn't even bothered by the epithet, "kid," which she had bitten Freeman's head off for using earlier that morning. That's when she realized her heart was racing and her breathing was hard. A gentle hand landed on her shoulder.

Claire looked up into the gentle eyes of the elderly man with the cane. His smile was subdued yet reassuring. As if he'd been in this situation before and knew that, while things looked grim now, all would be well in the end. Then, he turned his gaze on Freeman and asked in a voice surprisingly even for the situation they were in, "What do you need? I'm a doctor."

There was a sharp *crack* above them, and all four heads swiveled upward just in time to see The Electric Defender go flying horizontally into the side of the building and then bounce down onto the street nearby, her fall uncontrolled, the lights in her suit flickering. She crashed not even ten feet away from the group and didn't move. The slight hum from her suit died. Its exterior indicator lights went dark.

Claire felt like she'd been punched in the gut herself. *Am I about to witness my first Superhero death?* She willed the shamelessly cocky, publicity-hungry Superhero to stand up and make some quip about her last boyfriend hitting harder than that in the bedroom. Whatever she had imagined it would be like to be up close and personal with a Super-powered fight, it wasn't this. This was raw and smelled like dusty, crumbling concrete; acrid burning rubber and gasoline that was probably frying all her nose hairs; and the iron-tinged scent of blood.

Vengeance cackled as he floated down to the street to stand triumphantly over the fallen Superhero. The remaining civilians in the area froze. No one wanted to attract the attention of a gloating Supervillain. He propped his booted foot on The Electric Defender's head and looked around at the frightened populace.

All her hair seemed to stand on end, and Claire had just enough presence of mind to think, *It's probably from the charge of his electricity magic.*

"You think you can defeat me?" Vengeance snarled at Silver-and-Blue, who was slowly advancing on the Supervillain. "You're nothing but a snot-nosed brat fresh out of Superhero training. This is your training-wheels run with a seasoned Superhero. Well, young man, I have torn *off*—" here, he stomped hard on The Electric Defender's metal helmet, causing all the civilians in view to wince, "the training wheels!"

The new Superhero didn't respond as he continued to silently advance. Now that Claire could see the front side of him, she realized that his whole head was covered by a spandex hood that hid his eyes and nose. Only his mouth and jaw were free. In the back of her mind, Claire had the tiniest space to wonder how he could see through the silver mesh eye holes.

"You even made the classic rookie mistake," Vengeance spat. "You've left all these civilians unguarded right here in the street!"

Claire turned back to look at Vengeance only to realize that his eyes had landed on their little group—Claire, Freeman, the elderly man, and the blue-haired young woman who was bleeding out. He smiled an oily, cruel smile, and his fingers erupted in blue lightning again, the long, sharp, pointed nails almost touching. They lit up with a sickening blue glow. He struck a menacing pose, his arms outstretched toward the group still crouched in the street.

Claire's body moved before she even realized it. Her pulse hammered in her head, drowning out any thoughts that may have arisen, making it impossible to hear them over the steady drumbeat that now drove her forward. She pushed herself up on her knees, swiveled to face the Supervillain, and spread her arms wide, as if her tiny gesture would protect the others. It wasn't until her arms reached their full extension that her thoughts caught up with her body. *Oh shit*, flashed through her mind.

Vengeance threw his head back and laughed. "Oh, I like this one! At least someone in this city has some spirit."

Before the new Superhero could respond to Vengeance's taunt, the villain folded space; Claire was now sure that's what he was doing. She felt a gust of air whip around her, briefly sending the loose tendrils of her copper-red hair dancing. Then, a hand closed around her messy ponytail and pulled her to her feet. Her vision went red with pain, and she watched helplessly as Vengeance kicked the old man in the chest. Despite the chaos, Freeman had maintained the presence of mind to wrap the compression bandage around the woman's leg. Now, his eyes were wide with fear and locked onto Claire's.

What was it he'd said not even fifteen minutes earlier? Don't do anything stupid? Well, she'd certainly messed that part up.

Vengeance's other hand appeared in front of Claire's face, his sharp tongues of lightning inches from her. She could smell the ozone coming from it and the musty scent of old books emanating from the villain's robes. "What's your play now?" he snarled at the Superhero. "Call for backup? Try to distract me? Stall for time?" He tightened his grip on Claire's hair, and her eyes began to water. "Oh, I have an idea! You could learn something from this stray kitten. Offer yourself up to me in her place. Sacrifice yourself for her. Or is she the only one with any balls in this city?" He twisted Claire's neck painfully to the side, displaying her anguished face for the Superhero's view.

Silver-and-Blue stepped forward once more and then froze. His jaw worked furiously. Perhaps this was his first time dealing with a hostage situation.

Through her haze of pain and numb fear, Claire noticed that his lips were enticingly full, like a male model's. And yet, there was something oddly and unsettlingly familiar about him, something about his stance and the way his jaw moved even as he remained silent.

"Nothing to say?" Vengeance taunted, his over-the-top affected British accent echoing through the intersection, magically enhanced to carry to the crowds watching from a safer distance. "No pleading for me to let the girl go? No appeals to my sense of mercy for the innocent?"

The Superhero seemed to stare at Claire in shock—it was hard to tell through the mask—but said nothing. The entire intersection was still as civilians watched in horror, yet too afraid for their own lives to make a move to help her. Everyone was holding their breath, terrified of attracting the Supervillain's attention.

Claire could imagine this moment playing out on TVs and news sites all around the city—hell, all around the *world*—as the news helicopters that circled overhead struggled to get a good angle to capture the events. She'd gleefully watched thousands of such moments, thrilling as the Superheroes stepped in to save the day. Claire had a starring role in this particular little melodrama yet was ultimately unimportant. She was the bait, the damsel-in-distress, the hostage that the Superhero had to rescue in order to save the day. And yet, they were at an impasse, both Supers waiting to see what the other would do next. So, with a handful of lightning in her face, Claire decided it was time to take matters into her own hands.

Through the red haze of pain from Vengeance's sharp grip on her hair, she drew on all her years of martial-arts training—done in preparation for her future career as a Superhero once she was graced with powers of her own—and jabbed her elbow up and into Vengeance's jaw. He let out a yelp of pain and surprise, staggered, and slightly loosened his grip on her hair, though he didn't release it. But that loosening was all Claire needed. She allowed her arm to continue its movement, swinging up and over the arm holding her hair. The force yanked Vengeance's arm down, away from her hair, and she immediately locked it in an arm bar at her lower back. At the same moment, the old man swung out with his cane, hitting the back of Vengeance's knees. The Supervillain fell forward onto his knees, even as Claire's hold on his arm kept him twisted slightly back.

Claire hadn't seen him move, but suddenly, the Superhero was on Vengeance, his fist cracking across the older man's jaw as he went down. She heard the sickening *thwack*, and then, Vengeance slumped forward onto the grimy pavement. He didn't move; he'd been knocked cold by the Superhero's punch.

Claire released a slow, shuddering breath she hadn't known she'd been holding. The adrenaline was still coursing through her, and she began to laugh softly and slightly hysterically. She had just faced down her very first Supervillain at the age of twenty-two, and she didn't even have Superpowers. She bent forward slightly and placed her hands on her knees, hoping to dispel the dizzy giddiness she felt.

A whooping holler went up from nearby, prompting Claire to raise her head. "That's what I'm talking about!" a man in a hard hat and high-vis vest shouted from a few feet away. He stood beneath the temporary scaffolding that wrapped around the nearby building like an eggshell around an egg. He had probably been working when Vengeance attacked. "New York City's emergency personnel—the *real* superheroes around here!" He began applauding, and to Claire's horror and embarrassment, the other civilians in the area followed suit.

Her face immediately heated and became a bright red. She ducked her head, unsure of how to react in this moment. She wasn't supposed to be in the spotlight. That was the Superheroes' role. As much as she had imagined a moment just like this in the past, she had always envisioned her face being covered by a mask, not bare for all the world to see. She had pictured a spandex suit that allowed her to move easily, not a bulky, grime-covered EMT uniform jacket.

As the applause died down and people began moving around her again, Claire felt the world spin. Her feet were suddenly on unsteady ground. Strong arms caught her as her knees buckled, and they guided her gently to the curb. The pavement before her eyes swam, and her breath was suddenly shallow. A warm hand gently, tentatively touched her back, then withdrew as if scalded.

Slow, deep, even breaths, Green, Claire reminded herself.

A few moments later, after she felt like she was on solid ground again and not at sea, Claire looked up to thank whoever had caught her. She found herself staring into the masked face of Silver-and-Blue, who was crouching beside her in the street. She inhaled sharply, a tiny gasp of surprise, and her lips parted. "Thanks," she said weakly, lost in the face before her.

She couldn't see the Superhero's eyes through the silver mesh that hid them, but she felt them linger on her, studying her. Her heart rate had settled down, but it picked up again under his hidden gaze. The feeling of familiarity she'd had earlier was stronger than ever.

He licked his lips, and Claire couldn't help but stare, tracing the path of his tongue with her eyes.

With a jolt, she realized who this man reminded her of. It was the lips. They looked incredibly kissable, just like Jack's had been—and likely still were. Jack Elliott had been her high-school sweetheart back in Iowa. A tall, lanky young man, he was always painfully shy and awkward, following in the wake of the much brasher, much bolder petite redhead like a huge barge being pulled along by a tiny tugboat. Her breath caught in her throat at the memories—both fond and painful—that welled up for a moment.

But this man was even taller and far more muscular than Jack had ever been. And Jack had never been particularly interested in Superheroes. And despite how they had parted, Claire was sure Jack would have reached out to her if he were in New York now. She shook her head to clear the vision of the boy she had known, which was now threatening to distract her from the most exciting moment of her life. Jack was in her past and would remain so. This was the present.

Not noticing Claire's momentary flustered state, the Superhero leaned toward her and said, his voice pitched into a low, deep whisper that she struggled to hear, "You did well."

Then, he stood up and was gone. Time resumed its usual flow, and Claire was suddenly chilled bone-deep. She looked around, as if awakening from a dream. The NYPD's Super Containment Unit were already taking custody of the unconscious Supervillain. The International Association of Superheroes' Medical Unit were gathered around the still-prone Electric Defender. More emergency personnel were swarming the scene. Out of the corner of her eye, she spotted Professor Optimo, the leader of the New York Superheroes, escorting Silver-and-Blue toward the waiting horde of reporters and TV cameras.

Claire sat there for a moment, alone and disoriented. *What the hell was that?* she wondered, staring at the new Superhero. *Who the hell was that?* She looked up at the overcast afternoon sky hovering above the buildings.

Freeman approached and sat down on the pavement beside her. He dropped his head back to stare up at the sky and sighed. "I know I said you might have the best first-day-on-the-job story ever, but I didn't think you'd make it so... dramatic!"

Claire chuckled.

"You're gonna be on the news, you know," he continued. "Those reporters are busy fawning over the new Superhero right now, but what you did is the stuff of reporters' wet dreams. How'd you learn to do all that, anyway?"

Claire shrugged, suddenly too embarrassed to admit her youthful Superhero-adulation in such close proximity to actual Superheroes. "Martial arts classes. Self-defense stuff. You know..." She trailed off.

As she watched, Silver-and-Blue stepped in front of the cameras and raised his hand in a wave that would be comical on anyone but a Superhero. His back was to her, but she could still picture the way he nervously licked his lips before leaning in to speak to her.

Claire didn't know who this new Superhero was, but she was going to find out. It didn't matter how long it would take. She had plenty of time. All the time in the world.

Eight years later...

Chapter 1

Jack Elliott, the Superhero known as Silver Fist, yawned, scrubbed his jaw, and took another swig of his now-cold coffee. It tasted faintly of the Styrofoam cup it had sat in for entirely too long, and the mouthful of grounds at the bottom caused him to grimace. As beautiful as the facilities of the International Association of Superheroes' New York headquarters were, the free coffee was terrible.

The large briefing room in the heart of HQ was slowly filling with Superheroes for the daily briefing. Superheroes coming in from their night patrols, many sporting new bruises or bandaged lacerations, mingled with the Superheroes who preferred to work in the daylight. The grey, sterile room that reminded Jack of every military briefing room he had ever been in was awash in colored spandex and masks, flashy helmets, and big personalities. Loud voices bounced around the room as Superheroes swapped tales of altercations with villains, henchmen, and standard petty criminals.

Jack remained alone in the back corner, uncomfortably folded into his seat. The desks in the briefing room always reminded him of high school, not in their look but in their feel; it was like they were made for someone half his size. He had spent years with his knees bumping uncomfortably against the bottom of the desk until they no longer fit underneath at all. Then, he'd had to let his lanky body spill out into the aisle. The only comfort was the petite redhead beside him who also didn't fit into her desk, her legs swinging just above the floor—

Jack cut that thought off angrily. Why was he thinking of Claire now? They had parted ways over a decade ago, and she had made it perfectly clear that she wanted nothing more to do with him.

"Let's get started," Professor Optimo said from the front of the briefing room. The leader of the New York Superheroes stood behind a podium, the harsh overhead lights reflecting off his long salt-and-pepper hair pulled back into a ponytail.

As the Superheroes began to take their seats, the Professor fiddled with his custom tablet to project the briefing's agenda on the screen. He wrinkled his brow in frustration for a moment, and Jack chuckled despite himself. The Professor had been a Superhero since the 1970s, and his difficulties with modern technology reminded Jack of several of his older commanding officers in the army.

Moments later, the projector came on, the lights dimmed, and Professor Optimo looked satisfied as he raised his head to address the assembled Superheroes. "Good morning. As you all know, our top priority has not changed: apprehending the Supervillain known as Vengeance, who remains at-large. Since his escape from the super-maximum-security prison, Shadow Isle Asylum, two weeks ago, he—"

Before the Professor could complete his sentence, the large doors in the rear of the briefing room swung open with a grating squeak that seemed to echo with importance. All heads turned as Giada England, also known as The Electric Defender, walked in causally, clutching two large coffees in Moonbucks Coffee cups.

Unlike all the other gathered Superheroes, Giada did not wear her costume. Part of that was due to its unwieldy bulk—as an armored metal suit, it wasn't exactly ideal for sitting at a desk—but a large part of that was pure Giada. As usual, she was decked out in expensive designer items, from her black stiletto-heeled boots, to her ripped jeans—which, to Jack's Iowan eyes, seemed ridiculous to have paid for in that condition—to her bright-pink sweater that somehow managed to show off all her curves with its plunging neckline, to her dark, rich leather jacket, to the large sunglasses perched atop her glossy, bleach-blonde hair. A large designer bag swung from her shoulder as she tossed her hair and parted her perfectly painted lips in a smile. "Sorry I'm late," she said, looking around at the already-assembled Superheroes and holding up the two coffees, as if that explained everything.

Professor Optimo frowned. "Ms. England, we do not require punctuality for these daily briefings due to the... complicated nature of our work. However, standing in line at Moonbucks is not the same thing as apprehending a criminal."

"Oh, I wasn't standing in line," Giada said airily as she took the seat beside Jack. "I preordered by app, of course. But my favorite barista was out sick, and they put *way* too much sugar in my drink, so I had them remake it."

Several of the surrounding Superheroes chuckled. Even Jack grinned despite himself. Classic Giada.

Professor Optimo wasn't amused, though. "Yes, well, in the future, could you at least *try* to show up on time?"

"Of course," she said before taking a sip of her drink. As the Professor turned back to the briefing, Giada slid the second coffee over to Jack and said in a low voice, "Here you go, Jackie. I don't know why you insist on drinking the swill here."

Jack grinned and rolled his eyes even as he gratefully accepted the warm beverage. "Because the stuff here is free. I can't exactly afford your daily Moonbucks habit." The rich dark-roast coffee was just the way he liked it—no sugar, lots of cream. The fact that Giada always remembered his order still touched him after all these years. Despite her pretense of being a rich, spoiled airhead, her loyalty to those she liked and trusted shone through.

"Well, you're lucky we're friends, then," she said, patting his silver spandex-clad arm. She then leaned back in her seat, propping up and crossing her stilettoed boots on the desk. "Now, what are we talking about?" As the last-known photo of Vengeance, taken from a security camera at a bank, flashed up on screen, Giada groaned. "Him, *again*? Still? I *hate* that guy." She grimaced and sat upright, putting her feet back on the floor.

Jack noticed her free hand creep up to rub her midsection, as if the memory of the pain Vengeance had caused her had returned.

The broken ribs and severe concussion Giada sustained when they first captured Vengeance eight years ago had sidelined her for months, leaving her downright grumpy. Jack barely knew her at the time and still didn't understand why he'd been paired with her to make his Superhero debut, but the memory of her prone, unmoving form on the ground had haunted him—much like the memory of his fallen comrades in Afghanistan—and he made a point of regularly visiting her in the IAS's hospital. At first, she had done nothing but complain and order him around, but as soon as she was out and allowed to return to light duty—and her wild civilian life—she took him under her wing, offering to introduce him to her New York City socialite friends and all the best nightclubs in the city. He had declined on both fronts, but Giada continued to treat him as her pet project in many ways.

"We have reason to believe that Vengeance is behind the recent string of bank robberies in the Tri-State area," Professor Optimo said.

"Why would he be associated with such low-level stuff?" the always-logical Fiery Starling asked from the front row.

"I've had a team looking into that, and they've come to a fascinating conclusion," the Professor said. "From the outside, all these bank robberies appear to be random, with no pattern in terms of the location, timing, or even method. But then, we realized there actually is a pattern—one only we at the IAS would be able to recognize." He paused for effect, looking around at all the gathered Superheroes before delivering this new piece of intel: "All the banks that were robbed have, at one time or another in the past, held important items belonging to The Elite Five."

The room erupted in gasps and exclamations of shock.

The Elite Five were the very first Supers to overcome popular prejudice and protect the normal humans who had shunned them in the past. They donned costumes and masks to hide their identities and took on organized crime in New York City in the 1930s. At first, the people opposed them, deeming them just as dangerous, if not more so, as the criminals they fought. But with time, they won over the common people, and soon, the press turned a favorable eye toward them. Other Supers followed suit, and Superheroes sprang up in cities all over the United States and then, the rest of the world. The Elite Five established a partnership with the NYPD, which others emulated, so the Heroes could work alongside local law enforcement. In time, this led to the establishment of the International Association of Superheroes to oversee and regulate all Superheroes.

But just as Supers stepped up to stand on the side of law and order, others decided to use their abilities for their own gain. Supervillains were born, and thus, Superheroes had additional—and more dangerous—foes to oppose than just regular criminals.

Professor Optimo raised his hands to quiet the gathered Superheroes. When the room was again calm, he continued, "Obviously, none of these banks hold such important objects in their safe-deposit boxes anymore. Everything is gathered here at HQ. But the fact that Vengeance seems to know that these banks *once* held such important items is worrying. Only members of the IAS should know all this.""Are you concerned about a mole in the organization?" Agent Artifice asked.

The Professor didn't respond at first. He slowly scanned the room, locking eyes with each and every Superhero for just a moment before moving on. Jack returned his CO's gaze evenly. He wasn't worried about a mole, and even if there was one, they'd find them and root them out. Like everything else about being a Superhero, it was just a matter of time.

"That remains to be seen," the Professor finally said, "but that does bring us to our next order of business." He pressed a button on his tablet, and a new picture flashed up on the screen.

Jack felt like he'd been kicked in the gut.

The photo that covered the two-story-high screen at the front of the cavernous briefing room was of a serious-looking redheaded woman, her nose and cheeks dusted with freckles. She wore the uniform of a New York City EMT and stood in front of an ambulance, her arms crossed in a no-nonsense stance. What the photo didn't show was just how short and petite the woman was, nor how brilliantly her eyes sparkled when she laughed.

It was Claire Green.

Jack's face heated at the sight of his high-school sweetheart being flashed up in front of all his colleagues, though not even Giada knew of their past relationship. True, Jack and Claire were linked in the minds of any Superheroes who cared to remember by virtue of the fact that they had effectively worked together to take down Vengeance the first time eight years ago, but that was it. His heart pounded as he studied Claire's face, which now looked a little older and wiser than when he had last seen her up-close.

The scene with Vengeance hadn't been their last encounter, of course. He was a New York City Superhero; she was a New York City emergency medical technician. In many ways, they were fellow industry professionals, both rushing *toward* danger to help others when the occasion called for it. It was only natural that they would encounter each other from time to time. However, after that shocking encounter when Jack laid eyes on her for the first time in years as she was being held hostage by a Supervillain, her face twisted in pain, he had been careful to not speak to her. Officially, he told himself that he didn't want to risk her recognizing him, thus blowing the cover of his secret identity and exposing her to all kinds of dangers. But as he lay alone in bed at night with no mask to hide behind, he knew it was really because he didn't want to face the pain she had caused him. He didn't want to relive the hurtful words she had spat at him— *"You never believed in me"*—the accusations she had hurled— *"I can't trust you to have my back when it counts"*—or the mistakes he had made—*the ringing impact of his fist against Brian Butler's jaw.* Jack wanted to leave the past in the past, and having even the slightest interaction with Claire now would dredge up all that ugliness.

Just as her photo on display in the briefing room was doing now.

"This is Claire Green," Professor Optimo explained, "a long-standing IAS Person of Interest. She applied to the IAS Training Program a total of four times but was repeatedly rejected due to her lack of powers."

Beside him, Giada rolled her eyes and snorted. Giada herself didn't have any powers. What she did have was a bottomless bank account, a surprising aptitude for mechanics, and a stubborn streak than ran even deeper than her vanity. She had designed and built her own Super-suit and all but forced her way into the IAS Training Program.

Superpowers generally manifested during puberty, though they were occasionally activated later in life by trauma or intense stress. Professor Optimo famously displayed his Superpowers for the first time as a fourteen-year-old boy when he stepped in to stop the robbery of his mother's tiny diner. Panicking, he cut the two thieves' connection to the Earth's gravity and sent them flying high into the sky. The spectacle of two small-time crooks sailing past Manhattan's skyscrapers made headlines all across the country. In Jack's case, it took a tour in Afghanistan with the army and an encounter with an IED to gain his Superpowers.

The Professor continued his briefing: "Ms. Green has since become a New York City EMT and was present for—and assisted with—Vengeance's capture eight years ago."

"Oh yeah, EMT Girl!" someone shouted from across the room. "She was *good*."

Jack smiled proudly despite himself. Claire wasn't his and made it clear long ago that she didn't want to be his, but it still warmed his heart to hear the girl who had once been his praised for her obvious skills. For an instant, he was back in an Iowa high school gymnasium, grinning proudly as her athletic abilities—whether at a gymnastics meet, pole-vaulting competition, or martial arts sparring match—were on display for all to see, and he was able to bask in her reflected glory.

He shook his head to clear away such visions. A decade was long enough for her to have forgotten him, moved on, maybe even fallen in love and gotten married. She deserved happiness.

Jack often debated whether to look Claire up on social media. More than once, he had typed her name into the search bar on Facespace, only to hesitate and then backspace without hitting 'Enter.' A part of him wanted to know what she was up to personally and socially these days, but he didn't know how he would react if the profile picture that came up was of Claire smiling happily in a wedding dress, posing alongside a man who wasn't him. No, it was best not to know. If nothing else, it would make seeing her around the city at work less painful.

"Yes," the Professor said, oblivious to Jack's ambivalent anguish in the back row, "Ms. Green was instrumental in capturing Vengeance. However, she has come to our attention in a different capacity in the last few years. She runs a popular Superhero blog that covers a mix of current Superhero news and Superhero history. In the last six months, she has begun posting a great deal about The Elite Five, and much of her information is disturbingly accurate. She knows things that the general public would have no way of knowing."

Jack inwardly groaned, and he sank lower in his seat. He knew where Claire was getting her information. Her family secrets ran deep, but he had once been privy to them—or, at least, the ones she held closest to her heart.

"We've been monitoring her movements closely, and there have been no red flags," the Professor continued. "However, this has tipped us off to the fact that Vengeance appears to *also* be monitoring Ms. Green."

Jack's mouth went dry, and he took a large gulp of his forgotten coffee. He didn't want to recall the way his heart had seized up when he saw her face lit up with the reflected glow of Vengeance's lightning.

"We don't know if Vengeance is living up to his name or if he's interested in her recent Elite Five content, but after discussing it with the Council, I have decided to bring Ms. Green in for protective custody until this Vengeance situation is resolved."

Giada leaned toward Jack and muttered, "And to find out how she knows so much, no doubt." She sipped her coffee, scowling. "Typical. They're going to kidnap the poor woman off the street in the name of 'protecting' her."

Normally, Jack would argue with Giada, pointing out the logic of this step. But right now, his mind—and heart—were racing. Claire would soon be right here, in this very facility, and he had no idea what to do. He could probably find ways to avoid her, but did he really want to? On the other hand, if the IAS brought Claire in for questioning, she would probably reveal the source of her information about The Elite Five, thus relieving Jack of that duty. If he told Professor Optimo and the Council about Claire's family background and the source of her knowledge about The Elite Five, he would also have to explain *how* he knew all this. And while his teenaged relationship with a local EMT wasn't exactly a deep, dark secret, failing to mention it for this long increasingly felt like a lie of omission.

While Jack staggered through his confused thoughts and emotions, Professor Optimo announced the formation of two teams with orders for the day. The larger team, Team One, would attempt to identify which bank Vengeance would hit next and apprehend him in the process. The smaller Team Two would take Ms. Green into protective custody.

At that, Jack's head shot up. The meeting was already adjourning. Superheroes were standing up and talking amongst themselves as Professor Optimo struggled with his tablet. Claire's face still hovered on the screen at the far end of the room.

"Which team am I on?" Jack asked. He sounded—and felt—as if he were coming out of a daze.

"We're on bank-heist duty," Giada said, sipping her coffee. She still hadn't moved from her seat. Something must have shown on Jack's face because she suddenly turned toward him and propped her chin on her fist. "Oh, were you hoping to go see your little EMT friend?"

Jack schooled his features to remain as neutral as possible even as his heart beat faster. "What makes you say that?"

She grinned. "You're not exactly subtle whenever she shows up. You stare. A lot. Does Jackie have a crush?"

Jack weighed how best to respond, but Giada pushed on, turning away and leaning back in her seat to prop her heels up on the desk again. "Not that I blame you. She's cute. I have a bit of a crush on her myself, and I didn't even see her heroics in person—being unconscious and all. You should ask her out."

"No, I don't think—"

"Can I ask her out, then?" Giada cut in, raising an eyebrow at him.

"Why do you enjoy teasing me so much?" Jack asked with a sigh, hoping to sidestep her pointed questions and leave this entire conversation behind. He stood up, unfolding himself from the uncomfortably small desk. He was always faintly surprised that, despite being a facility dedicated to Superheroes, all of their furniture was fairly normal-sized.

"Because you're so much fun to tease," she returned. Sighing herself, she swung her legs back down to the ground and stood up, picking up her designer purse and nearly empty coffee cup. "Come on. Let's get to work. First one to catch this Super-powered bank robber gets to ask out EMT Girl."

Too bad, Jack thought, *that ship has already sailed.*

Chapter 2

Claire was more than ready to call it a day... or a night, depending on how one looked at it.

Her twelve-hour overnight shift had been an endless round of calls. She hadn't gotten a meal break the whole shift. And Ramirez, the new guy in their crew that Claire was technically training, had decided it would be hilarious to make fun of Claire's height—or lack thereof—so she'd overcompensated and pulled a muscle in her back trying to lift something that she knew perfectly well should always be lifted by two people.

Fortunately, Claire had no shortage of admirers around her to put the new guy in his place. "You watch your mouth," Carbonneau had snapped. "Green took down a Supervillain all on her own on her very first day. Show some respect."

That shut Ramirez up, though Claire didn't bother to correct Carbonneau on the details of her encounter with Vengeance. At this point, The Legend of Claire Green had grown to almost epic proportions in the telling and retelling of the story. Freeman didn't help matters, being one of the worst offenders when it came to exaggerating Claire's exploits. He seemed equal parts amused by and in awe of her, and Claire suspected that he was trying to have her elevated to sainthood before he retired just so he could laugh at her bemused expression and bask in the glory of being The Guy Who Saw It All.

But now, as Claire made her way up to her fifth-floor walk-up apartment, she didn't feel particularly saintly or heroic or even cool. She felt tired and sore and every one of her thirty years. She longed for an ice pack and some ibuprofen and a long, deep sleep, in exactly that order. It was mid-morning, but she could easily pull her black-out drapes and crash until her roommate, Ramona, got home from work at the bank.

The steep wooden stairs creaked with every step, as did the knee she had dislocated two years ago while on the job. The whole building smelled dusty, like it had been packed away in storage for too long. It felt like a metaphor for something in Claire's life, but she wasn't sure what. Superheroes probably didn't feel this way. They almost certainly didn't live in old, rent-controlled buildings that they had to sneak into through the back stairs so the landlord wouldn't catch them.

Neither Claire nor her twenty-seven-year-old roommate looked like Ramona's eighty-year-old grandmother, who was supposedly the one still living in their bright, sunny, run-down, and shockingly cheap apartment. Fortunately for all of them, the grandmother had relocated to Florida with her new girlfriend, allowing her granddaughter and her friend to live in the apartment at 1960s rent prices.

Claire sighed. One flight of stairs to go.

On the bright side, two of the night's calls had been "Code 1938"s—the official designation for scenes involving Super-powered beings. Some emergency medical personnel disliked having to deal with the damage caused by Superheroes and Supervillains, but to Claire, it was still the highlight of her day. Many of her colleagues were surprised that her near-legendary encounter with a Supervillain hadn't put her off the experience. But being up close to Super-powered beings was like basking in the sun's rays. It was a reminder of why she did what she did day-in and day-out. Plus, it gave her additional material for her blog.

That blog had been doing well lately by almost every conceivable metric: hits, unique visitors, comments, and social media shares. It seemed that people were especially interested in her latest series on Superhero history and The Elite Five. It even looked like she might be able to spin this whole venture off into a new career—as a writer. *The New York Times* had invited her to write an op-ed on Superheroes, and she was currently talking to an agent about a possible book about The Elite Five.

Of course, this all raised a new problem. If she went down that path, sooner or later, she'd have to reveal her sources regarding the shadowy 1930s Superhero team known as The Elite Five. She clearly knew far more than she ought, and this would raise questions in a number of organizations. Claire wasn't particularly worried about protecting those individuals' secret identities—so far as she knew, they had all passed away years ago—but her grandmother had been sworn to secrecy as a young woman, and she had in turn sworn Claire to uphold that secrecy. While simply writing a blog and judiciously sharing a few details here and there, Claire could convince herself that she was still upholding those family secrets. But if she had to show her hand... *that* felt more like a breach of trust.

At last, Claire reached the top floor. Grimy light spilled through the dirty hall window and washed over the worn red carpet, which had faded to a pink along the sun's path over the years. There was no one in sight, but she could hear the sound of televisions playing behind the whitewashed doors of her neighbors, many of whom were elderly, retired, and at home during the day.

She turned to the first door on the right—hers—and despite being nearly asleep on her feet, Claire immediately noticed something off about her front door. It was still closed, but the strike plate was bent at an odd angle, catching the midmorning light from the hall window, and the wood around it was splintered.

Claire instantly went into high alert. Adrenaline shot through her, pushing away her fatigue and pain. The world became vivid again as her brain woke up, and her hyperfocus took in all the details around her. She gripped the set of keys in her hand harder and fanned them out so she had one key sticking out between each of the fingers of her right hand. Then, she dropped into a slight crouch and pressed her ear to the door.

If there were robbers in there, she didn't want to blunder into anything.

The apartment was silent. All Claire could hear was her neighbors' TVs, the traffic coming from five stories below, and the pounding of her own heart. Still, something itched in the back of her mind. Someone was in there. She could *feel* it, just like when she came home from a shift at one in the morning and could sense Ramona silently sleeping in her own room.

Claire slid her backpack off her shoulders and placed it on the hallway floor by the door. She needed to be ready for action. Taking a deep breath, Claire steadied herself and sank into a fighting stance, her legs wide, knees bent, and feet slightly turned out so she could easily move in any direction. Then, she threw the door open.

The main room was empty.

The sun pooled on the purple velvet couch in the middle of the room, the dining table was covered with junk mail that neither of them ever bothered to go through, and Ramona's dishes sat in the sink. It all looked perfectly ordinary, and nothing appeared to be out of place. Their large flat-screen TV—the most obvious target for thieves—still hung on the wall.

Maybe Ramona had problems with the lock when she went to work, Claire thought. *She could have at least texted to warn me.* Even as she had the thought, she knew that wasn't Ramona's style. Her roommate misplaced her phone more often than she had it on her.

Claire let out her breath in a deep sigh, and her shoulders drooped in embarrassment and relief. At least no one had been around to see her completely unnecessary action-movie entrance into her own apartment. She grabbed her backpack from the hallway, dragged it into the living room, and closed the door behind her. The chain lock was undamaged, even though the handle was bent at a strange angle, so Claire slid it into place and made a mental note to replace the door handle. One of the drawbacks of illegally living in a rent-controlled apartment was that she couldn't go to the landlord about such things.

As the adrenaline leeched from her body, her fatigue washed back in to replace it. She'd fix the door handle later. For now, she needed a nice, long nap. As she made her way to her bedroom, her senses were already quietening down again in anticipation of several hours of blissful, uninterrupted sleep. She kicked off her sneakers, leaving them on the floor in the hallway. *Later, later, I'll tidy up later.* As Claire stumbled into her darkened, messy, purple-hued bedroom, she pulled her hoodie over her head and prepared to toss it to the floor. *Later*, she thought.

Suddenly, *Later* vanished in a flash of coppery shimmer as something hit the balled-up hoodie still in her hands. She dropped the hoodie and spun toward the copper-colored shimmering lines just as a bulky man muttered "Shit" under his breath and hit some kind of release on what looked like a gun. *A taser*, she belatedly realized.

Claire's senses roared back to life, though her thoughts remained sluggish and dull. There was no time to think, no time to feel the natural fear of being caught flat-footed by a robber. Her heart was again pounding in her ears, and her adrenaline was pumping. That was all she needed. Her fists balled, and one snapped out to connect with the man's face before she was even aware that she was moving. He went down with a yelp and a gush of blood from his nose.

"Get control of her!" a woman's voice roared from Claire's mirrored closet.

Apparently, it was *robbers*, plural.

In an instant, two other men were on her, punching and grasping and kicking and trying to subdue her. But whoever these people were, they had missed one very important fact: she was Claire Green, and despite appearances, she would not be taken down by mere street thugs. Fifteen years of formal karate lessons in her childhood and twelve years of MMA training as an adult flowed through Claire's body without her having to summon them. Her muscle memory engaged, and she dropped into a defensive fighting stance and danced away from the men. She was able to block most of their punches, in part because their aim was off. They were far too used to fighting other street toughs like themselves, rather than a five-foot-nothing woman. This fact also left them wide open where it really counted.

Claire ducked back into the living room, creating a natural chokepoint in the doorway. They had no choice but to come through one at a time. From there, it was almost comically easy to stomp on their toes, kick their shins, and—most effectively—drive her knee into their sensitive groins. The first man toppled over within seconds, moaning and clutching his crotch. The second was so close behind him, he actually stumbled over his comrade and went down on top of him. A sharp jab of Claire's fist to the first's head left him unconscious. A sharp kick took care of the second.

The guy Claire had sucker-punched wasn't as easily taken in, though, probably because she'd already drawn blood. He emerged from the shadows of Claire's bedroom wiping blood from his upper lip with his grimy shirt sleeve. "You didn't say the little bitch could actually fight, Zoe," he tossed over his shoulder to the woman who had been hiding in Claire's closet.

"Stop your whining and get the girl," the woman, Zoe, responded.

Until now, Claire had assumed that she'd walked into the middle of a regular burglary, but at Sucker-Punch's complaint, her fatigued mind whirred to life like an old dial-up modem. Why would robbers have a taser? Why would they need a four-person crew to rob a small two-bedroom apartment occupied by two perennially broke women? And if they were robbers, why were they so intent on fighting, rather than running, when caught in the act? No, something else was going on here. Maybe it was time for a change of tactics.

Claire took a step back and lowered her fists, taking a calculated risk. "Let's make a deal. The TV in the living room and our laptops are the most expensive things here, though that's not saying much. Ramona's has a cracked screen, and mine's several years old. You can take them, and I won't call the cops for another fifteen minutes so you can make a clean getaway, okay? Our renters insurance might even cover the cost of getting new ones." As she gestured around the room, Claire belatedly realized that her hands were shaking. She crossed her arms over her chest to hide that fact. Fatigue plus hunger was doing a number on her, but she didn't want her uninvited guests to know that.

The woman—tall, thin, and raven-haired—stepped past Sucker-Punch and sneered at Claire. "Don't play stupid. You and I both know that we're not here for your cheap shit." She walked through the doorway of Claire's bedroom and entered the living room. Her black leather jacket, leggings, and combat boots contrasted with her pale skin in a way that seemed more goth hacker than robber—or whatever she was.

Claire stood her ground, refusing to back up even an inch.

"I propose a deal of my own," Zoe continued. "We'll take *your* laptop, you'll come along quietly, and we'll forget this whole ugly incident and release you once we have what we need. Understood?"

Claire tilted her head to one side, as if considering. She tried to imagine herself as a secret agent and schooled her face into a calm, cool expression appropriate for the role. Inside, a headache began pounding in her temples.

Zoe took a few steps to the right, moving farther into the living space. Claire was almost offended by the obviousness of the plot. *She's going to circle me, trying to get me to turn my back on Sucker-Punch. Not likely.*

"Do you know who I work for, Ms. Green? Vengeance is coming for you."

Ice water froze Claire's veins. For a moment, she couldn't breathe, couldn't think. All she saw was blue lightning before her eyes. She forced a laugh out, but it sounded weak and breathy to her own ears. "Vengeance? Are you talking about the person or the noun?" The world spun around her, and her headache pounded in time with her pulse. *I must be asleep on my feet and dreaming. This has to be a dream. Wake up, Green. Wake up!*

Sucker-Punch took advantage of Claire's momentary distraction and crashed into her, sending her sprawling on the ground. He knocked the wind out of her, her head bounced against the floor with a loud *crack*, and his considerable weight pinned her as he flipped her onto her stomach. The world spun, and the portion of Claire's brain that was still operable noticed just how dirty and dusty their wood floor was. Someone was laughing in the distance. Was Ramona watching a sitcom on her laptop in the other room?

No, it was Claire who was laughing.

"Don't scramble her brains into next week!" Zoe hissed.

Claire laughed louder. She was being kidnapped by a Supervillain's goons, her apartment was filthy, and she couldn't stop laughing. *Possible mild concussion, though stress and exhaustion may also play a role*, the professional in Claire assessed, as if watching herself from a great distance.

But it was when she felt her arms being tugged behind her back that things started to get… weird.

Sucker-Punch yanked her arms behind her, but Claire didn't feel the pain. She felt him chuckle above her, but she didn't hear him. All she could hear was a roaring that drowned out even the pounding of her heart that echoed through her head. Her eyes were locked on a shallow gouge in the wood floor, and she couldn't look away. It was like the minor imperfection was drawing in her, and she was caught in a whirlpool of space dust circling around and around a black hole, slowly descending into the churning vortex. Her fingers and hands went numb. She wasn't even sure if she was breathing anymore. Time seemed to both slow and stretch, becoming infinite and compressed. Sucker-Punch moved impossibly slowly as he secured her hands behind her. Zoe said something, but it was distorted and unintelligible over the roar. Claire's heart beat faster and faster, like the pet rabbit she'd had as a child.

The gouge in the floor beckoned. She fell in.

When reality returned, Claire was breathing heavily, gasping for air. There was an odd taste in her mouth, like black licorice, but not quite. She sat on the floor of her apartment, her back against the door. Zoe and Sucker-Punch lay unconscious before her. Claire stared at the pair for a long moment, unsure of what she was seeing. She raised a shaking hand to brush away the stray lock of red hair that stuck to her jaw and felt something wet. Her knuckles were bloody.

The sight jolted her into action again. She scrambled to her feet as Zoe's words came back to her: *Vengeance is coming for you.*

Claire had seen on the news that Vengeance had escaped from prison. She'd been disappointed, of course, but when her colleagues joked that the Supervillain was going to come after her seeking revenge, she'd laughed it off. Vengeance was known for his animosity toward Superheroes, not mere mortals like her. If anything, he would likely focus his ire on Silver Fist, the silver-and-blue-clad Superhero who had earned notoriety by taking down Vengeance in his debut appearance.

Claire had always felt an odd kinship with Silver Fist—and not just because he reminded her of an old flame. They'd both been on their first day on the job when they inadvertently worked together to subdue and capture a dangerous Supervillain, and since then, their careers had both prospered in part due to that early fame. She'd seen Silver Fist around the city in the eight years since, of course. After all, there were only so many Superheroes and so many EMTs, even in a city the size of New York. But they had never spoken again. Claire doubted that he even remembered her face.

And now, the dangerous Supervillain that they had both pissed off was free. And that Supervillain knew her name. And her home address.

Claire moved without thinking. She grabbed her backpack, which always contained a fresh change of clothes, a water bottle, and some protein bars. To that, she added the three energy drinks from the fridge and her laptop in its purple plastic case. Zoe had been interested in it, so Claire wasn't about to leave it behind.

As Claire started toward the door, she realized that she needed to warn Ramona not to come home after work. She didn't want her roommate to walk right into the same trap she'd just narrowly avoided. She pulled out her cell phone and hit 'Call' on her top emergency contact.

Within seconds, she heard a harsh vibrating sound come from somewhere under the pile of junk mail on the table. She sighed and rolled her eyes as she turned toward the disaster area that was more of a catch-all than a table used for eating. Sure enough, Ramona's phone was there, under several envelopes containing credit card offers.

"Typical," she muttered.

Claire's thoughts raced. She didn't know the number for Ramona's bank, but it was only a few blocks away. She could head straight over there and warn her roommate in person. Then, she'd find a safe place to hole up and figure out her next steps.

Chapter 3

The lines for the tellers at the First Resolution Bank of New York were annoyingly long, and Ramona's line was the longest of all. Claire considered going to find a manager and explaining the situation, but she was loathe to draw more attention to herself. So, she unzipped her black, fleecc-lined waterproof jacket, adjusted the straps of her backpack, and got in line in the vast marble hall. The reflection of her sneaker-clad feet drilled down into the polished floor beneath her, as though she were a statue and part of the bank.

In normal circumstances, Claire loved New York's art deco buildings. She had grown up in a rather bland small city in Iowa, and a part of her was still overawed by the majestic architecture of marble floors, gilded domes, ornate archways, magnificent statues, and fabulous woodwork. Even after eight years in New

York, she never got tired of glancing around such buildings, filing away details in her mind for her small-town self to delight in later. But now, as the adrenaline sparked by her encounter with a Supervillain's goons slowly ebbed away, Claire was blind to the opulent flourishes in the building constructed during the Roaring Twenties.

Claire knew she needed to alert the authorities, both the police and the IAS. In fact, that's what she should have done right away, as soon as she was out of immediate danger. And yet, a part of her—a large part—was hesitant to make that call. For one thing, she didn't know how to explain what had happened when she blacked out. She must have knocked Zoe and Sucker-Punch out, but how? She'd been pinned, her hands and arms immobilized by a much larger opponent. And she was good, but she wasn't *that* good. Plus, there was the fact that Vengeance and his crew knew her home address. Claire wasn't exactly in the witness protection program, but she scrupulously scrubbed any and all secure personal information, like her home address and cell phone number, from the internet. She'd briefly had a problem with overly enthusiastic admirers—stalkers, as her roommate at the time had called them—immediately after the Vengeance incident, so she'd fallen into the habit of keeping such identifying data private. So how, then, did Vengeance find her?

Someone behind her cleared their throat loudly, drawing Claire out of her thoughts. Her line had advanced slightly, and Claire took a few steps forward, then flashed an apologetic grin over her shoulder. The older couple behind her were clearly tourists—actual New Yorkers would have said something rude or just cut in front of her—and they both smiled back. Their University of Wisconsin jackets and exceedingly sensible shoes screamed "Midwestern tourist," and Claire briefly worried that she was giving her fellow Midwesterners a bad impression of the Big Apple.

Or an accurate one, a part of her silently quipped.

Now, as she looked around, Claire realized why the lines were moving so slowly. They appeared to be short-handed behind the teller desk, and only four of the six windows were open. Ramona had repeatedly mentioned how busy their branch always was, complaining about the line of customers whenever someone called in sick and hadn't been able to get someone to cover for them in time.

Out of the corner of her eye, Claire noticed two men standing at the private check-signing station. They had been there when she first walked in and hadn't moved since. They were talking to each other, though they never looked up. They simply faced each other, heads down, eyes focused on their own documents, only occasionally glancing around. They must have had a lot of paperwork to get through before they got in line for a teller.

Then, the security guard by the west door clutched his stomach, hurried over to his nearest colleague, who hovered around the middle of the lobby, and said something. The central lobby guard nodded and smiled briefly, and the west door security guard hurried off—presumably to the bathroom. Maybe a stomach bug was going around the bank. That would explain the dearth of tellers. Something in the back of Claire's mind idly observed the fact that there were now just two security guards in the crowded lobby—one by the north door and one in the center of the room. The west door was uncovered.

Moments later, the two men by the check station left, one through each door. They never got in line for the teller.

She should have seen it coming. Later, she would kick herself for not putting it all together: the reduced staff, the security guard suddenly taking ill, the two suspicious men casing the place. But at the time, she didn't *see* it. So, when almost a dozen heavily armed men wearing Halloween costume masks rushed in through the west door, she was as surprised as everyone else.

A man in a vampire mask held a rifle over his head and sent a single shot into the air. Plaster rained down, and the resulting blast echoed through the high-ceiled lobby, followed immediately by the terrified screams of over two dozen people. Two other armed and masked robbers covered the two remaining guards and ordered them to put their hands in the air. They quickly complied. Still others fanned out around the room, pointing weapons at everyone in the lobby. Bank patrons clustered together in a panicked mass. A woman screamed, and a child started crying. The Midwestern tourists behind Claire crouched down slightly, their hands in the air and their eyes wide.

Definitely giving them a bad impression of New York, Claire thought grimly.

Three more robbers rushed from somewhere within the bank and hopped behind the counter with the tellers, ordering them away from any panic buttons. They complied, stepping away, their hands in the air. Claire could just see Ramona's panicked face through the gathered throng. Her long pink nails pointing toward the ornate art deco ceiling caught the light, and her wide brown eyes didn't move from the barrel of the gun that was pointed toward her.

In a mere three seconds, the bank lobby had gone from busy, yet peaceful to a site of fear.

For the third time that morning, Claire was hit by a rush of adrenaline. It swept away the cobwebs again gathering in her exhausted, sleep-deprived brain and flooded her world with vivid color. But by now, her tank was running on empty. She'd inhaled a protein bar on the walk over to the bank and washed it down with an energy drink, but that didn't change the fact that she'd been awake for nearly twenty-four hours straight. She didn't have the reserves to deal with this new threat, and this wave of energy left her dizzy and almost reeling. Her heart started racing, and her palms grew sweaty. She consciously tried to even her breathing and focused on not locking her knees. This would not be a good time to pass out, especially since she still wasn't sure if she'd sustained a concussion earlier.

Good grief, she thought as the bank swam before her eyes, *what a day. First, a Supervillain's henchmen. Now, bank robbers. What's next, an alien invasion?*

"Good people," the apparent leader in the vampire mask bellowed, "we don't want to cause you any trouble. So, as long as you cooperate, I think our time together here can be short and pleasant."

A goon wearing a banana mask holstered his weapon and pulled out a large, blank canvas tote bag, the type usually used at farmers' markets and covered with the NPR logo. He stepped toward the bank patrons as Vampire Mask continued, "My friend here will be coming around to collect your cell phones. You will get them back at the end of this. Failure to comply will result in unpleasant circumstances for you."

Banana Head circulated through the crowd, and everyone dropped their cell phones in the bag. No one resisted. Everyone was silent, though muffled sobs of fear still echoed through the lobby.

When Banana Head reached Claire, she held up two cell phones in a shaking hand and focused on the holes that she assumed were for his eyes. He cocked his head at her, and she explained in a voice that was far calmer than she felt, "One of these belongs to my roommate, who's a teller. She won't have a phone on her. She's not being difficult. She forgot it at home. Okay?"

Banana Head nodded gravely, and Claire dropped both phones into the bag. She glanced in Ramona's direction, hoping to catch her eye, but the tellers were all fully focused on the robber with the gun that was practically pointed in their faces.

Once he had collected all the phones, Banana Head and his colleague, Scarecrow Face, herded all the patrons toward the back wall, away from the windows. The security guards had by now been disarmed, and they and the tellers joined their frightened customers. The robbers ordered their hostages to sit on the floor, their hands on their heads.

Claire gratefully sank to the ground before her knees could give out. As she laced her fingers together over the top of her head, she let out a deep sigh and tipped her head back slightly. Her eyes slipped closed, and she sensed motion all around her as everyone else followed her lead. She swayed slightly in place, as if she were sitting on a boat at sea and not on a firm marble floor. Her mouth was painfully dry, and the lemon flavor of the energy drink she'd consumed only made her thirstier.

When she opened her eyes, she saw even more masked goons herding a troop of personal bankers and loan officers down the stairs from the second floor, their hands also on their heads. *What is going on?* she wondered in a numb haze. At this point, there were almost twenty robbers in the bank. Based on Claire's knowledge of bank heists—which, admittedly, came entirely from movies—this was a truly massive amount.

At this point, though, the hostages became very much beside the point. A few robbers stood guard over them, a handful guarded the doors, and two others began emptying the contents of the cashiers' drawers into large sacks, but the majority of the Halloween-masked criminals headed back, deeper into the bank, where the safe-deposit boxes were.

Seeing this, there was a stir among the bank employees.

"Everybody keep quiet," Banana Head said with a nasally voice that didn't match his imposing, muscular build. "No talking, no heroics. Let's just stay calm, and we'll all part as friends, okay?"

Claire's heart was still racing, and everything had taken on a glassy, crystalline quality. All around her, Midtown businessmen and women in suits, a handful of tourists in jeans and hoodies, and a few wealthy housewives in LuluLemon activewear looked around, wide-eyed. They looked a bit unreal, like Claire was watching a scene play out on an old TV. She didn't want to draw attention to herself by having a panic attack or passing out, so she focused on her breathing, trying to slow it and her racing heart.

Beside Claire, a woman who appeared to be dressed for yoga class, her jet-black hair tied up in a messy ponytail, cradled a three-year-old on her lap. The little girl was crying, and her mother was frantically trying to calm her while still keeping her hands on her head, as ordered. Banana Head noticed and came over. Claire cringed in anticipation of a potentially bad scene, and another spike of adrenaline shot through her.

To her—and everyone else's—surprise, Banana Head spoke to the mother in a level tone: "You can take your hands down. Just shut that kid up and keep her calm. We don't want any dramatics." Then, he turned and walked away.

Claire noticed that the woman was shaking as she lowered her hands and wrapped her arms around her daughter.

Ramona had finally spotted her roommate. She was huddled with her coworkers on the other side of the group of hostages, sitting awkwardly due to her tight pencil skirt. She caught Claire's eye and raised her eyebrow the way she always did when asking her friend if she was okay. Claire swallowed and nodded. Hoping to reassure her friend, she even offered a weak smile. Ramona nodded in return.

Claire had lived in New York for ten years now, and this was her second active crime scene as a witness/victim. Sure, she'd experienced or heard about her fair share of muggings and break-ins, and she'd responded to the scene of many, many more crimes than she could count as an EMT, but this was her first bank robbery. Thus far, the experience was a walk in the park compared to her encounter with Vengeance.

Vengeance, who was after her.

Vengeance, who knew where she lived.

With a gasp, Claire forcefully shoved the thought aside. She would not think about that now.

She closed her eyes and imagined how this scene was playing out on TV. She pictured the news cameras setting up outside the bank, the faces of serious-looking news anchors narrating the facts they knew thus far. She envisioned footage of the police cordoning off the block, SWAT teams coming in to capture the building, and Superheroes formulating a plan to rescue the hostages. She was aware enough to realize that she was disassociating, but at that moment, she didn't care. She just wanted to mentally escape this moment. Hell, this *day*.

Envisioning the scene from the outside, as though she wasn't actually there, calmed Claire. Her breathing slowed. Her heart no longer raced. Her fingers still felt numb on the top of her head, but there wasn't much she could do about that right now.

Both Claire and the little girl in her mother's arms beside her calmed down at about the same time. The child's sobs quieted, and Claire glanced in their direction. The mother's mascara was running slightly. The little girl had curled into herself on her mother's lap, hiccupping and staring at Claire, her large black eyes boring into her. Claire offered the girl a smile, but she recoiled, curling deeper into herself and her mother.

Time lost all meaning. Claire didn't know how long they waited, but it felt like forever. The guards paced. The hostages shifted uncomfortably on the cold, hard floor. And coming from outside were the ever-increasing sounds of sirens, choppers, and people shouting.

Then, the large mass of robbers came out from the back of the bank, hauling large sacks filled with what Claire assumed were valuables from all or even just a few safe-deposit boxes. The hostages stirred, as if waking from a poor slumber. They knew the end of this scene was drawing near. The robbers gathered in the middle of the bank, with several conferring quietly. Claire assumed they had come into this with plans for their getaway, but they weren't making a break for it. They were just hanging out, waiting. The goons standing guard over the hostages and doors were just as vigilant as ever. *Is the operation not done?* Claire wondered. *What are they waiting for? Don't they want to get away before a Superhero shows up?*

The three conferring in the middle of the bank's lobby—Vampire Face, Werewolf Face, and Rat Head—seemed to be getting antsy. They were speaking quietly amongst themselves, but Rat Head was gesticulating wildly. There was some kind of problem. Claire looked around at her fellow hostages and saw that they noticed it, too. Something was happening. Claire sat up straighter and focused all her lagging energy on listening to the apparent leaders of this heist.

At that moment, Rat Head exploded, "Then where is he?" Everyone's heads swiveled in his direction, and Vampire Face slapped him upside the head. That seemed to quiet Rat Head down.

"He'll be here," Vampire Face promised quietly, though his voice carried through the cavernous lobby. "The boss promised."

That's when it happened, the event Claire was secretly waiting for: a man dropped down from the second floor and landed in the classic three-point Superhero pose in the middle of the bank lobby. Claire always internally winced when she saw such a pose. It was terrible for the knees, but all the Superheroes seemed to do it. Perhaps Supers were also blessed with superior knee joints. However, this time, she felt nothing but excitement. Her face widened into a grin despite her best efforts.

As the Superhero stood up, Claire recognized the familiar form of Silver Fist decked out in blue and silver. He had added a silver cape recently—capes were all the rage among Supers at the moment—and his hood had been refined in the last few years, probably to allow him better vision through those eyeholes.

Silver Fist looked around, surveying the situation. The robbers didn't move as he turned 360 degrees, taking in the whole scene. Claire didn't understand why they weren't closing in on him.

Vampire Face spoke up. "So good of you to join us, Silver Fist. We've been waiting for you."

The Superhero said nothing is response.

Silver Fist was known for never speaking to anyone: the press, those he saved, or the Supervillains he took down. Some speculated that he was actually mute. So far as Claire knew, she was the only person he had ever spoken to in his Superhero persona. The memory of his soft, low-pitched words, "You did well," never failed to fill her chest with warmth, as if her heart were expanding and floating higher and higher within her. She often replayed that moment, a flush creeping into her face as she pictured the way he licked his lips before leaning toward her. That brief exchange was the one part of her experience with

Vengeance that she had never shared with anyone. It felt too private, too intimate.

For a moment, everything in the bank lobby stood poised in perfect balance. Even the slightest movement on anyone's part could send the whole place into a chaos of fists and bullets—and bullets could easily go astray and hit the hostages. Claire was sure that's why Silver Fist hesitated. Based on what she'd seen on the news, he had gotten better at dealing with hostage situations over the years, but he was still far more cautious when civilians were around than many of his colleagues.

"Nothing to say?" Vampire Face asked, his voice muffled yet mocking through his mask. "Well, I'm sure you'll change your mind when you meet my employer." He raised his arm and gestured dramatically toward the back of the bank, where there were countless private offices and hallways.

A tall man with cropped white hair, a short white beard, and stern features was suddenly at Vampire Face's side. He didn't walk out of the offices to join the henchmen. He didn't fade into being, like a slow dissolve in a movie. It was more, *blink*, and he was just there, as though he had always been there. Several of the hostages gasped, but none of the robbers responded in awe. They must have seen this before.

Claire's heart thudded to a sudden, intense stop. Her blood turned to ice water. She knew this man. His face had been occupying her thoughts all morning.

Vengeance.

The Supervillain who had sent goons to her apartment to kidnap her stood less than ten feet away, his familiar purple robes replaced with an all-black three-piece suit. Prison had apparently been good for him. He stood taller and straighter than he had eight years ago, and his manicured facial hair gave him a distinguished air. He had gone from an evil version of Merlin in *The Sword in the Stone* to cool James Bond villain.

Claire had to remind herself to breathe. Vengeance never even glanced at her. *He's not here for me*, she told herself. All of his attention was focused on the Superhero. It was pure coincidence that the three of them were all here again. All she had to do was remain inconspicuous, and she might still get out of this in one piece. She slowly, subtly sank down, slouching slightly to better hide her face.

"Hello, Silver Fist," Vengeance said, his affected British accent booming through the bank lobby. "So good to see you again and meet you properly. I'm afraid I didn't catch your name at our first encounter, but I've taken pains to follow your career since then."

His words broke the spell holding everyone in place. The hostages shouted warnings, though several of them just screamed. The robbers' guns came up, some pointed at the civilians and some at Silver Fist.

The Superhero himself charged at Vengeance, becoming a blur of blue and silver. Vengeance raised his right palm toward Silver Fist and muttered a single word. A bolt of green flame shot from his hand, raced toward the blur that was Silver Fist, and encircled him. The Superhero stopped dead in his tracks and dropped to the ground face-first, not moving. His silver cape slowly settled over him like a blanket. And just like that, it was over.

Several hostages screamed, hands flying up to cover mouths that hung agape.

A lump formed in Claire's throat, and tears sprang to her eyes. *Get up*, she silently willed. *Get up!* Her eyes were fixed on Silver Fist's back, and while it continued to rise and fall evenly, he did not otherwise move.

"Good job, sir," Vampire Face said.

Vengeance ignored him and stalked toward the unconscious Superhero. "Turn him over," he ordered, his voice rich and full, like a Shakespearian actor's.

A few months earlier, while safely ensconced on the couch in their apartment, Claire had wondered aloud to Ramona, "Why do Supervillains try so hard to sound refined?"

Ramona had responded, "Because they're always thinking about who they want to play them in the next Superhero biopic! There's nothing quite like having a former James Bond playing you on the big screen—even if you have to watch that big screen from behind bars."

The two women had descended into peels of laugher.

Now, three robbers jumped to do Vengeance's bidding. They lifted and turned Silver Fist over onto his back, his limbs splayed out like a doll's.

Several hostages leaned forward, intrigued to see how this would play out. Civilians so rarely got to take part in the cat-and-mouse games of the Supers, as Claire was all too aware. Her own experience was unique enough to make her a minor celebrity of sorts among the Superhero fan community. To most people, though, Superheroes existed among the rest of the populace, but they were beyond and above mere mortals like Claire—sometimes, literally. Now, these mere mortals had forced front-row seats to a Super face-off. And unlike Silver Fist—and Claire—they weren't the object of a Supervillain's vengeance. They could afford to be curious. Only Claire buried herself deeper in her jacket, trying to disappear into her clothing.

"Remove his hood," Vengeance boomed. "I want to see his face."

Scarecrow Head complied. He reached behind the unconscious Hero's head, loosened some unseen fastener, and pulled the mask off. The man's uncovered head lolled to the side, facing toward the gathered hostages.

For a moment, the entire universe froze. Claire couldn't breathe. She struggled to draw oxygen into her lungs, but it was like they had collapsed. A ragged, raw, white-hot pain stabbed her in the chest. Pain mixed with joy in a combustible solution that threatened to explode, tearing her heart into pieces.

Directly before her was the face of a man she thought she would never see again. A man she thought was gone from her life forever: Jack Elliott.

His eyes were closed, and his mouth hung loosely open. His strong chiseled jaw was clean-shaven, and his dirty-blond hair was cut short in a military crew cut. He looked older than when Claire had last seen him—which made sense, given that it had been twelve years—and the beginnings of a web of crinkles spread across his forehead. But it was still the same Jack she had fallen in love with as a starry-eyed teenager who dreamed of one day getting out of their small Iowa world and making a difference in the big city.

Claire managed a ragged, painful breath in. It felt like she was breathing ice crystals or as if each molecule of air were sharp as glass. They shredded her insides, leaving a bloody trail of twisting agony that both burned and froze her all the way down. With that breath, the world sped up again, and she was back in it.

Without pausing to think or feel, she reacted. Claire sat up on her knees and gasped, "Jack?!"

She recognized her mistake the second the word left her mouth. Everyone—hostages, robbers, Supervillain—turned to stare at her.

Banana Head approached and shoved his gun in her face. "You know this guy?" he demanded.

Claire's eyes darted back to Jack. She shook her head and lowered her eyes to the ground. "N-no," she stuttered, sinking back down into herself, trying to make herself look small and unimportant. "I was mistaken. He just looks like someone I know."

"Are you sure?" He lowered his gun and grabbed Claire's hair, hauling her to her feet. "Take a closer look." The pain in her scalp was intense, and she stumbled as he dragged her forward. She tried to get her footing, but he quickly threw her down on the cold, hard floor right beside Jack. "Take a good, long look."

Claire was mentally kicking herself. She had done the unpardonable, the unthinkable: she had revealed a Superhero's true identity. There was a reason why they wore costumes and masks, a reason why they went by code names. They had to protect their true identities as well as their friends and families. If Supervillains knew who these Heroes were in real life, they could manipulate and blackmail Heroes into doing their bidding. The risk was too high. And now, Claire had unthinkingly spilled a tiny portion of Jack's true identity. On top of that, she had called attention to herself right in front of the very Supervillain who was after her. She had essentially signed both of their death warrants.

Claire crouched on the marble floor, the cold seeping into her legs. She bent over Jack's unconscious form, careful to turn her face away from Vengeance. She could feel Jack's soft breath on her chest and tried to suppress a shiver. "No, I don't know him," she said, her eyes on his jaw. "He just looks like an old friend—"

Another, even more powerful hand closed around Claire's ponytail and lifted her into the air. She let out a sharp yelp and grabbed onto the hand that held her aloft, trying to take some of the pressure off her scalp. She recognized the scent of ozone mixed with old books that sometimes haunted her nightmares. Claire opened her eyes through the red haze of pain and saw Vengeance standing before her, his arm extended, holding her a few inches off the ground.

"Stray kitten!" he purred. "I thought I recognized you, Ms. Claire Green. I sent Zoe to collect you at your domicile, but it seems she just missed you. How fortunate that we ran into each other here."

Claire's eyes watered, turning Vengeance into a blurry portrait of white, black, and pink. She tried to scratch at the hand that held her, but all that did was put more pressure back on her hair.

Vengeance continued, "I was hoping we could have a nice chat, you and I, so this is marvelous. And it seems you know our mutual acquaintance, Silver Fist—or should I say, 'Jack'?—as well. You really are full of surprises, kitten."

"Go to hell," Claire managed to grind out between clenched teeth.

"Oh, I've been there and back again," he said, his smile melting into the rest of his face as Claire grimaced and twisted in his grasp. His other palm came up, he muttered something Claire didn't understand, and then, everything was a bright green before fading to black.

Chapter 4

Jack woke up freezing cold and with a throbbing headache. He also woke up completely immobilized, his whole body wrapped in an electric-blue glow. There was a cold, damp stone wall against his back, but he couldn't so much as shimmy against it. His feet dangled in the air about a foot above the cracked concrete floor, and his arms were stretched out beside him, spread-eagle. When he turned his head to the right, the muscles in his neck spasmed painfully.

A metal door slammed open, sending a jolt of pain through his skull. His headache pounded even harder. Try as he might, even with his Super-strength, he couldn't raise his hand to massage his temples. They were frozen in place. He had as much control over them as he did over another person's limbs.

"Oh, good, you're awake," Vengeance's theatrical British accent boomed through the small room.

Jack groaned in renewed pain. The dramatics were completely unnecessary.

He lifted his head to study his surroundings. They were in what appeared to be the break room of a warehouse. Everything was cinder-block walls, metal shelving, poor lighting, dust, and the stale scent of cigarette smoke. Three men who looked like regular working-class laborers, dressed in jeans, hoodies, and jackets, sat around a folding table near the door eating delivery pizza. Apparently, even henchmen got hungry. Vengeance stood just inside the doorframe. He looked out of place in this scene. His meticulous three-piece black suit belonged at a socialite's party or a Broadway show, not in this dirty cavern of a room.

The Supervillain strode into the room, past the pizza-eating henchmen, and right up to Jack's face. Jack didn't see the man levitate into the air, but he must have been floating. At six-foot-six, Jack wasn't exactly a small man, and the fact that he was hovering above the ground only added to his distance from the floor. Vengeance leaned in close. Close enough for Jack to smell his slightly oily breath. Close enough to notice the red lines that ran like spider webs through the whites of his eyes. Close enough to hate the way his carefully manicured white beard pulled up at the corners in a smile that didn't meet his eyes.

And that's when Jack realized that he was no longer wearing his hood. He had been unmasked.

If Jack could slump right now, he would. Instead, he settled for a sigh of defeat. He'd correctly identified the next bank

Vengeance was going to hit, but he'd failed to stop the bank robbery and was actually defeated, captured, and unmasked instead, partially revealing his true identity. If he made it out of this alive and in one piece, Giada was going to give him the hardest time about this. And that was a big *if*.

"It's been some time since our last little tête-à-tête," Vengeance said, drawing back slightly. Jack couldn't see the other man's feet, but he was now sure he was levitating. "I understand you've made quite a name for yourself these past few years—in large part, no doubt, to having defeated me." He turned away slightly, gesturing airily, as if showing off his outfit for a crowd.

The pizza-eating henchmen seemed unimpressed. They continued eating and watching, but said nothing.

Jack swallowed hard. His headache was intense and threatened to drown out everything else. Even Vengeance's voice was hard to focus on, and Jack struggled to make sense of his words. The room swam in and out of focus, making it difficult to count exits and access points. He needed an escape plan, but the buzzing in his head made it almost impossible to think.

"But wait," Vengeance said, suddenly turning back to face Jack again. "You *didn't* defeat me. Not on your own. You had the help of that stray ginger kitten and her elderly friend with the cane."

Jack gritted his teeth and hoped Vengeance would take it as a sign of pain or defiance and not for what it was: the rage that bubbled at the Supervillain's mere mention of the girl he had once loved long ago. Unbidden, the image of Claire's face contorted in pain as Vengeance twisted her head toward Jack surfaced. It pushed away the throbbing pain that engulfed him, like the sun coming out from behind the clouds, and filled him with energy and a white-hot anger that caused his chest to heave.

"But I'm not here to talk about the past." Vengeance turned away and hopped down from whatever floating platform he had been standing on. "At least, not our past. In general, I find history fascinating, don't you?" Jack maintained his silence, and Vengeance continued, "I'm particularly interested in Superhero history. All those grand deeds and heroic stories... and all those deaths. Superhero deaths. So-called 'Supervillain' deaths. Civilian deaths." As he spoke, Vengeance's voice turned to stone. He turned a level gaze on Jack that would have frozen him with its intensity, were he not already immobilized.

For just a moment, Jack's whole focus turned to the Supervillain. *Who or what hurt you?* he wondered. *Who did you lose?*

And then, the spell was broken. Vengeance turned away, and his voice again took on the tone of a history professor giving a lecture to a bored class. "The Elite Five in particular fascinate me. Why did they come out of the shadows and step up to help their fellow citizens who feared and despised them? It's an interesting question, no?"

At this point, it was clear that Vengeance wasn't expecting an answer. He barreled on with his monologue: "But allow me to get to the point. After a great deal of searching, I have found the hidden location of the headquarters of the Elite Five. What I don't have is the access codes. I had been hoping to find them in one of the Elite Five's safe-deposit boxes, but you just dropped into my lap and, well, beggars can't be choosers, as they say."

Jack ground his teeth together. At least the Supervillain need to grandstand answered a few of the questions that had come up in that morning's briefing. He glared at Vengeance, communicating his refusal to cooperate with what he hoped was a steely gaze.

"I see the rumors are true: you're not much of a conversationalist," Vengeance said. "But then again, perhaps we got off on the wrong foot. In that case, I have a gift for you that might loosen your tongue."

His smile made Jack's stomach drop. In his experience, the phrase, "Beware Greeks bearing gifts," would more appropriately be, "Beware Supervillains bearing gifts."

Over his shoulder, Vengeance ordered, "Felipe, Gus, go get her."

Two of the men—one with messy blond hair and a reddish five o'clock shadow, and the other, a hulking man who looked like a bodybuilder—stood and exited the room. Two others continued to eat pizza as if this were a normal Wednesday night.

Vengeance turned on his heel and retreated to the shadows at the far side of the room. Jack could feel the Supervillain's eyes on his face, studying him. He could have sworn he saw Vengeance's eyes glow.

They were apparently waiting for someone, and Jack suspected it was a hostage taken from the bank. Jack ached with sorrow and regret for whoever this "she" was. He imagined a terrified young bank teller or a middle-aged tourist who just wanted to go home to her family. He hoped that whoever she was, she wasn't too badly injured or traumatized—and that he could get them both out of there before they came to any more harm.

A few minutes later, the two men returned. The large bodybuilder carried a small woman over his shoulder as though she were a sack of potatoes. Her black uniform pants were splattered with mud around the cuffs, her feet were bare, and her ankles were zip-tied together, as were her hands.

"You can put her down there," Vengeance said from the shadows. His voice sent a tremor of revulsion down Jack's spine.

The bodybuilder threw the woman down onto the hard cement floor as if she were a ragdoll. She landed facedown directly underneath Jack, and the crack when her head hit the floor caused Jack to flinch. She wheezed, as if the air had been knocked out of her. The flash of blazing red hair that hung from a messy ponytail made Jack's breath catch in his throat. *No, it couldn't be.*

"Now, let's try this again."

Vengeance's voice sounded distant over the roar again growing in Jack's ears. Even though he was held immobile by Vengeance's magic, his world tilted.

Still struggling to breathe, the woman rolled to her side and looked up at Jack.

It was Claire.

She lay on the floor, her eyes wide and fixed on his. Her long-sleeved black T-shirt was torn at the shoulder, and her long red hair escaping from her ponytail framed her face. A strip of silver duct tape covered her mouth. Her nostrils flared as she struggled to breathe through her nose. Blood leaked from her right cheekbone where she'd hit the floor. Jack was relieved that it appeared to be her only injury.

Vengeance's voice sounded very far away. "You will give me the access codes to the Elite Five's base, or I will kill this woman. The choice is yours... Jack."

A cold wind rushed over Jack's body, and something near his heart twisted like a knife—cold, hard, and metallic. He felt disoriented, like he was trapped in a bad dream. He was running through a house of mirrors, the world coming back to him distorted and chaotic. Too many thoughts crowded his mind. Why was Claire here? Did Vengeance know of their past relationship and was trying to use her against him? Or was this just revenge against the two people who had taken him down eight years ago, and their past was merely a coincidence? And how did Vengeance know his real name?

Jack couldn't tear his eyes away from Claire. Her bright-blue eyes shone with fear, but also determination. And something else. Regret? Why would she look at him like that right here and now? And more importantly, why did she not seem shocked to see him dressed as Silver Fist, yet without his mask? Did she already know his secret identity? Had she tracked him down with her Superhero-fangirl resources and raw intelligence? Or was she just in shock after being kidnapped, zip-tied, and throw around like a doll?

Jack's mind raced. He couldn't focus, couldn't settle on how to best respond to this situation. This was all too much. He forced himself to look at Vengeance lurking in the shadows.

The Supervillain was enjoying himself. His eyes darted between his two prisoners, and an expectant smile covered his face. He looked like he was about to sit down to a particularly exciting movie on a Saturday afternoon. All he was missing was some popcorn and a large soda.

Jack took a deep breath and schooled his face into a stony, impersonal expression of disapproval. He made his voice forceful and strong and pitched deep—the voice of a Superhero—and said, "You really are vile. You again threaten a random civilian, an innocent bystander, just to get me to cooperate?"

"'A random civilian,'" Vengeance echoed, reemerging from the shadows and advancing on the pair. He chuckled. "Oh, no. Ms. Claire Green seemed to know you earlier... Jack. And I've had my eye on her for quite some time."

The saliva dried in Jack's mouth. His identity had been revealed, his cover blown. Even if he were able to escape, if this information got beyond this room, his career as Silver Fist was over. He'd have to leave New York, start a new life somewhere else, and adopt a whole new persona. Even worse, based on the look of regret that still shone in Claire's eyes and Vengeance's leading tone, he suspected that she had been the one to reveal his secret.

He dismissed the thought almost as soon as it appeared. No, Claire wouldn't purposefully, knowingly reveal a Superhero's true identity to a Supervillain. It would go against everything she stood for.

You don't know her anymore, a traitorous voice whispered in his mind. *It's been over a decade since she kicked you to the curb and left you behind in her pursuit of her glorious destiny.*

Jack forcefully redirected his thoughts to the issue at hand. Vengeance had used Claire's full name, but only Jack's first name. Perhaps Vengeance didn't know as much as he wanted Jack to *think* he knew.

"You know, Ms. Green is even more interesting than I first thought!" Vengeance paused beside Claire's prone form. With a flick of the Supervillain's wrist, she was suddenly floating in the air before him. The movement was so abrupt that her hair whipped past her face. He reached out to caress her cheek, but Claire flinched away. She struggled, but her movements were futile. She looked like a drowning person trying to break the surface of the water, but could only flail with her bound hands and feet. The blood on her cheek caught the light.

Jack's gut twisted at the thought of Vengeance's thin, bony fingers on Claire's soft white flesh. Without any conscious thought on his part, all the muscles in his body tensed, and he threw himself at the magical bonds that held him in place. It was no good. He could move nothing below his neck.

Vengeance continued, his eyes still on Claire, "This stray kitten is actually descended from one of the Elite Five! Can you imagine? Her computer is full of scanned letters and documents from The Shadow to her family back home in Iowa. It's sweet, really. Letters about life in the big city and taking down the bad guys, to be read on the front porch while sipping iced tea after a hard day's work on the farm, no doubt."

Jack sighed. Yes, he knew. He knew about the letters and Claire's famous great-aunt and everything that had driven her into this life.

"Why do you want to be a Superhero so badly?" sixteen-year-old Jack asked, caressing Claire's hair. They were cuddled on her twin-size bed in her childhood bedroom. Posters of Superheroes lining the purple walls gazed down at them under the illumination of strings of twinkle lights.

Claire wiggled against him, sending fire into his groin that he was already struggling to contain. Her breath was warm on his neck as she looked up at him and asked, *"Can you keep a secret?"*

"Of course," he said. *"For a price."*

"What price?"

"A kiss."

She smiled and obligingly tilted her head up. Her lips were warm and soft and tasted of her beloved Dr. Pepper lip gloss. He inhaled her, wanting to bury himself in her scent, in her arms, in her. But Claire pulled back, ending the moment with a giggle.

"There, a kiss. The contract is sealed," she said.

"Your secrets are safe with me," he responded solemnly.

Claire chewed her lip for a moment, and Jack wished he were the one doing that. He thought about diving in for another, deeper kiss, but Claire finally said, *"This is supposed to be a family secret, but my great-aunt—Grandma O'Neill's sister—was a Superhero back in the day."*

Jack was impressed despite himself. He wasn't particularly interested in Superheroes, but he knew that having one in the family was probably a point of pride. It would be like having a great war hero in the family. *"That's so cool. Anyone even I might know?"*

Claire looked into his eyes, her expression serious. *"Yeah. One of the Elite Five. The Shadow."*

Jack whistled. Being related to one of the Elite Five went beyond having the equivalent of a war hero in the family. It was like saying that George Washington was your great-grandfather or something.

Claire then shared what she knew of her great-aunt Lillian Donoghue, the black sheep of the family who ran away from home to join the circus and become an acrobat at age thirteen. No one heard from her for five years, and her family worried that she had been murdered or sold into prostitution or forced into a marriage to a horrible man.

But then, five years later, in 1938, Lillian contacted her family. In her letter, she explained that she had gained Superpowers and was now working in New York City with a group of Supers to take down a group of mobsters preying on innocent people.

"Grandma was much younger than Aunt Lillian and only had vague memories of her before she ran away," Claire explained. "She thought her sister was doing the coolest thing imaginable, and she wrote back. The two stayed in touch throughout The Shadow's career as a Superhero. Grandma let me read all the letters a few years back. And they're amazing! Aunt Lillian doesn't say much about the dangers she faced, but just imagine!"

Claire's eyes sparkled and took on a faraway look. She wasn't seeing him anymore. She was looking into another world, a world of Tommy guns and car chases and mobsters in suits. A world of skyscrapers and zeppelins and reporters with flashbulb cameras. A world of danger and adventure. A world of Superheroes.

In that moment, Jack felt his heart break for the first time. It shattered like glass, yet maintained its form, held in place by surface tension alone. Without it being said, Jack knew that he didn't belong in that world. And someday, Claire would leave him and Iowa and the safe world they had always known to go in search of that other place. Her eyes were on the dazzling future before her. His eyes were on her back, already watching her walk away. Even though he lay pressed against her, their bodies touching from head to toe, Jack felt very, very far away from her.

Vengeance's voice drew Jack out of his memories and back to the present: "I had hoped that she might know the access codes to their base, but it seems she doesn't. And so, her usefulness has come to an end... almost."

The Supervillain waved his hand as if brushing away a fly, and Claire flew across the room. She sailed past Gus, Felipe, and the two men still eating pizza and crashed into the far wall. Claire's head hit the wall with yet another sickening crack. For the first time since Jack came to, the four goons looked alarmed. One dropped his slice of pizza. Gus and Felipe took a step back and glanced at each other nervously.

Claire slumped to the ground in a heap. She was still for a moment that stretched into eternity, then raised her head and glared death and destruction at Vengeance. If she had a Superpower that enabled her to shoot literal daggers out of her eyes, she would have.

Jack struggled against his invisible magical bonds. His heart pounded in his chest, and his limbs strained and flexed as he tried to rip apart the forces that held him helplessly in place. *No, not like this...*

Vengeance turned a poisonous smile on him. "I'm afraid Ms. Green's only remaining value is as a hostage. I have no intention of keeping her alive... unless you give the word," he sneered. "You see, I'm not fond of cats."

Not like this, Jack screamed internally. *Things can't end between us like this.*

Vengeance instantly transported himself right into Jack's personal space, again hovering before him, his nose inches from Jack's. All good humor and false pretensions to an upper-class British refinement were gone. His eyes were green pools of hatred. His voice could cut steel. "Give me the access codes to the Elite Five's base, or I will kill this woman. Slowly. Painfully. In front of you. And you will know that it was your fault. You could have saved her. I am merely the instrument of your failure."

Jack's chest heaved with indecision. Almost any other Superhero would know what to do and say in this situation. Giada would handle such threats with a laugh and a cheeky one-liner. There was a reason Jack chose to never speak in public in his Superhero persona. He could never match the star-power of many of his colleagues. He grasped for a response, but his tongue was paralyzed with uncertainty.

A muffled shouting from the other side of the room broke the spell.

Vengeance must have been just as surprised as Jack was, because the Supervillain drew away from Jack, and they both looked toward the source of the noise. For the second time in the last eight years, Claire ended a standoff between Jack and Vengeance.

Seeing that she had their attention, Claire began kicking and shimmying her zip-tied feet, as if trying to loosen her tight plastic bonds. Her muffled shouting from behind the duct tape increased in volume. Rather than looking frightened or even dazed and injured, Claire looked *mad*. Mad as hell. And Vengeance had no idea what an angry Claire Green could be like. A small part of Jack that had lain dormant for many years smirked internally.

Vengeance chuckled. "I'm sorry, it seems the lady has something to say. Gus, remove the tape. Let's hear what Ms. Green would add to our negotiations."

The man with messy blond hair stepped forward and tore the duct tape from Claire's lips without kindness or gentleness. Before he could complete the movement, he was rewarded with the harsh *chomp* of Claire sinking her teeth into the meat of his hand. He screamed—really more of a high-pitched shriek—and tried to tug his hand loose, but Claire bit down harder. Blood appeared around her lips. Vengeance took a step forward in an uncharacteristic display of concern, and the pizza-eating henchmen jumped to their feet in support of their fellow. But only Felipe the bodybuilder had it in him to save his colleague from the literal jaws of the bound five-foot-tall woman. He kicked her in the stomach, and Jack winced in sympathy.

The kick had the intended result: Claire released the man's hand. But she wasn't done expressing her thoughts on her captivity. She inhaled sharply and then let loose a string of expletives directed at Vengeance and his goons, the likes of which Jack had never heard. He was pretty sure that some curses, such as "elitist fuck canoe," "pompous taint waffle," and "atomic donkey-pickled duck-licker," were Claire Green Originals. The force of her words was only enhanced by the trails of blood dripping from her mouth and running down her chin.

Any normal person would have kept silent in such a situation. Jack *wanted* her to keep silent in this situation, though a small part of him silently delighted in her display of spirit. *Just like old times*, he thought. This was Claire Green, and she had been taking on all-comers in fights since she was five. She didn't know how to back down. This was no exception.

When she was done with her list of creative insults, Claire turned to the matter at hand. "Listen, you rusty fuck fiddle," she spat, "don't use that tired blaming-the-hero-for-your-actions line on me. No one's forcing you to murder anyone."

She's going to get herself killed.

Jack couldn't keep his admiration out of his eyes. The fiery determination he saw blazing from every pore of her body was so familiar, it made his chest ache. It was the same fire he'd seen the day he'd met her freshman year, when she'd been a tiny, scrawny spitfire defending a silent, awkward giant—him—from the school bully. It was the same fire that had drawn him to her. It made Claire who she was. She could never tame it.

"My, kitten, what a mouth you have on you," Vengeance said, but his tone was more taken aback than his breezy words would suggest. "Boys, muzzle the beast."

Felipe and the guys who had been eating pizza rushed to subdue the now thrashing, biting, and kicking hostage who screamed insults the likes of which they had probably never heard in all their years of henchman-ing. Gus cradled his bleeding hand and stared at her in confusion, likely wondering how someone so small could inflict so much damage. Jack privately hoped the guy would need stitches.

"Boss, a little help?" one of the pizza guys shouted. He was immediately rewarded with a barefooted kick in the face from Claire.

Vengeance sighed. "I thought you were supposed to be good in a fight! And you can't even control a tiny, bound girl?" Under his breath, he muttered, "I have to do everything around here myself." He waved a hand, and a shimmering blue glow enveloped Claire's entire body. She went limp, and her shouting was immediately silenced. Her eyes darted around wildly, and her chest heaved with exertion, but otherwise, she was completely incapacitated.

Vengeance spun back to Jack. "So, what's it going to be, *Jack*? This hissing street cat in exchange for some information? Or..." He let the word trail off suggestively.

Jack's eyes traveled back to Claire's. They were wide with confusion, but when they met his, they softened. She held his gaze for a moment, then blinked both eyes slowly. In her frozen state, it was the only signal she could send him, and he recognized it as a nod of acknowledgement. She was letting him know that she understood what he had to do—and what she would certainly do in his place. Claire probably knew better than most civilians exactly what would happen next.

Jack looked up at Vengeance. "Go to hell," he ground out between clenched teeth.

"Where do you think I got my powers?" Vengeance crossed to where Claire lay on the floor. He spread his palms wide above her and began chanting, though Jack could not identify the words or even the language. A sickly green flame erupted from his hands and shot downward, enveloping her body in tendrils. It replaced the shimmering blue glow that had held her immobile, and her pale skin took on a ghastly greenish tint.

Claire's back arched violently, as though she were being bent backward in half. A scream was wrenched from her, but it was unlike any scream Jack had ever heard before. It was a scream not just of pain but of damnation, of physical, mental, and spiritual agony. It pierced his ears, and the four goons in the room covered theirs. Her eyes rolled back until only the whites of her eyes were visible, and she began shaking violently on the hard cement floor. Foam started to collect on her mouth.

Jack couldn't bear to watch, but he also couldn't look away. This would have been hard enough to watch happening to a random member of the public, but with Claire, it was tortuous. Jack felt like he was the one being torn in two. His heart raced, he was panting, and tears leaked from his eyes.

Claire's screams and the sight of her body spasming with pain washed away every last shred of anger he still felt toward her. He had once promised to love her for all eternity. That may have been the silly vow of a sixteen-year-old boy who didn't know what love or eternity actually were, but it didn't matter. He had once felt that way and believed he really could stand by her side forever.

As her whole body convulsed, Jack saw and embraced his own failure. He couldn't do it. No matter what had happened between them twelve years ago, no matter what she may or may not have done to betray his secret identity now, Jack couldn't let Claire suffer and die like this.

"*Enough!*" Jack's voice cut through the room.

Everything immediately stopped: the green glow, Claire's screaming, the fist clenching Jack's heart. Claire's arched back released, and she flopped down onto the ground. She gasped for breath, and her eyelids fluttered weakly.

When she managed to open her eyes to meet his, they were glassy and dim. She mouthed the words, *I'm sorry.*

Jack let his head droop forward and his eyes slip closed. The tears that had gathered in the corners of his eyes cascaded down his cheeks. "I'll give you the access codes. Just let her go." His voice came out subdued and pained.

Across the room, Claire let out a weak croak of protest. *She would have fought to the end,* Jack thought. *She's always been the strong one. She should have gotten these powers. She would have known how to handle them.*

"Of course," Vengeance said. Jack looked up, and the Supervillain's satisfied smile made him want to throw up. To Vengeance, torturing a defenseless woman was probably as much fun as a Saturday afternoon at Disney World; his expression certainly gave that impression. "Though I should warn you: if these codes prove to be fake, she will pay the price with her life."

Jack looked over at Claire. Her eyes were fixed on him, and she gently rocked her head from side to side. *No*, her expression said. *Don't do this. I can take it.*

Another tear leaked from the corner of Jack's eyes and trailed down his cheek. "I know," he said in a low voice.

Chapter 5

A great many things seemed to be happening all around Claire. Movement. Light. Noise. Her eyes were so heavy that she couldn't open them. The world was a blur, and she was a ship at sea, beating against the waves.

The last few functional brain cells in Claire's exhausted, pain-encrusted mind registered Vengeance sweeping out of the room, his goons following behind him. She and Jack would probably be kept there under heavy guard while Vengeance and his minions went off to confirm that whatever access codes Jack had given them actually worked.

She no longer cared about all this Super posturing. She just wanted to sleep. She was chilled down to the bone, her clothes felt damp against her clammy skin, her muscles and joints all ached the way they did the day after an unusually intense day of physical training, the worst headache of her life pounded in her skull, and her hands and feet were going numb from the zip ties binding them tightly. The loss of her shoes, socks, and jacket didn't help matters.

Jack's defeated expression was the last thing she saw before the world went dark and she finally sank into blissful unconsciousness.

Claire awoke some time later, slumped in a metal folding chair in the corner of what looked like a warehouse. She wasn't sure how long she had been out, but the grill-covered windows high up on the walls showed nothing but darkness outside.

Her head continued to throb painfully, and she quickly found that if she turned her head too quickly, the world spun. *Patient continues to exhibit signs of a concussion*, she assessed. *Great, just great. That's exactly what I need right now. That'll make escaping SO much easier.* She licked her dry, chapped lips and tasted blood. Her tongue felt like sandpaper. She tried to work up some saliva to wet her mouth, with limited success.

That done, Claire tried to move her limbs one at a time, testing to see if anything was broken. She was unbearably stiff and sore from having been thrown around and bound in an uncomfortable position, and her wrists were raw from the tight zip ties holding them, but that was about it. Everything seemed to work, though moving was agony as her muscles screamed in protest.

Claire looked around to see if her backpack was nearby. As memory flooded back, she slumped in defeat. Vengeance had mentioned finding the letters between her great-aunt Lillian and Grandma on her computer, which meant the Supervillain now had her laptop—and, likely, everything else she'd left the apartment with, including her keys, wallet, and cell phone. If she'd had her backpack, her next step—escape—would have been much easier. Claire had a small, portable cannister of pepper spray in her bag, with a retractable switchblade attached. She'd never needed to use either one in all her years in New York, but it was better to be safe than sorry. Of course, the one time she could have actually used these items, she was sorry not to have them.

So much for safe, Claire thought with a grumble. *I ran straight from the frying pan and into the fire. At least Ramona's okay… hopefully.*

At the thought of her roommate, Claire's mind flashed to how the story of her own kidnapping was likely playing out on the news right now. She and Ramona, a fellow Superhero fangirl, often sat on the couch, devouring such news stories and speculating about the Superheroes involved. Claire could easily picture the two of them flopped on their purple velvet couch, its stuffing slowly leaking from the sides, watching the news over a bowl of popcorn.

"The Supervillain known as Vengeance," the imaginary news anchor in her head reported, *"recently escaped from Shadow Isle Asylum, held up First Resolution Bank of New York today. He stole an estimated five million in gold and cash and held over twenty-five people hostage in the bank for several hours. Local sexy Superhero Silver Fist attempted to subdue Vengeance, but he was instead defeated and captured himself. Also taken prisoner was kick-ass New York City EMT, Claire Green, who was already having the worst day of her life. The IAS is currently working to*

locate both hostages and have no comment at this time. More at eleven."

Claire prayed that they used a good picture of her. Her current Facespace profile picture was from Halloween and featured her and Ramona dressed as sexy versions of Chip and Dale from the 1990s cartoon show, *Chip 'n Dale Rescue Rangers*. They wouldn't put that on the news. She hoped.

Shrugging these unproductive thoughts off, Claire examined her surroundings to see if any possibilities for escape presented themselves. There were no obviously sharp rocks or chunks of concrete on the floor, no shards of broken glass lying around. She turned her attention to the rows of metal shelving nearby. This appeared to be some kind of auto parts warehouse, and the shelves were filled with various mechanical parts and tools, none of which Claire had the slightest idea what they were used for. *Come on, Green, they're not gonna lock you up with anything you can obviously use to free yourself.* Still, she had to try.

The muscles in her back rippled and screamed in pain, but Claire engaged her core and executed her slowest, most awkward move from seated to standing. The world swam before her eyes, and her feet were still zip-tied together, so she had to move with precision. If she fell down, she wasn't sure she would be able to get up again.

Once she was standing and sure she wasn't going to immediately topple over, she began hopping toward the nearest set of tall metal shelves. Her first objective was simple: find something she could use to cut through the zip ties that bound her. *One thing at a time,* she reminded herself as her thoughts began to race away to what she would do once she could move more freely.

Unfortunately, everything Claire found looked blunt. She hopped down the length of the shelf, looking high and low and trying not to let the fact that she probably looked like a bunny hopping around a garden distract her. When she reached the end of the shelf, she turned down the next one, hopping and hoping as she went.

The only thing that kept her from laughing at how ridiculous she looked was the fact that she started to feel better as she moved. The ache in her muscles decreased, and while they were still sore and tight, they felt better with each little hop. Her headache still pounded, and the icy cold cement floor burned her bare feet, but she was moving and gaining speed with each hop.

The warehouse was poorly lit, with overheard lights spaced fairly far apart. The narrow windows nearly eighteen feet up likely provided the bulk of the illumination during the day. But now, in what was probably the middle of the night, everything on the shelves was dim, cast into shadow by the shelves above.

I could easily be missing something, Claire thought, coming to a halt. She turned around and started running her bound hands along the shelves she could reach, trying not to knock anything over and make a noise in the process. She wasn't sure how long her minders would leave her to her own devices, especially once they learned the results of whatever access codes Jack had given them.

Jack. The thought of him brought her up short and froze her in her tracks. *Silver Fist is Jack.* Something hard settled in her chest. Her mouth tasted bitter. Claire suddenly understood why Silver Fist had seemed so familiar the first time they met, back on the corner of Broadway and Wall Street. Now, with this newfound knowledge, she saw that whole encounter in a new light. Jack froze not because he didn't know how to respond to a Supervillain taking a civilian hostage but because that civilian hostage was her.

Claire blushed as she recalled how she'd noticed his lips at such an inappropriate moment. She and Jack had worked together to do something incredible, and that knowledge warmed her frozen core.

But then, his words came back to her and cut her like a knife: *"You did well."* Those words had fed daydreams and more than a few nighttime fantasies for eight years. They seemed to come from someone she admired and respected—and possibly even had a crush on. They were an acknowledgement of her worth from someone she wanted to emulate. But now, they felt condescending and even cheap. Of course she had done what she did. Jack should have expected no less from her. Once again, he had underestimated her.

Claire tried to refocus her mind on the task at hand. She continued her hop-search-repeat routine, running her hands along the shelves she could easily reach. But her thoughts drifted back to Jack and the way he had licked his lips before leaning in to whisper to her on that day eight years ago.

Is he seeing anyone? Claire wondered despite herself. The thought of someone else kissing those lips sent an unexpected stab of jealousy searing through her. But it had been twelve years since they broke up. It would only make sense that he would have moved on by now. *For all I know, he's married to another Superhero, and they have cute little Superbabies waiting for him at home.* Claire put the brakes on that thought even as a vice tightened around her chest. *Green, you're being weird and irrational. I blame the concussion.* No one carried a torch for their high-school flame at thirty. Jack had clearly moved on; it was high time she did as well.

And yet, admiration had burned so clearly in his eyes when she'd stood up to Vengeance back there. It was a familiar look, one that took her back to a time when the world seemed simpler and Superheroes were a distant dream, found only on the news and in Claire's imagination.

"Look at this nerd," an older boy sneered loudly. "He's so scrawny, he'll disappear if he turns sideways!"

The late-August Iowa heat was finally starting to dispel as night moved in, but the bright lights of the Roosevelt High School football stadium still lit up the sky as if it were day. Claire was standing under the home-team bleachers, sipping her Mountain Dew, and listening to her best friend, Annie, describe in minute detail her latest interaction with her crush, a senior boy who definitely didn't know the freshman girl existed.

Claire loved her friend but was honestly bored by the conversation. She was grateful that the shadows under the bleachers, the occasional roar of the crowd overhead, and the announcer's voice over the PA system negated the need for her to react much. However, at the sound of the mocking jeers nearby, her head shot up, and she scanned the area.

About fifteen feet away, near the edge of the bleachers, a group of older boys had surrounded the tall, gawky, painfully awkward freshman who always seemed to stand out due to his height, despite his best efforts to hunch his shoulders and disappear silently into the woodwork. Claire had English and geometry with him and even sat beside him in the latter, since their teacher assigned seats alphabetically by last name and there was no one with a last name that started with an 'F' in that class. Despite that, their only conversation had occurred when Claire dropped her eraser one day. They both bent down to pick it up at the same time, and their fingers brushed. The tall boy—Jack—immediately drew back as if she'd burned him. "Sorry," he'd muttered, turning away as his face heated to a brilliant red the color of Claire's hair.

Now, as the older boys circled him like a pack of wolves sensing easy prey, Claire knew what she had to do. "Just a second, Annie," she said to her best friend, placing her hand on the other girl's arm. "I gotta take care of something." Before Annie could respond, Claire was moving toward the bullies surrounding the shy, quiet freshman.

"You gotta be careful with this one," the pack leader said, gesturing to his victim. "He'll blow away in the wind." He reached out and shoved Jack, who stumbled backward and landed hard on the ground. The whole pack laughed.

Claire stepped up behind them, pitched her voice loud enough to carry over the cheering crowd overhead, and said, "Why don't you pick on someone your own size?"

The pack leader turned around and stared down at her for a moment before chuckling. "Go back to your parents, kid. This doesn't concern pint-sized shrimps."

"I'm actually a freshman at Roosevelt," Claire answer evenly, a slight smile hovering around her mouth. "And I was talking about the size of your dick."

The pack leader's eyes went wide. His followers all erupted in "Ooooooh!"s. Unnoticed behind them, Jack scrambled to his feet.

The bully's mouth opened and closed for a few seconds, as if struggling for a response that would allow him to regain control of the situation. Then, his eyes hardened, and his mouth twisted into a sneer. "Normally, I like fucking freshman girls. You know, pop their cherries first, before the other guys spoil them," he said. "But don't worry. You're safe. I don't go for girls with no tits. What would even be the point of fucking you? It'd be like fucking a dude."

"And what would be the point of fucking you?" Claire shot back. "It'd be like fucking my own little finger." She held up her hand, showing off how small and slender it was and waggling said digit.

The pack leader darted forward in a threatening move, but Claire was ready for him. In a single, smooth motion, she ducked to avoid his fist and drove her own into his stomach. He doubled over with a grunt, the wind knocked out of him. Claire finished him off with a knee to the groin. He collapsed to the ground, clutching himself and moaning softly.

Nobody moved for a moment. The other bullies stood frozen in place, not quite sure what just happened. Then, Claire stepped back and gestured to their fallen comrade. "Go ahead and help marshmallow balls here."

That did the trick. The other boys surrounded their leader and helped him up, carefully staying out of Claire's reach. They *hurried away, almost at a run, a few looking back in fear at the petite girl who had taken down their leader with just two moves.*

Claire called after them, "And remember: there's more where that came from, you idiotic shart tool bags!" She then turned and looked back at Jack, who lingered nearby. Even in the shadows under the bleachers, his eyes were bright with admiration. "Are you okay?" she asked.

He swallowed and nodded. "Yeah... yes," he said, clearing his throat. A gust of wind blew the scent of popcorn around them. "Thanks. That was incredible. You just swept in out of nowhere... like a Superhero!"

It was the most words she'd ever heard Jack string together at once, and the compliment warmed her heart. She grinned and winked. "Well, you never know where you'll find a Superhero. We're everywhere!"

Jack unconsciously licked his lips and said, "I'm glad you found me, then."

Three shelves away from her chair, Claire stumbled and fell, finally bringing her Bunny Hop routine to an end. The floor was dusty and cold, and she tried to stifle her gasp as she crashed down onto it. Her cheek landed on the edge of the bottom-most shelf. There was a gash in the metal there, and it tore her flesh just below where she'd gotten cut earlier on the harsh cement floor. She could feel the blood well up and quickly start running down her cheek; the warmth stood out in the cold air.

Despite her stinging cheek, excitement welled up within her. Claire twisted around awkwardly to get her bound hands to the sharp gash in the metal. It was a single rough edge the size of a quarter, but it was enough to break the skin on her cheek. It would have to do.

She started raking the zip ties back and forth across the metal and immediately froze at the loud grating noise it made. She listened hard, but could hear nothing beyond her own heart pounding in her head. No footfalls echoed through the warehouse. *Did they leave me alone in here?* she wondered for a moment. *No, it's more likely that the guards left behind are simply lazy. It can't be fun babysitting an unconscious prisoner.*

She resumed her work, going slowly to avoid making much noise, though her efforts weren't entirely successful. Claire raked her wrists and hands against the sharp metal edge several times, and her wrists were soon sticky with blood. Still, she could tell it was working.

After several minutes of sawing, she felt a *ping* against her wrists, and the thick plastic ties broke free. Claire immediately sat up and set about doing the same with the ties that bound her ankles, always keeping her ears trained on detecting even the slightest sound. Her wrists were sore and stiff, and she was sure they'd be bruised in the morning, but she kept going. She couldn't afford to stop now.

As soon as her feet were free, Claire stood up. So, of course, it was at that exact moment that she heard voices echoing from the far end of the warehouse.

These knuckleheads couldn't give me five more minutes to make my escape? she grumbled internally.

Claire slowly backed up and headed deeper into the warehouse, trying to get farther away from the entrance and the chair that the voices were heading toward. The one bright side of having her shoes and socks taken from her was that her bare feet were silent, so she was able to move quickly and lightly in the dark. When she reached the warehouse's far wall without ever once having found a door, she turned right and followed this wall. Every time she hurried into a trot, propelled forward by the need to get outside before the guards discovered she was gone, she forced herself to slow down.

Silence and stealth are more important than speed now, Green.

"Damn it, where'd she go?" a man's voice echoed through the large warehouse.

Shit. Too late.

"We gotta find her. Maybe she's still in here. She can't have been gone long. The boss'll kill us if we lose her now," the same voice said.

Claire couldn't make out what his fellow said, but she did detect a second voice. *Okay, so there are at least two of them. I can sneak past two numbskulls like these.*

And then what? a harsh voice within asked. *You don't know where you are, you're mixed up in Super business that's way above your pay grade, and you're barefoot without your cell phone or even a credit card. You're way out of your league here, Green.*

But there was Jack. That fact alone trumped everything. And when she had last seen him, he'd looked so lost and empty. Like he was drained of all purpose and hope. First, Claire had to save herself. Then, she would save Jack... Silver Fist... a Superhero.

By the time Claire was halfway across the room, it was so dark that she had to move at a snail's pace to avoid bumping into anything and knocking it over. As she felt her way forward, casting her arms out blindly to navigate her surroundings by touch, her fingers brushed across some kind of metallic shaft sticking out from one of the shelves. She paused, curious, and ran her hands along it.

Claire initially assumed the object was a wrench; it was about five or six inches long, with round openings at both ends, one much larger than the other. She could easily wrap her hand around the shaft and lift it. As she brought it close to her face to better examine it in the dim light, Claire realized with delight that she had stumbled upon a connecting rod for a piston. She had helped her dad work on his old muscle car enough as a teenager to recognize it. And now, it would serve as an ideal weapon.

Grasping the connecting rod, Claire continued down the aisle, but she was closer to the shelf than she realized and almost immediately stumbled into it. She cringed, dreading the loud noise that was sure to follow and give away her location, but to her surprise, there was only a muffled creak that didn't carry. She bent down and discovered what she had missed earlier: the shelves were bolted into the floor. Claire grabbed her newfound weapon and continued on. By the time she reached the wide central aisle that almost certainly led to the doors, she had a plan.

Claire could now hear both guards—there were definitely two of them—bumbling around among the shelves. The beams of their flashlights gave them away. She scurried to the far end of the warehouse and confirmed that the shelves were indeed bolted down here as well. Moving as quietly as possible, Claire slipped the connecting rod into the large pocket in her uniform pants and began climbing up the shelves by straddling the narrow walkway between the rows. When she reached the top, she had to crouch to avoid hitting her head on the ceiling, but from here, she had a clear view across the entire warehouse. As she'd suspected, the guards were between her and the door. *I really should have climbed up here from the start and made my way across the tops of the shelves*, she thought.

When Claire was satisfied that the two guards were far enough apart, she knocked several screws to the ground and then stood up on top of the shelves, straddling the walkway. She wiped her sweaty, bloody palms on her shirt, pulled her new weapon from her pocket, and gripped it tightly in her right hand. And waited.

As she'd hoped, the nearer of the two flashlights started to approach. Based on the direction of his beam of light, he was proceeding carefully, peering down each row before advancing, but he wasn't looking up. *Perfect.*

At long last, he turned down Claire's row. Tattoos snaked down his arms, emerging from his rolled-up sweatshirt sleeves, but his round, tan cheeks made him look young—too young to be doing this. He looked like he should still be in high school, not working for a Supervillain. Claire felt a little bad about what would happen next, but she had already committed to this path and had to see it through. Maybe her actions would be the wake-up call the kid needed to get out of this life and onto a better path.

He slowly advanced toward Claire, peering left and right but never up. She had to time this just right, and her aim had to be perfect. There would be no second chances.

When the young guy was directly beneath her, Claire braced her legs on the shelves, tightened her core like she never had before, and swung her right fist downward. The thick end of the piston rod in her hand connected squarely with his temple, as she hoped it would. He crashed to the ground, knocking things off the shelves around him, and lay still, unconscious. Years of martial arts training and EMT work told Claire that she had almost certainly given him a concussion. She just hoped it wasn't too severe.

Unfortunately, because Claire's palm was slick with blood, the piston connecting rod flew out of her hand as well and followed through its arc, launching itself past the face-down guard and clattering into another shelf. The resulting crash was truly impressive.

"Benny?" the guard who had spoken earlier called out. "That you?"

Now you've gone and done it, Green. Claire tried to silently scramble down the shelves, but her blood-slick right hand slipped, and she fell the last few feet, landing with a thud right beside the unconscious young man.

"Benny, you got her?" the man called out. His steps advanced quickly.

Claire scrambled up, grabbed her connecting rod, double-checked the direction the second guard was coming from, and dashed to the end of the shelves and around the corner. Her breathing sounded loud and ragged to her own ears, and she tried to hide it by holding her breath—which didn't work, of course. She transferred the rod to her left hand to wipe her right on her dirty, dusty EMT uniform pants. It came away sticky. She pressed herself against the back of the shelf and tried to prepare for whatever might happen next.

The second guard's flashlight beam turned down the row she had just exited, and his gasp rang out. "Benny, what happened?" There was some shuffling, and Claire could imagine him turning the younger man over. This was followed by, "Okay, lady. I know you're around here. You got a lucky shot on Benny, but you're not gonna get one on me. Come on out, and maybe we'll go easy on you."

His steps slowly advanced toward Claire's position, and she swallowed, trying to wet her parched mouth. As good as Claire knew she was—and she *was* good—she felt way out of her league. Sure, she had decades of martial arts experience under her belt, but at the end of the day, she was used to fighting in adjudicated matches with rules, protective equipment, time limits, and a clear scoring system. Once a match was called, everyone shook hands and walked away. But here, there were no points, no referees. This was a real fight with real consequences. This was what real Superheroes had to do almost every single day. This was what *Jack* had to do.

Jack, I'm coming for you, Claire thought, steeling herself.

When the man was inches away from rounding the corner and spotting her, Claire stepped out and spun in one motion, swinging the rod toward the guard. He must have suspected she was there, though, because he jumped back, narrowly missing getting hit. The connecting rod again slipped from her bloody palm and crashed to the ground behind her opponent. She was now weaponless and face-to-face with a large man with a... That's when it registered: he didn't have a gun. This whole time, Claire had assumed he would.

They stared at each other for a moment, then both moved at once, closing in toward each other. He reached out to grab her, but Claire used her shorter stature against him by crouching and slamming into his hips with all her might like a football player. She didn't have a lot of weight on her side, but given his height and higher center of gravity, it wouldn't take much to throw him off-balance.

It worked. The second guard tipped over backward and landed on top of Benny. Claire came crashing down on top of him, and they were caught in a tangle of limbs. The guy hadn't showered in a while and smelled strongly of BO and taco sauce—probably spilled on his New York Jets sweatshirt. Claire tried to scramble up, but he grabbed her hair, holding her in place. Her fingers reached out, grasping for something, anything, she could use as a weapon.

The guard sat upright and drew her up with him, tugging painfully on her hair, just as her fingers closed around something large and metallic. She had no idea what it was, but she grabbed it, brought it up, and smashed it against the larger man's temple with all her might. He roared in pain and released her hair, and Claire pushed herself back and away from her opponent. This was not going as planned. The element of surprise was gone, as was any hope of a stealthy escape. She simply needed to get out. Now.

Claire turned and raced toward the exit, but the second guard was already moving as well, in hot pursuit. She was lighter and faster, but he had longer legs. Still, she charged ahead with everything she had, not even feeling the cold floor on her bare feet. Her ragged breath ached in her dry, parched throat. She was almost to the wide double doors that signaled her freedom. She reached out, ready to shove them aside and burst through.

Then, suddenly, something grabbed her hair and yanked her backward. The bile of frustration rose in her throat as she crashed into the guard coming up behind her. *I was so close! I was so damned close!* A sob escaped her lips despite herself.

The guard yanked her head back painfully, forcing her to look up at him as he loomed above and behind her. Whatever Claire had hit him with had opened a large gash in his forehead, and blood ran freely down his face. "You little bitch," he barked. "I'm gonna make you pay for this." He slammed her forward into the cinder-block wall beside the door, and the cut on her cheeked reopened and started to bleed again.

Claire struggled, pushing against the cinder-block wall with all her might, but it was no use. This guard was physically large and experienced at dealing with prisoners. She had caught him off guard once, but she wouldn't be able to again.

Tough luck, Green. You gambled, and you lost. Now, you have to pay the price. Claire squeezed her eyes shut. Tears leaked out. *Sorry, Jack. I wasn't fast enough. I guess you were right... I really can't do everything myself...*

There was a cool breeze, and then, something solid impacted the man behind Claire. He released his grip on her hair and went flying backward. He landed with a heavy thump and did not move.

Claire spun around to see who had come to her rescue. *The cavalry has arrived! The other Superheroes have come to...*

The thought trailed off into embarrassed nothingness. Standing there before her, bruised and bloody, was Jack. His bare fist was still clenched from punching the guard, and he glared down at the man for a moment before turning toward Claire. His eyes softened when they met hers.

Claire took one step toward him and said the first thing that came into her mind: "Jack, are you okay?"

His mouth fell open ever so slightly. "I—am *I* okay?" he echoed incredulously. "Are *you*—"

She cut him off. "I was coming to rescue you," she said in a rush, gesturing uselessly at the guard. "I was having a bit of trouble with this guy, but I took care of the first one, no problem."

Jack blinked once. Twice. "I swear to god, Claire Green, you're going to be the death of me," he said and then quickly stepped forward and pulled her into a sudden warm embrace.

Claire was surprised at the contact but immediately and gratefully sank into it. He was dirty and bloody and sweaty, and yet, he smelled familiar. His arms around her were large and muscular—far more so than she remembered—but Claire fit into them just as well as she had when she'd been a nervous sixteen-year-old undressing in front of him for the first time at her parents' lake cabin. Unbidden, the word *home* danced through her mind. She allowed her exhausted eyes to drift closed, and a soft sigh escaped her lips.

That was apparently too much, because Jack stepped back and broke the spell. "We can't stick around. We have to get out of here before Vengeance and his men get back," he said, grabbing her hand and tugging her through the double doors that had represented her salvation. They emerged in a long, dark corridor, and Jack raced down it, dragging Claire in his wake.

Claire struggled to keep up with him. Jack had always been tall with a long stride, but he had grown taller in the intervening years, and his stride had only increased to match. Claire yanked her hand out of his to better jog after him. He glanced back when she did so, but didn't complain or try to retake her hand. It was probably hard for him to move as well, towing a woman a foot-and-a-half shorter than him behind him. They were better off moving on their own.

And don't you forget it, a voice in her head cautioned.

Claire shook the voice away. "Where are we? How do we get out of here?" she asked as she jogged along behind him.

"A warehouse out on Staten Island," he said.

"Staten Island? How did we get out—" Claire cut herself off. "Never mind. Supervillain powers. Folding space. The whole deal. Got it."

The hallway ended with a sharp right turn. Jack paused, pressed his back flat against the wall, and put an arm out to stop her. She matched his posture, making herself flat against the painted cinder-block wall beside him. He peered around the corner, checking for enemies. Apparently, he saw none because he advanced down the corridor, beckoning for Claire to follow him. "That also means he'll probably be back any minute now," Jack said. "We have to find an exit."

This hallway led to a dirty, run-down office area. Claire assumed that one of the doors led to the dingy break room they'd been in earlier. It looked like they would need to investigate at least some of the doors to find the way out. Claire was about to sigh in frustration when she noticed a broken unlit red 'Exit' sign.

She beckoned for Jack to follow her, but he quickly put himself in the lead. Claire bristled at the motion, and her mouth turned down into a frown, but she settled for following behind him—for now. He may have reverted to being just Jack in her eyes, but he was still Silver Fist, and they were still in his world.

The door opened onto an alley, and they slipped out into the night.

Chapter 6

J ack stepped outside, inhaling a lungful of air that smelled
equally of diesel and the ocean. The stars shone overheard,
and a full moon illuminated their position far better than he had
anticipated. Jack took a half-step back into the shadows of the
warehouse doorway and considered their position.

They had come out into an alley that ran between long
rows of warehouses. Dotted with metal dumpsters, rubbish,
chunks of concrete, and various other debris, the alley looked
like any in an industrial area. But the brisk November night
air sent a shock wave through Jack and reminded him of
where they were: outdoors in New York in the winter with
minimal protective clothing. Jack was warm enough, thanks to
the thermal additions to his costume, but Claire was already
shivering beside him.

Jack glanced back at Claire and realized that he'd have to get her to safety—and warmth—quickly. She was barefoot and without a coat. Her practical heavy-duty uniform pants looked warm enough, but her shirt was torn wide-open at the shoulder. She stood on the uneven concrete on her tiptoes to protect her feet from the freezing ground, even as she craned her neck to scan the alleyway. He wasn't used to having to look out for someone while on the job, and he knew for a fact that Claire didn't want to be "looked after" like a child. In fact, even the slightest hint that he was doing so was sure to send her into paroxysms of anger.

And we don't want to go through that again, he thought bitterly. *Once was enough to last a lifetime.*

Noticing Jack's hesitation, Claire turned her face up toward his. She raised her eyebrows and tilted her head to the side, as though to say, *Are we going or what?*

Steeling himself for Claire's almost-certain protest, Jack bent down and swept her up into his arms. He was surprised by how light she felt. He hadn't held her in his arms in over a decade, and he had forgotten just how petite she was.

As he set off down the alleyway, Claire squirmed in protest, and Jack whispered, "You're barefoot. We won't get far if you slice your foot open on a piece of glass or break your toe on a cinder block."

To Jack's surprise, Claire simply nodded and wrapped her arms securely around his neck. He'd assumed she would put up more of a fight at being carried like a damsel in distress. Perhaps she was more seriously injured than he thought. He certainly didn't want to entertain the notion that she actually *liked* this close physical contact. That would only lead to traitorous thoughts and impossible hopes, all of which would bring him back to where he'd been twelve years ago as an eighteen-year-old watching what he thought was the love of his life walk away. Her parting words echoed in his head: *"Get out of my life. I don't need you to fight my battles for me."* Jack swallowed the growing lump in his throat and pushed the memory away.

Still, feeling her small, yet muscular arms creep up and around his neck made something tighten in Jack's stomach. He shook his head as if to clear it and forced himself to focus on their surroundings as he made his way down the alley. He couldn't afford to get lost in the sensation of Claire's cold fingers grazing the sensitive skin at the nape of his neck. Or the warm puffs of her breath against his jaw. Or the fact that his fingers were just brushing the side of her breast. Or—

They reached the end of the alley, and Jack heard voices bouncing off the sides of the industrial buildings that ran along the street before them. One of the voices had a British accent. In an instant, the warm feelings that had been creeping up from his stomach were doused with ice water, and he came to a halt.

Claire must have heard them, too, because she tapped his shoulder and pointed to a large rusty dumpster to their left. There was just enough space between it and the brick wall behind it for two people to squeeze into. Hiding there would make escape difficult if they were spotted, but it would also provide ample cover.

"Hold onto me," he whispered, lowering her legs and wrapping both arms around her waist. Her feet dangled above the litter-strewn ground, but she tightened her core, making it easy for him to hold onto her, especially with her arms wrapped tightly around his neck. As one, they slipped behind the dumpster.

The dumpster was not perfectly parallel to the brick wall, and the angle got tighter as they moved deeper into the shadows. Jack squeezed them into the narrow space, and when he could go no farther, he lowered Claire to the ground. "Stand on my feet," he said, keeping his voice low. She nodded and slid down his body until her weight rested on his booted feet. Despite the cold and the imminent danger they were in, he silently groaned at the feeling of her warmth slowly gliding down his torso, her breasts pressed against his chest. His athletic cup grew very tight; this wasn't the first time he was grateful for it, but it was the first time he'd needed it to preserve his—and someone else's—modesty. He was sure that his cheeks were blazing, and he silently thanked the darkness that enveloped him.

Not wanting to look at Claire while his heart still beat a wild rhythm inside him, Jack peaked out between the wall and the dumpster. He only had a few inches of visibility, and the dim light on the street wasn't helping matters, but he could tell that the voices were indeed getting closer.

The warmth of Claire's body pressed closer as she wrapped her arms around his waist. Her icy-cold fingers came to a rest against his lower back, but they burned his skin like a brand. He turned his head to look down at her. He couldn't see her face clearly in the dim light, but he could see the dried blood on her cheek and chin, darker than the rest of her skin. It looked like she'd gotten a second cut on her cheek at some point since Vengeance had tortured her in front of him, and as his eyes landed on it, an iron band tightened around his chest, making it hard to breathe. As if sensing his gaze, she looked up at him, and their eyes locked. He realized that their breathing had synchronized, flowing in and out together. His body seemed to be reacting to her presence and her pain in a way he couldn't control. It made him nervous. He didn't like feeling out of control.

Claire shivered, and her teeth rattled together aloud. Jack's arms came up to wrap around her shoulders before he even knew they were moving. By the time they settled around her, pulling her even more firmly against his chest, Jack was mentally kicking himself. *I'm just keeping her warm*, he told himself. *I don't want her to give away our position before we can retreat. That's all*. Of course, that didn't stop his fingers from gently caressing her upper back. The cotton of her long-sleeved T-shirt was thin, and when his hand grazed the bare skin of her shoulder, it was like ice.

Claire buried her face in his chest as another shiver traveled down her spine, and Jack wasn't entirely sure if it was due to the cold or to his caresses. *I'm just keeping her warm*, he repeated to himself, tightening his arms around her. He prayed that she hadn't noticed how his heart rate picked up when she pressed herself against him.

He had thought that watching Claire being tortured earlier was difficult. This was a million times worse. He tried to remind himself that Claire had broken his heart and stomped on it as she walked away, that he wanted nothing to do with her, and that they were in the middle of a daring escape from the lair of a Supervillain. But his body wouldn't listen. With the cold brick wall behind him and Claire's warmth in front of him, he wanted to relax and melt into her embrace. He wanted to enjoy this stolen moment.

Jack lowered his face to as close to the top of her head as he could get and quietly inhaled her scent. If this moment was all they would have together, he wanted to store it up as best he could. It needed to last for the rest of his life. He closed his eyes and focused on the feeling of her in his arms, rememorizing the way she fit against him. He had grown taller in the intervening years and bulked up quite a bit, but she had also changed, feeling more muscular and firm against him.

Vengeance's voice boomed from close by, quieting the tumult of emotions and sensations that threatened to overthrow Jack. "The second we get back, bring the girl to the conference room and execute her in front of that damned liar. He needs to know that we mean business!" Vengeance thundered.

Jack turned his head to look out of the crack between the wall and the dumpster. He felt Claire's head, still resting against his chest, turn as well.

Vengeance and five henchmen passed within six feet of the dumpster. Claire silently sucked in a breath, and Jack's arms tightened around her. The group passed out of his field of view as quickly as they had entered it. He and Claire probably had about five or ten minutes at most before the Supervillain and his goons discovered that Jack and Claire were missing.

Claire started to pull away as soon as Vengeance and his group had passed, but Jack held her in place against his chest. "Wait," he whispered. "They need to get a bit farther away before we move." He kept his gaze on the street beyond, and Claire settled back against him, wrapping her arms around his waist again. She leaned into him just as another shiver racked her body.

As immediate danger retreated, awareness crept back into Jack's body. He and Claire were still breathing in unison, but their breaths had become somewhat shallow and rapid. She was warm and soft against him, and his hands again started to move, caressing her back. Her hands began tracing tiny circles on the small of his back, mirroring his motions.

He glanced down again and saw that her eyes were closed as her head rested against his chest. As if sensing his gaze, her eyes fluttered open, and she pulled back to meet it. As dark as the alley was, Jack could see the gleam of her eyes. He raised his hand and was relieved that it didn't shake as he cupped her cold, bloodied cheek. The stickiness of dried blood under his thumb stopped him from rubbing it along her skin.

Claire tipped her head ever so slightly to lean into his touch. She licked her lips—unconsciously, he hoped—and his eyes darted down to them. His stomach clenched, and a warmth rushed through his body. Despite being in peak physical condition, his heart was racing like he had just run a marathon, and his pulse thundered in his ears.

In that moment, their surroundings vanished. Jack was no longer aware of the cold, his aching muscles, or his pounding headache. He couldn't think. He didn't want to think. His mind and lungs were full of Claire. Her name escaped his lips in a soft puff before he was even aware of opening them.

Later, neither of them would be able to say who moved first. Claire pressed herself up on her tiptoes at the same moment that he leaned down to capture her lips.

Her lips were chapped, like his, and she tasted of smoke and blood and warmth and home. The kiss was chaste, but in the brief moment where their lips met, time stopped, and the cold, dirty alley outside of New York City melted away, replaced by the dense July heat of an Iowa summer and the taste of blue-raspberry slushies from the gas station and Claire's lips on his as they sat on an old quilt in Ellis Park along the Cedar River, waiting for the Fourth of July fireworks to start.

With a gasp, Claire broke away, and the sensation ended. Time resumed its normal flow, and they were back in the cold and grime of the wintry city. Oddly, her cheek still felt hot under his cupped palm, as though it had been warmed by the Iowa summer sun. She looked up at him, her eyes wide. She was breathing heavily—much more heavily than the light kiss warranted.

Jack could have kicked himself. Claire was injured and freezing, they were just steps away from the warehouse they were trying to escape, and they were still in danger. They could have been caught, yet he'd thrown caution to the wind and let his guard down. Such behavior showed a major lack of caution—on both their parts. It was unprofessional, undisciplined, unadvisable. Plus, it had been more than a decade since Claire made it clear that she was done with him, yet here he was, delighting in the sensation of holding her in his arms like they were teenagers behind the bleachers of a high school football game.

He dropped his hand from her face. "We should move," he whispered, praying his voice wouldn't break. "We aren't safe here."

Claire nodded and released her arms from around his waist. He immediately felt colder out of her embrace. She threaded her arms around his neck once more so he could pick her up and carry her out of their narrow hiding place, but her motions felt professional, all-business. As they slipped back out into the alley, he scooped her up again, but it wasn't the same. It was like carrying a ghost who was no longer there.

Jack paused at the edge of the alley, ensuring that the coast was clear. As he peered around the corner onto the larger road, Claire asked quietly, "Where to now?"

"We need to lie low," he said, starting down the road. "Luckily, I know a place nearby. Hold on tight." He started to jog and quickly picked up speed despite the extra hundred pounds in his arms.

Blood thundered in Jack's ears as he ran, but not due to the exercise. *We just escaped a dangerous situation*, he assured himself. *Our adrenaline was running high. We were carried away by the moment. That kiss was simple animal urges in the face of death. That's all.*

Claire tightened her grip around his neck. *She's only holding on so tightly for safety's sake. She isn't doing it because she enjoys being in my arms. And neither do I. That kiss meant nothing.*

But another, quieter voice whispered in response, *Liar.*

Chapter 7

After about fifteen minutes of Superpowered running, they reached a rundown area of crumbling brick storefronts and row houses, all of which flew past Claire in a blur of neon signs and broken and flickering streetlights.

They eventually came to a stop in an alley that ran between rows of rowdy bars and smelled of urine and vomit. Jack was barely even breathing hard. The loud thrum of a deep bass beat echoed up and down the alley, and the cheers of men having a good time followed in its wake. Before them was a dingy metal door with a sign that read: "Trixie's Lounge—Employees Only."

Claire raised her eyebrow at the sight of the sign but said nothing. She pushed lightly against Jack in anticipation of him releasing her, but he tightened his grip and held her in place against his chest. "Too much broken glass out here," he said in response to her unasked question. "Don't worry. I got you."

He walked up to the door and kicked it three times. A moment later, it swung open, letting the deep thumping bass spill out into the alley. A tall man with thick arms, lot of tattoos, and a red beard stood in the doorway, partially blocking the light, for which Claire was grateful. After running through the darkened streets, the bright lights inside were almost blinding. The man looked them both over carefully, raised an eyebrow, and cocked his head inward, motioning them inside. Jack hurried past him, and the bouncer—for that's what Claire assumed he was—looked both ways up and down the alley before bolting the door shut behind them.

As Jack released her, finally allowing her feet to touch the ground again, Claire found herself in a tiny back hallway. To her left was a door propped slightly open by a brick. Through it, Claire could just make out a large room filled with makeup mirrors, lights, and a half-naked woman reapplying her lipstick.

Jack had brought her to a strip club.

Before Claire could tease Jack about his choice of hideout, a red-painted door on the other side of the hallway swung open, and a tall, lean woman with a shaved head, dressed in a black business suit, and sporting colorful, glittery makeup and long hot-pink nails that didn't really match the rest of her no-nonsense appearance stepped out. She took one look at both of them and said, "Inside," in a light Caribbean accent that Claire couldn't quite place.

The woman waved them into what was apparently her office. A large desk was covered with a brand-new expensive-looking laptop as well as piles of receipts, order forms, and forms with official seals from the City and State of New York. In sharp contrast to the businesslike desk were the walls covered with posters featuring scantily clad women promising cheap drinks, shelves full of lingerie in every imaginable shape, size, cut, and color, and a liberal amount of glitter sprinkled everywhere.

"Regina, this is Claire. Claire, Regina," Jack said by way of introduction once the door was closed.

"Trixie's my stage name," she with a smile, as though that explained everything.

"We need to lie low for a bit. And I need to make some calls," Jack said, walking toward the back of the room. "I'm glad I caught you here tonight."

Regina groaned and rolled her eyes. "You never come by just to see me," she said, turning to her desk. "And you know where the gear is. You don't need me to give you the grand tour." She pulled out the bottom drawer, which was filled with hanging folders, pushed those back, and revealed a hidden compartment completely filled with cell phones. She pulled one out at random and threw it to Jack. "This is all going on your tab," she said, straightening.

Jack waited at the back of the room by a large standing wardrobe. "As always," he said with a charming grin that made Claire's insides churn with an emotion she refused to call jealousy.

Regina stalked toward Jack and paused immediately in front of him—far closer than seemed necessary to Claire. The club owner looked up into his eyes and reached toward him, her fingertips just brushing his forearm. Claire's heart thudded to a halt in her chest, and she couldn't breathe. She felt her face heat, and her scalp prickled. She wasn't sure what she was seeing, but she knew she didn't want to see it.

Before Claire could avert her eyes, Regina's hand continued forward, past Jack, and she pulled open the wardrobe door behind him. Pushing aside a variety of trench coats, many of which had liberal amounts of glitter coating the insides, she fumbled with something Claire couldn't see. Then, the back of the wardrobe swung open, revealing a dusty opening with a set of steep stairs going up.

"Thanks a million, Gina," Jack said with a smile as he crossed the room, heading back toward Claire. He grabbed her hand and dragged her into the secret passageway.

The space was all brick, with no lights. Before she closed the door behind them, Regina handed Claire a flashlight. It was all they had to light their way up the rickety stairs. The thump of the bass beat in here as well.

"What is this place?" Claire asked, starting up the stairs.

"A safehouse. Regina has Superpowers herself, so we'll be okay here."

Claire made the mistake of looking back at Jack in surprise. She stumbled on the steep steps and had to grab the railing so she wouldn't fall backward onto him. After seeing his little exchange with Regina downstairs, her heart and her mind were in a tumult, and she feared that touching him now would crack something open inside her that she didn't want to address. She turned around and kept climbing.

Jack continued, "She discovered that her powers involved enticing others. Specifically, others that are attracted to women.

That's all she needed. It got her out of the slums in Haiti and into the US. Today, she owns sixteen strip clubs all across the city. Every single one of them is a safehouse for Superheroes who need to lie low for a bit."

When Claire reached the top of the flight, the stairs turned 180 degrees and continued on up to the third floor. She was tempted to ask whether Regina had ever *enticed* him, but she also knew she didn't want to hear the answer. She remained quiet and climbed.

At the top of the stairs, there was a heavy metal door. Claire pushed it open to reveal a small, but surprisingly tidy room. She stepped inside, and Jack followed, flicking on a light switch to illuminate the space. A large futon occupied one wall. Opposite it stood a tall wardrobe, several chests of drawers, and a mini fridge. Jack advanced on that and pulled out two bottles of water. He handed Claire one and then closed the door behind them, drawing the four bolts closed. With the door closed, they could barely hear the beat of the music two floors below.

We're tucked in tight, Claire thought.

She hadn't realized how thirsty she was until she held the cold, sweating bottle in her hands. Claire twisted off the cap and drank greedily, letting the chilled water dribble down her chin. She didn't care how undignified she looked; the crystal-cold water felt amazing on her parched throat.

When she had quenched her thirst, Claire lowered the bottle, sighed, and tipped her head back in relief. Her eyes locked with Jack's, who lowered his own bottle at the same moment. A jolt ran through her, just like when she first recognized him in the bank. Claire couldn't believe that had only been a few hours ago. It felt more like years.

Seeing Jack like this, standing here in a normal-looking room, dressed in his Superhero attire—minus his mask—released something in Claire that she'd been holding back. A dam broke inside, and thoughts, ideas, questions, and worries rushed to the surface en masse, all demanding immediate attention. She advanced on him, her mouth already open, though she had no idea what would come out first.

He must have seen the look in her eyes because he raised his hands in defense. "I can explain," he started.

"You're Silver Fist!" she snapped. Jack cringed. "You're a Superhero! You—who never gave two shits about Superheroes! *You* got powers!" Her chest heaved with anger and resentment. She let the unspoken *and I didn't* hang in the air. "And you never reached out, never told me!"

"I know. And I'm sorry. I should have—"

"And it's not like you didn't know how to find me! My god, Jack, I was literally standing right in front of you! I elbowed a Supervillain in the face, and you still couldn't—" she cut herself off. She wasn't sure where this diatribe was going, but she knew she didn't want to follow it all the way to the end. Just as she knew it wasn't really about Jack at all.

"I know it's a lot to take in, and I can explain everything," Jack said, approaching her with his palms out, as if she were a wild animal that might attack him at any moment.

You're still protecting me, she thought bitterly, eying him up and down. She crossed her arms and turned away to gather her thoughts.

As she did so, Jack sucked in a sudden harsh breath.

"What's wrong?" Claire started to turn back to him, but Jack's hand on her shoulder stilled her.

"Step into the light a bit more," he said, guiding her toward the middle of the room.

Gentle fingers on her scalp parted her hair, and a sharp stinging sensation shot through her. She hissed.

"That looks nasty," Jack said, crouching to examine the back of her head. "There's a lot of blood here. I was worried when I saw your head hit the ground more than once."

At his words, Claire's headache roared back into her awareness. It had been there all along, quietly thrumming like annoying background noise. But now, she couldn't ignore it any longer. "Head wounds do bleed a lot, but I may have a concussion," she acknowledged. "Of course, that could be from my fight with Vengeance's goons back at my apartment.""Your what?" Jack asked, sounding alarmed. He gently spun her around to face him again.

Claire quickly detailed her encounter with Zoe and the hired muscle and her decision to go to the bank and warn Ramona. Jack's face drained of color as she spoke. His jaw worked furiously in that familiar way it did when Jack was upset about something but didn't want to voice his thoughts.

The only part of the story she left out was the disturbing moment of lost time, when she went from being pinned to sitting before an unconscious Zoe and Sucker-Punch without the slightest idea of how she got there. She still needed to analyze that gap in her memory and figure out what happened. Memory loss was a common symptom of concussion, but something about this seemed…different. That missing space had what Claire could only describe as a flavor, one akin to black licorice. It was almost like a gap in time that had been sewn shut, rather than being the result of head trauma.

Green, you're not helping your case. It's definitely a concussion… right?

Regardless, given how stricken Jack already looked, Claire doubted that hearing about her missing memories would help matters.

When she had finished, Jack nodded once, though his eyes took on a faraway look. "That does explain matters," he said, though Claire noticed that he didn't elaborate. Then, his eyes returned to her face. He seemed to be studying her, and Claire realized he was examining the size and movement of her pupils. When he was done, he nodded again. "Looks good. Pupil size and movement are normal. And you clearly aren't struggling with loss of coordination or confusion. Still, we should get you to a hospital, but I don't want to move you until I'm sure it's safe. Vengeance and his henchmen will likely be combing the immediate area, so we need to lie low for now."

Claire nodded and felt the fight go out of her. She was exhausted, running on pure adrenaline, beaten, bruised, bloody, cold, sore, barefoot, and probably concussed. She had been threatened, abducted, and tortured. She had escaped, overpowered one of her captors, discovered that her ex-boyfriend was a Superhero, and shared a highly inappropriate kiss with him in a filthy alley behind a dumpster—a lapse of judgement that was probably due to the concussion. Her emotional reserves were tapped out, and all she wanted at this point was to sleep for a million years. Supervillains and explanations could wait.

Jack must have seen at least some of this in her eyes because he stepped forward and enveloped her in his arms. "It'll be okay. You'll be okay," he murmured into her hair.

For some reason, that undid Claire, and she started dry sobbing into his chest. She was so dehydrated that she couldn't produce any tears, but that didn't stop her from trying. Her chest heaved, her fists pulled at and clenched around his spandex suit, and she buried her face fully in his chest, using it to stifle the sounds of her shuddering sobs. Her knees felt weak, but Jack wrapped his arms more firmly around her, holding her up and to him.

"It's okay," he whispered. "Let it go."

She unleashed all of the past day's terror and stress, her body convulsing around the huge waves of emotion that passed through her. All the while, Jack rubbed soft circles into her back and muttered reassurances that all would be well.

Eventually, Claire's sobs died down. Everything in her seemed to go quiet for the first time all day. She didn't want to move from her place nestled against Jack's chest just yet, so she kept her eyes closed and basked in the comfort of his strong arms around her. She could hear his heart pounding under her ear, and to her surprise, it seemed to be beating unusually fast.

Claire pulled back and looked up at him. He smiled down at her, and there was no judgement in his eyes. If anything, they were soft and warm and reminded her of home.

This was the first time Claire had been able to really study Jack's face. Despite the bruises, it was an even more handsome face than it had been twelve years ago. His jaw was stronger now and more defined. His nose had been broken at some point since then, but it just made him look more dangerous. His bright-blue eyes hadn't changed a bit, though. They were still the same pools of emotion they had always been. They now glistened suspiciously as he gazed down at her.

"I'll tell you what," he said, his voice deep and low. It sent shivers of anticipation down her spine. "You take a shower and get cleaned up. I need to make some calls. Then, when you're done, I promise I'll tell you everything."

Claire studied Jack's face carefully. It was completely open and honest. "Calls to your Superhero buddies?" she asked as neutrally as she could.

He smiled and nodded. "We now know what Vengeance is after: the Elite Five's headquarters. We need to organize to take him down."

Claire nodded in return and swallowed the lump rising in her throat. "We" didn't include her; her part in this story was over. Once the coast was clear, she would go to the hospital and get checked out while all the other Superheroes in New York converged in a huge, glorious mission to take down Vengeance once and for all. And she would get to watch it on TV in the ER. As usual.

She gave Jack a tight smile and stepped away from him. "You better be here when I come out," she cautioned, pointing a stern finger in his direction. "I want to hear the whole story. I don't often get to talk with a real Superhero about how they got their powers, you know."

He smiled back, but his was full and open. "I promise."

Claire ducked into the bathroom, trying not to think about that smile or about how good it had felt to be in Jack's arms. She tried to focus on the bright side: Vengeance would soon be in custody, and it would be safe for her and Ramona to return home. She'd have to buy a new laptop, but she had a birthday coming up and could always use her birthday money from her parents. And maybe she and Jack—

Claire cut that thought off sharply as she turned on the bathroom light. She refused to go down that road. It would only lead to heartache and regret. Again.

Claire looked around the small bathroom. It wasn't much, but it had a surprisingly large tub/shower combination, probably to accommodate all the random needs of different Superheroes.

As she stepped toward the vanity mirror, Claire gasped at what she saw; she looked even worse than anticipated. Her top was dirty and torn, and much of her long hair had escaped her ponytail, which had been yanked around so much that it was almost pulled to the side of her head. The two lacerations on her cheekbone were a dark maroon color, and her entire right cheek and chin were stained red with blood. She had also acquired a large bruise on her forehead somewhere along the way, which would probably be a goose egg the next day. Looking down, she saw that her feet were filthy—almost black—and that the big toenail on her left foot had been ripped clean off, leaving the whole toe bloody. Her wrists and ankles were also lacerated where she had tugged on her bindings.

Green, you look like hell, she thought.

She carefully stripped off her clothes and removed her hair elastic, hissing when she brushed the wound on the back of her head. Her hair was sticky with blood.

The warm water of the shower felt unbelievably delicious on her body, though it stung wherever it touched an open cut or wound—and there were a great many of those. There was soap, shampoo, and conditioner in the shower, as well as a large stack of clean washcloths. Claire took her time and carefully cleaned all her cuts and abrasions. That done, she washed her hair, scrupulously avoiding touching her scalp. As it was, the shampoo sent shockwaves of pain through her as she slowly massaged her hair, trying to wash the dried blood out.

She took longer than she meant to in the shower, but by the time she stepped out, Claire felt like a new woman. Her headache had all but disappeared, her sore muscles were somewhat soothed, and she was more relaxed than she had been in over twenty-four hours.

As she toweled off, Claire spotted a pile of clean, neatly folded clothing sitting just inside the door. Investigating, she found that it contained a pair of black leggings, a black tank top with a shelf bra, a red T-shirt bearing the Hard Rock Cafe logo, and a pair of panties that appeared to be her size. Claire smiled as she looked over them. She hadn't even heard Jack come in.

Jack... She let the thought linger and trail off into nothingness for a moment. *Maybe when this is all over... when I'm not exhausted and strung out... Maybe then, we can have a coffee and talk and...*

She didn't know how she wanted to end that thought, so she let it go, unfinished.

Chapter 8

Jack's heart was still beating faster than it ought when Claire closed the bathroom door behind her. He released a breath he didn't know he was holding and slumped down onto the futon, cradling his head in his hands.

Oh, Jack, you're really in it now.

His head and heart were a mass of confusion. He could still feel her in his arms, coming unraveled in a way he knew she hated for others to see. Even after everything that had happened between them, she trusted him enough to sob on his chest.

And what was that look in her eyes downstairs when he was talking to Regina? Jack refused to call it jealousy because that would imply she felt something for him that could merit such emotions. He wouldn't, *couldn't* let himself believe such things. Claire was his past, and while fate—and Supervillains—had brought them together again in the present, that didn't mean she was his future. Their paths had diverged long ago.

Then why are you still thinking about her? a voice asked from deep within.

Traitorous fingers rose to his lips and ghosted over the spot where she had kissed him. He wanted to store that moment in the alley in a velvet-lined box in the back of his mind so he could take it out and revisit it whenever he felt alone in the dead of night—which was, admittedly, often. In such moments, Claire frequently appeared in his thoughts, and he basked in the bright sunlight of the good times they'd shared.

There had been other women, of course. Jack wasn't a monk. He was tall, fit, and good-looking, and women often passed him their number in a variety of creative ways. But nothing ever went beyond a handful of dates and maybe a few nights together. Part of the problem—a large part—was that he couldn't talk about his job. Secret identities are secret for a reason, and Jack didn't enjoy having to lie to the woman he was sleeping with about where he went all day and how he earned a living. But another part of him—a part he tried to keep hidden even from himself—knew that the real problem was that none of those women were Claire.

He had a type, and he knew it. Most of the women he did date were athletic, on the petite side, and often with red or blonde hair. When one of his buddies in the army had jokingly pointed out that Jack "went for the short chicks," he'd laughed it off. By the time Giada was teasing him about "being into redheads," he knew he was in trouble. He had to move on, but Claire had imprinted herself on him in a way he could never wash away.

The sound of the shower turning on in the bathroom drew Jack out of his thoughts. He scrubbed his face with his hands and sighed. He needed to put on his business face and make that call.

The burner phone he'd left on top of the mini-fridge taunted him. Anyone else would have missed the bitterness on Claire's face and in her voice when she'd asked about his "Superhero buddies," but Jack didn't. He recognized the tightening at the corners of her mouth and the way her voice seemed strained, as if she were fighting for control.

He realized the unfairness of it all. Claire had been hoping for—expecting, even—Superpowers since she was a kid. She'd spent her whole life training and preparing for such an outcome. She chose sports and activities in high school that would benefit her as a Superhero: martial arts, gymnastics, pole vaulting. Unfortunately, she had never developed Superpowers. Meanwhile, Jack had little interest in Superheroes. He preferred books and video games. Sure, he had always been tall, but he disliked sports and anything that put him too obviously on display. Their high school basketball coach approached him every year, trying to convince him to try out for the team, but he always declined. He preferred the behind-the-scenes roles: newspaper staff, prom-planning committee, and running the lights in theater productions. And yet, he was the one graced with Superpowers. Truthfully, he still had no idea what to do with them.

Sighing, Jack picked up the burner phone and dialed the only number saved in the contacts field: IAS's New York HQ. The agent who answered immediately transferred him to Professor

Optimo, whose undisguised relief at hearing Jack's voice made him wonder just what had been going on in the twelve or so hours since his capture at the bank.

"Tell me everything," the senior Superhero said. "Start at the beginning."

Jack knew this call was being recorded both for posterity and to use in immediate briefings for his colleagues, so he paused, collected his thoughts, and launched into his tale, beginning with his arrival at First Resolution Bank of New York.

When he reached the part about Claire being dragged into the warehouse break room, he realized that he was at an impasse. Claire didn't just know his face; she knew that Silver Fist was Jack Elliott from Cedar Rapids, Iowa. She was also trustworthy. Jack was certain she would take any Superhero secrets she harbored to her grave. Still, this knowledge had implications for his career and future as an active Superhero. He drew in a deep breath and confessed, "Sir, I haven't been entirely honest with you."

Professor Optimo paused for a moment, then asked carefully, "How so?"

"I know Claire Green. I mean, I knew her before... before I gained Superpowers and we took down Vengeance together. We went to high school together." He swallowed and felt his face heat. He couldn't believe he was about to share these personal details with his boss. "Actually, it's more than that. We dated. For all of high school. We broke up senior year and went our separate ways after graduation."

Professor Optimo was quiet for a long moment. When he finally spoke, he asked, "Why did you not share this sooner?"

"It never really seemed relevant."

"Until now."

"Until now," Jack echoed, nodding even though he knew Professor Optimo couldn't see him. Before his boss could start asking questions, Jack found himself rambling, assuring the senior Superhero of Claire's honesty and trustworthiness in keeping his identity a secret. He wasn't sure if he was worried more about protecting his job or Claire's honor, but his voice rose with intensity as he warmed to his subject. Before he knew it, his chest was heaving with emotion, and his face felt warm. His eyes never left the bathroom door, which was all that separated him from the woman he found himself describing to his boss.

When Jack finally paused to take a breath, Professor Optimo inhaled audibly and slowly let it out. "Pause recording," he said, and there was a soft click.

Jack furrowed his brow. "Sir, why—"

"Son, I've been in this game for a long time, and I can see that you're headed for a world of pain right now," Professor Optimo said, cutting him off. His tone reminded Jack of his CO in the army attempting to give personal advice to the young men away from home for the first time, deployed to a desert thousands of miles from the girls they loved. "You say you trust Ms. Green with your secret identity, and that's good enough for me. After eight years behind the mask, you know what you're about. But you're clearly still carrying a torch for her, and while there are no rules against relationships with civilians—"

Now it was Jack's turn to cut him off. "Sir, I am certainly not 'carrying a torch' for Claire. We broke up more than a decade ago and haven't spoken since. In fact, at the time, she made it clear that she wanted nothing to do with me anymore." The memory stung, but it was the truth.

The Professor was silent for a moment, and Jack thought he had gotten through to the older man. But then, after a beat, he said, "That doesn't mean you don't still have feelings for her. They shone through in your voice clear as day just now when you were talking about Ms. Green. Jack, I'm saying this as a friend, so... just be careful. Don't mistake a shared secret—your true identity—for a renewed connection. You may trust this woman with your life, but that doesn't mean you can or should trust her with your heart."

His words punched Jack in the gut harder than anything had since he'd gained Superpowers. His gaze finally dropped from the bathroom door to the floor. Professor Optimo was right. Jack was letting himself get sucked into a fantasy of reconnecting with Claire, despite his best efforts. Why else would he have kissed her? Why else would he have been so ready and eager to hold her and comfort her? If he truly believed they were a thing of the past, why was he fighting so hard to remind himself of that fact?

"You're right, sir. Thanks. I'll give it some thought," Jack murmured.

"Very good. Now, let's get back to the subject at hand," the Professor said.

The recording resumed, and Jack dutifully related every detail of the evening—every relevant detail not related to Claire and kissing Claire and holding Claire and thinking about Claire and worrying about Claire, that is. He tried to be professional and keep his mind on the matter at hand, but it kept drifting back to the woman who was currently showering just a few feet away from him.

What does she actually think and feel? She's injured and likely concussed. It's possible that she's only acting this warmly because she's out of it and vulnerable. And if that's the case, you're taking advantage of her with all your hugs and kisses and caresses.

That thought caused Jack to pause and physically recoil. He turned around and put his back to the bathroom. Maybe he could pretend she simply wasn't there.

"Silver Fist, you still there?" Professor Optimo asked, cutting through his thoughts.

"Yes, of course," he said. "Sorry. As I was saying..." He continued with his description of Vengeance's base of operations, forcing his mind to focus on details like the number of henchmen he saw, security systems, and potential civilian collateral in the area that Vengeance could use against them. These were the kinds of details Jack was good at gathering and remembering. His Superpowers may have been Super-strength and Super-speed, but his real skillset lay in nuance, logistics, and planning.

By the time he had completed his report, Jack felt fully in control of himself and his emotions again. Even Professor Optimo's instructions to stand down and remain in hiding with Claire while other Superheroes moved into the area to defeat and capture Vengeance didn't faze him. He would do what he had to do to protect a civilian asset and then escort her to the hospital once they were given the all-clear. Until then, he just had to manage his own emotions and not push his impossible hopes—for that's what they were—onto a woman who, in all likelihood, didn't share them.

Professor Optimo's words echoed in his mind: *"You may trust this woman with your life, but that doesn't mean you can or should trust her with your heart."*

As the Professor wrapped up his orders, Jack pulled himself back to the present once more. "Yes, sir," he said formally, acknowledging his instructions. In a softer voice, he added, "And... thank you for what you said earlier. I'll give it some thought."

"Good," the older Superhero said. "I hope it helps. I can't have one of my best Superheroes getting distracted by personal matters." With that, he ended the call.

Jack stood in the middle of the room for a beat, staring at nothingness, the burner phone still pressed against his ear. The sound of the shower in the bathroom continued. Jack shook his head as if to clear it and lowered the phone. As good as it sounded to simply "protect a civilian asset," in practice, that still meant spending the rest of the night in this small room with only one bed with a woman who had once broken his heart and stomped on the pieces.

Clothes, a voice whispered in his mind. *She'll need clothes. Unless you want her naked in bed beside you...*

He silenced the traitorous thought with a grunt and slammed the burner phone down on top of the mini-fridge harder than he'd intended to. He would *not* go down that mental path.

Jack opened the tall wardrobe and started looking through it, but his brain didn't register anything he laid his eyes on. His mind was occupied with other things.

The image of Vengeance reaching out to caress Claire's pale cheek dusted with freckles...

He pulled out a T-shirt that seemed small enough for her and moved on to the chests of drawers, opening them one at a time and peering inside.

Claire looking up at him, her eyes wide, and speaking her first words to him in years: "Jack, are you okay?"...

He blindly grabbed a pair of leggings and a tank top and threw them on the bed beside the T-shirt.

The feeling of Claire's body warm against his as she slithered down him in their hiding place in the alley...

He selected a pair of underwear at random, not even looking at them. He didn't want to see or even think about a garment that would be so close to her most intimate parts.

Claire's lips against his...

"Enough!" Jack barked aloud.

"You may trust this woman with your life, but that doesn't mean you can or should trust her with your heart."

Jack would trust Claire Green to have his back in a fight against anyone, anytime. But she was too proud, too hung up on her inability to accept help from others for him to trust her with his heart. Not again.

"Hey, you hear about Claire and Brian Butler?" Ashlee Lawler asked as she slid into her desk behind Jack in math class. Before he could respond, Ashlee gleefully continued, "He picked a fight with her in gym class. Again. They're gonna fight after school in the parking lot."

Jack groaned, rolled his eyes, and sank down into his uncomfortably small desk-chair combination seat. They were two weeks from graduation. Couldn't Claire get through these last ten days in the classroom without needing to fight every trash-talking prick who made a crack about her size? And why did all these guys still think they could take Claire in a fight? No one could take Claire in a fight, outside of a few other black belts in her division at state- and national-level competitions.

Despite himself, Jack asked Ashlee, "Did you hear what Brian said this time?"

Ashlee shook her head no. "I was running laps with Kelsey. But I know it had something to do with you."

"With me?" Jack sat upright in his seat and spun around to face the blonde girl behind him. "What about me?"

Ashlee shrugged. "So, you gonna go watch? I always enjoy seeing Brian eat his words."

"Yeah... I'll be there..." Jack said, trailing off. He would always be there to watch Claire kick the ass of whatever guy she needed to in order to prove herself to the world. But what did he have to do with it this time?

This question nagged at Jack all through math class, keeping him from focusing on a subject he normally enjoyed. Thoughts of what Brian had said to get Claire so riled up—and why she simply couldn't let things go—plagued him.

When the bell rang, Jack gathered this things and followed the throng of fellow students out into the hall, which was alive with the high spirits that always accompanied the end of the school year. Loud voices and laughter bounced down the hall. Jack slouched as he walked, as if he weren't a full head taller than almost everyone else in the hallway.

He paused to get a sip of water at the water fountain just outside the bathroom. That's when he heard it.

"If you ask me, Jack's a fucking pussy," Brian Butler said, his voice echoing out of the bathroom. "Lets his little girlfriend do all the dirty work while he just stands there and looks cool."

Jack straightened and glanced around the crowded hallway. Based on the wide eyes and shocked whispers nearby, he wasn't the only one who'd heard Brian. Heat flooded his face, and he ducked his head.

"What kind of man just stands there and lets his girlfriend fight another guy? Fucking loser," Brian continued to his silent buddy in the bathroom.

His heart pounding in his chest, Jack turned on his heel and strode away. He knew his face was bright red, and his hands shook as he clenched them into fists at his side. He wanted to march in there and give Brian a piece of his mind, but he didn't know what to say or how to say it. Claire would know exactly what to do in such a situation. Hell, for all he knew, Brian was repeating verbatim what he'd said earlier that so upset Claire.

Without seeing or hearing anything around him, Jack shouldered his way through the crowded hallway toward his last class of the day, English. Brian's words haunted him. What kind of man was he? Was he hiding behind Claire too much, always letting her handle things? But Claire always knew how to handle things, ready with a snappy comeback or a quick, definitive answer. Put Claire on the spot, and she could handle anything. Jack needed more time to think things over, to plan and consider his responses.

But was it really fair to rely on Claire so much? Maybe it was time to start being a different kind of man. After all, in just a few weeks, they would be graduating. In a few months more, he would be shipping off to boot camp, and Claire would be moving to New York. He'd have to stand up for himself, think for himself, answer for himself. When challenged, how would he react without Claire?

As Ms. Lane, the English teacher, droned on about something, Jack's thoughts were in a tumult. But by the end of class, he had a plan. He knew what he had to do.

When the final bell of the day rang, Jack practically raced out of class. He stopped at his locker just long enough to drop off his books and grab his backpack. Then, he ran toward the parking lot behind the building, ignoring the shouts of teachers behind him, telling him not to run in the halls.

Jack reached the familiar designated fight spot in the parking lot first. It was hidden from view behind the theater, with a tall chain-link fence and several massive utility systems closing off the space in a perfect U shape. Kids often smoked here before and during school, but after school, it became their own personal Fight Club, where students could duke out their differences with fists. He had stood at the edge of the U many times with a gaggle of curious students, watching as his girlfriend took on guys twice her size.

But not today. Today would be different.

"Where's your little girlfriend?" Brian Butler's voice from behind him caused Jack to spin around. To his surprise, several students had already gathered, their eyes darting between Jack and Brian nervously.

Jack squared his shoulders, raised his chin, and forced his voice to remain as steady as possible. "You got a problem with me, you talk to me. Leave Claire out of it."

Brian stared at him for a second, then threw his head back and laughed. "You finally grow a pair?" he sneered. "Get tired of letting Mighty Mouse wear the pants in the relationship?"

A few of the students behind him chuckled, but most just watched the pair silently. This wasn't the usual eager-for-a-fight crowd. They kept their distance from Brian and eyed Jack warily. He was an unknown in the ring, known more for being soft-spoken and shy than for confronting bullies. And yet, his height—six-foot-four this year—meant he probably wouldn't go down easily.

Jack spread his hands in a questioning gesture. "Why do you have to be such an asshole, man? Just leave me—and Claire—alone. She's kicked your ass every time you've fought the last four years... and I'm prepared to kick your ass now if you don't drop this whole thing and walk away." His heart pounded as he spoke. He prayed Brian wouldn't call his bluff. Jack had never actually been in a fight in his life.

Brian eyed him for a long moment that seemed to stretch on forever. Perhaps he was trying to gauge just how serious Jack was. Perhaps he was sizing him up, looking for weaknesses. Perhaps he was trying to decide how to respond to this new, unexpected challenge. Finally, Brian stepped forward. He spit on Jack's shoe and sneered, "Fuck you and your whore girlfriend."

Jack's fist started moving at the word "whore." He didn't even put any thought into it. He swung out, and his fist cracked against Brian's jaw with more power than Jack knew he had.

Brian spun in place like a cartoon character for a moment. Jack could practically see little animated stars twirling around his opponent's head. Then, Brian crashed to the ground in a heap, unconscious.

No one moved for a second. No one even dared to breathe. The crowd stared, open-mouthed. Jack flexed his hand, wondering what he was supposed to do now.

"What the fuck?!" The shrill exclamation shattered the moment.

Jack looked up to see a bright-red Claire, her jaw hanging open, her brow furrowed in confusion and shock. The crowd parted in an instant, and Claire marched forward, her backpack slipping from her shoulders onto the pavement.

Jack said the first thing that came into his mind: "I took care of him for you."

"You... you what?" she hissed, her eyes moving between Jack and the prone Brian who lay on the ground between them. "I didn't need you to take care of him! I can handle him on my own!"

The venom and hurt in her voice was audible. Jack cringed, and the crowd started to drift away, reluctant to watch this kind of drama. They'd come for a fistfight, not an argument between a pair so well-established, they were practically like an old married couple.

"I know," Jack said, "but you're always standing up for me. I decided it was time I stand up for you for a change."

If Jack thought this would defuse her, he was wrong. Her hands clenched into fists at her sides, and her eyes flashed dangerously. "I can take care of myself," she said through gritted teeth.

The surge of adrenaline still running through Jack's veins must have made him stupid, because he blurted out, "And so can I! You don't need to do everything yourself, you know. You can't *always do everything yourself! Why don't you try relying on others for a change, instead of taking on the world on your own? Why don't you try relying on* me?"

Claire looked like he'd slapped her. She reeled back for a moment, then pointed at Brian. "Because apparently, I can't trust you to have my back when it counts." Jack opened his mouth to respond, but Claire pressed on, "This was my *fight. Brian challenged me, not you." Her chest heaved as she spoke.*

"But he was talking shit about me, too!" Jack roared, surprised at his own vehemence. "He was talking shit about both of us, and I'm sick of it! I'm sick of having to watch you deal with the bullies for me—for both of us."

"So what, you want me to just stand on the sidelines and watch you save the day?" she shot back. "Not gonna happen!"

"You don't trust me, then?"

"Trust you? You just stole my fight out from under me!"

"'Stole'?" Jack snapped. "I didn't 'steal' anything. I didn't know you were doing this for the glory." His chest heaved, and he realized he was shouting now. The crowd had vanished, and it was just the two of them, yelling at each other behind the school. Brian Butler still lay unconscious between them. Jack's anger got the better of him, and he spun away, throwing his hands in the air in a mocking gesture. "Oh, it's the great Claire Green, UFC champion of Cedar Rapids, Iowa!"

"I do what I do because I need to be ready for anything!" she retorted. "When the time comes, I won't be able to rely on anyone else to—"

"Claire, give it up!" he shot back, temper flaring dangerously. "You're not gonna be a Superhero, okay? You don't need to take on the entire world. You *can't* take on the entire world. Not by yourself. Let it go!"

Claire was silent. When she didn't respond, Jack turned back to face her. That's when he realized his mistake.

Her head hung low so he couldn't see her face. Her arms were tense at her sides, and she let out a long, slow breath.

Jack took a step forward. "I'm sorry. I—"

"You never believed in me," Claire said, her voice low. "Were you just humoring me all this time, playing along?"

"No, Claire—"

She continued as if he hadn't spoken. "You're just like everyone else. I thought you were different, but you're not. All you see is this tiny, helpless, petite little girl who needs to be protected from the world." She turned and started walking away.

Jack stumbled over Brian's body in his haste to follow her. "Claire, that's not what I meant!" he shouted.

Claire paused but didn't turn back to face him. "Get out of my life. I don't need you to fight my battles for me." With that, she continued to walk away.

Jack stood there, unmoving, for long enough to watch her get into her car and peel out of the parking lot.

Claire didn't speak to him again for four years. And then, it was on a city street in New York, and she didn't even know it was him.

Jack shook his head to clear it of the painful memories that threatened to overwhelm him. The sound of the shower running in the next room helped draw him back to the present, but the remembered pain of that final, decisive argument still thrummed through his veins.

As he picked up and folded the clothing he'd selected for Claire, he grasped onto that hurt, winding it around him like a scarf. That pain would serve as his armor for the next few hours, protecting him from Claire's proximity and from his own impossible longings.

He slid the bathroom door open ever-so-slightly and placed the fresh clothing on the floor for her. He didn't even dare look toward the shower cubicle. He feared it would shatter any resistance he'd just built up by reviewing the past.

Remember what the Professor said, he told himself, turning away.

But then, his eyes landed on Claire's pile of discarded clothing on the floor. They were all black, so they hid any blood well, but he had apparently pushed the pile a few inches with the door, revealing a smear of blood on the floor. He couldn't tear his eyes away from it: Claire's bright-red blood under the harsh white lights of the bathroom. She was injured. She had been injured escaping from a Supervillain. She had apparently also been injured by taking down a whole gaggle of Supervillain henchmen. Superpowers or no, Claire Green was incredible.

Her moan of pleasure coming from the shower broke the spell, and Jack quickly withdrew, ducking back into the main room. He scrubbed his eyes with the heels of his hands and sighed.

It was going to be a long night.

Chapter 9

When Claire emerged from the bathroom fully dressed, clean, and with wet hair, she felt more relaxed than she had in over twenty-four hours. She stretched her arms over her head and announced airily, "The bathroom's all yours."

Jack was laying out various items from an extensive first aid kit on the dresser. At the sound of her voice, he nodded but did not look up. "Just a second," he said, his voice distant, as if he were concentrating on something else. He pulled out a few more items, then turned toward Claire. The look in his eyes and the tone of his voice were professional and cool as he said, "Have a seat." When Claire didn't move, he added, "I need to bandage you up."

Right. Of course. Can't have me bleeding all over the place. Or at least more than I already have.

Claire sat down on the futon, trying to act natural. In truth, she was quaking inside, and she was sure her jerky motions gave that fact away. She was alone in a room—*A room with only one bed*, her mind traitorously reminded her—with a man whom she had once loved with every fiber of her being and whom she hadn't seen in twelve years. And now, he was going to touch her.

"I'm glad the clothes fit," he said as he walked into the bathroom to thoroughly wash his hands. "Regina keeps all kinds of civilian clothes here for when we need a quick disguise, and while she's pretty good about having lots of different sizes, there aren't exactly a lot of..."

"Short Superheroes?" Claire offered with a grin.

"I was going to say 'petite,' but yes." He returned, his hands clean and his eyes on the floor. "Now, let's start with those cuts on your cheek. I hope they don't need stitches," he said, squatting down in front of her.

Jack's face was mere inches from Claire's as he studied the gashes on her cheek, but it felt like he was a million miles away. He could have been studying a piece of modern art in MoMA for how dispassionate his gaze was. He may have been looking at her wounds, but he wasn't *seeing* Claire, and it unsettled her, especially after how warm he'd been toward her earlier.

I wonder if he got bad news from his Superhero buddies, she thought. "So, do you want to start at the beginning of the story?" she asked, hoping to draw Jack out of whatever funk he had fallen into.

Finally, he met her eyes, but the look in them was confused.

"You know, the story of how you got your Superpowers," she prompted. "You promised."

"Oh, yeah. Of course," Jack said, sitting back his heels. He got up and turned to gather his medical supplies on the dresser. "It won't need stitches. I would say you should make sure your tetanus shot is up to date, but given your profession, I'm sure it is." He returned to kneel in front of her, but his eyes immediately darted back to the cuts on her cheek, staying far away from her eyes. "I deployed to Afghanistan pretty soon after I got out of boot camp." He began dabbing her cheek with a stinging antibiotic.

Claire winced but didn't pull away.

"I ended up deploying over there twice during my four-year contract. During my second tour, there was an accident."

"An accident?" Claire echoed stupidly, blinking hard against the tears that rose unbidden from the harsh ointment.

Jack turned away to grab a large bandage that would likely cover her whole cheek. "It was a regular supply run out to another post. We were in a pretty secure area. We didn't expect anything to happen." He opened the Band-Aid's wrappings and smoothed it across her cheek, his fingers never touching her flesh and his eyes never meeting hers. "There was an IED in the road. It blew our truck sky-high."

Claire fought down the gasp that tried to escape her lips. Images of soldiers in fatigues toting heavy guns—images she had imbibed from watching the news for hours on end—danced through her mind, but she struggled to put Jack's young face on one of them. The Jack before her now—older, wearier, more confident in himself—would fit into such a scene conjured from the news, but not the shy, awkward, gawky young man she had known in high school.

In truth, Claire had never really understood his decision to enlist. Most of the kids in their school who did enlist fit one of two profiles. Many were athletic, enthusiastic about everything but school, and eager to prove themselves to the world. Others were serious and driven but from poor backgrounds, viewing the army as their only path toward college. Jack was neither of these things. He claimed that it simply didn't make sense to go straight into college because he didn't know what he wanted to study or what he wanted to be when he grew up. This seemed logical, but Claire's questions of "But why the army specifically?" never received a satisfactory answer. It just seemed to her like he was going through the motions.

As he was now.

Jack's eyes remained focused on her bandage, smoothing it down so it would adhere to Claire's cheek without any wrinkles. The heat of his fingers seared her, even through the layers of latex and cloth. "Somehow—I don't know how—I was thrown clear. I tried to run back, to pull the other guys out before the gas ignited and exploded, but I wasn't fast or strong enough. I was the only one to survive," he said in a low voice.

Claire moved without thinking. She placed her hand over his, pressing it to cup her cheek. He reacted as if she'd scalded him, drawing back sharply. He finally met her gaze, but his eyes were distant and haunted. "Sorry," she murmured, dropped her own gaze to the floor. "I didn't mean—"

"It's okay," he said, sounding like his old self for the first time since she'd come out of the bathroom. Claire risked glancing back up, and the bright-blue eyes she saw staring back at her were full of unshed tears. "It's okay, Claire," he repeated. She couldn't tell if he was reassuring her or himself. But at least now he was actually *looking* at her.

I could drown in those eyes, she thought, surprising herself.

Fortunately—or unfortunately, depending on how one looked at it—the moment ended before it began. Jack dropped her gaze and stood up, returning to his medical supplies and putting distance between them again.

Claire gnawed on her lower lip as she studied Jack's profile. The stubborn set of his jaw and the downward hunch of his shoulders told her everything she needed to know: Jack was holding himself back, keeping something from her. And despite wanting the full story, she couldn't blame him. She knew he couldn't let her in all the way. He was sharing painful memories, memories she had rejected the right to know.

When he sat down beside her with gauze and bandages for her wrists, he again didn't meet her eyes. "Soon after, I started exhibiting signs of Superpowers. Specifically, Super-strength and Super-speed. My enlistment contract was coming to an end anyway, and since the military doesn't trust anything it can't control, and Supers are notoriously hard to control..." He trailed off, letting the end of that thought linger.

"They sent you on your merry way?" Claire asked.

He smiled sardonically, picked up her right hand, and started rubbing more of the harsh, stinging ointment onto her wrist. His grip was light, yet Claire's heart began to race as his fingers ran along the raw, sensitive flesh. "More like, they passed me along to the IAS. I went into Superhero training, and my planned 'graduation' and debut coincided with Vengeance's attack. Giada and I just happened to be the closest to the scene."

Realizing his slip, Jack's eyes widened and darted up to meet Claire's. "Umm, you didn't hear that last part."

"Hear what?" Claire asked with a wink, even as her stomach dropped and her pulse thundered in her ears. Her smile felt frozen on her face. *Giada... He's good enough friends with the Electric Defender to automatically call her by her first name. It just slipped out like it was nothing, like he calls her that every day. Like he calls her that every night, in bed...*

Claire bristled and cut that train of thought off before it could go much further. She tried to retract her arm, but Jack held onto it and began wrapping a gauze bandage around her wrist. Claire prayed he wouldn't notice how her pulse raced in her veins or how bright her cheeks had gotten.

It's been twelve years, Green. He's a thirty-year-old man, and he is allowed to do whatever he wants with whomever he wants. And if what he wants is to fuck this "Giada," his colleague, one of the most famous Superheroes in New York, that is his right. You gave up any right to complain over a decade ago.

Jack turned to Claire's left wrist, and a tense silence fell between them. Claire chewed on her chapped lower lip again, trying to decide what to ask next, how to ask it, and whether she had any right to ask. For his part, Jack seemed comfortable with the lengthening silence between them.

As he has been for the past eight years, Claire thought bitterly. *Ah! At least that's a less personal question.* Aloud, she asked, "So, why didn't you reach out and let me know you had Superpowers, especially after we ran into each other that first time? I wasn't exactly hard to find. I was all over the news and social media."

Jack focused on bandaging her left wrist. He even dipped his head slightly, studiously avoiding her gaze. "I thought about it. I thought about it a million times. But I was never sure how to open, what to say. I wasn't sure you'd even want to hear from me. And as time passed and we continued to see each other at crime scenes around the city, it just seemed increasingly impossible."

Claire put as much emotion as she could into her next words. "Jack, I would have *loved* to hear from you. At any time. I know we ended badly, and that's my fault. But we're both adults. I think we could be mature enough to grab a coffee and share our news and maybe swap stories about saving the city and its people. You know, as fellow industry professionals."

Jack actually chuckled at that and looked up at her. His eyes were warm again, and Claire realized that their faces were so close, she could feel his breath on her forehead. She willed her eyes not to drift down to his lips, which were tantalizingly close. His thumb started rubbing distracting circles in the palm of her left hand, sending a tingling sensation down her arm. Claire felt herself being drawn into his presence, into his eyes that were whirlpools of emotion.

But then, his eyes clouded over, like a storm rolling in off the sea. He dropped her hand and asked softly, "How's your head?"

Claire felt like she was getting whiplash just from his changing moods. "I've still got a slight headache, but it's died down a bit. I actually feel a lot better now that I've showered. Finally getting some sleep should knock the last of it out of me." *I hope*, she added silently. "You know, I was just coming off a twelve-hour overnight shift when this whole episode with

Vengeance and his goons began. I could use some quality shut-eye."

Jack turned back to his medical supplies, nodding. He shifted away from her, and Claire's stomach clenched in disappointment. Or maybe it was hunger. "Hey, is there anything to eat in here?" she asked. "I don't even know when I last ate."

Without a word, he got up, walked over to the dresser, and pulled out the top drawer. "Looks like we have Staten Island's finest assortment of protein bars," he said, rummaging through the drawer. "Regina needs to restock this a little. You still like peanut butter, right?"

At Claire's affirmative response, he turned back to her, tossed her a dense protein bar, and returned to sit down beside her, immediately drawing one foot into his lap. Claire tipped back slightly at the unexpected motion and let out a surprised gasp.

"Sorry," Jack said, studying the bruises and cuts around her ankle. He was back to all-business, it seemed. "I just need to treat these lacerations around your ankles and whatever you did to your big toe and take a look at your head injury. Then you can get some rest."

Claire nodded, unsure of how to read Jack's changing mood. She had to wonder, in spite of his familiar face, did she really know this man in front of her? For more than a decade, he'd been living a life she could only imagine and watch from the sidelines. Sure, she was sometimes called to the same scenes he was, but she was a background character, the EMT dutifully cleaning up in the wake of the Superheroes' fights. She had been a Superhero fangirl her whole life. She read about them, followed their blogs and social media accounts. She had spent her entire childhood and youth preparing to be one someday. But the reality was far, far away from what she had always imagined. Sure, there were daring acts, dramatic fights, and exciting adventures—all the things Claire had imagined as a girl working on her gymnastics and karate skills. But there were also secret back-alley escapes, ugly wounds, and hiding out above strip clubs in Staten Island. How much had this life changed Jack?

"So, how do you like being a Superhero?" Claire asked as he got to work on her ankle. Jack's head shot up, and she quickly waved her hands in front of her. "Don't worry, this isn't like an interview for my blog or anything. I'm just curious. What's it actually like?"

Claire took a bite of her protein bar—which tasted like peanut-butter-flavored cardboard—while Jack rubbed ointment on her ankle and appeared to gather his thoughts. He had that focused look she recognized that meant he was searching for the best way to present information.

"It's a lot like the army, actually," he confessed.

This surprised Claire. With all the different Superheroes' unique costumes, individual flair, and big personalities, it seemed a far cry from the structured, regimented world of uniforms and the chain of command. Sure, they had to work as a team and often dealt with things like group battle tactics and maneuvers, but most Superheroes presented themselves to the media as lone wolves who took care of matters solo. Individual Superheroes even often had archnemeses and sidekicks—as Vengeance and Claire were starting to turn into for Silver Fist.

"Professor Optimo is kinda like our commanding officer," Jack continued. "He's even got the same dorky mustache as my first CO and calls me 'son' when he's attempting to give personal advice."

Claire chuckled and took another bite of her protein bar. She was trying to focus on Jack's words and not his hands ghosting over her feet. *This man is touching me everywhere tonight*, she thought half-cheekily. Instantly, heat flooded her face, and she banished the smirk that threatened to appear.

Luckily, Jack was too focused on bandaging her ankle to notice her blush. "We go on missions and patrols. There are assignments. There are rules and regulations and standard operating procedures. The main difference is that the uniforms are flashier and the personalities even bigger—if that's possible. Oh, and the healthcare is easier to access than at the VA."

Her ankle bandaged, Jack turned his attention to her big toe and its missing toenail. The whole area was angry, red, and slightly throbbing. Jack doused it with stinging antibiotic, and Claire hissed at the searing sensation.

Trying to keep her mind off the mix of confusing sensations in her foot, she focused on their conversation. "I guess I can see that. But do you *like* it?"

Jack chuckled, keeping his eyes on his work. "It's my job. Does anyone actually like their job?"

"I do."

At that, Jack finally paused and looked up at her. His eyebrows lifted in disbelief. "You like being an EMT? It doesn't burn you out or upset you in some way? After all, you see a lot of the world's ugliness."

Claire thought for a moment, her mind going back to all the calls she'd been summoned to over the years. The gunshot wounds from arguments that went too far. The domestic violence that erupted into serious bloodshed. The rapes. The car crashes. Admittedly, those were difficult days. She saw sides of people that she didn't necessarily want to see.

But she also knew that she was spending her days—and often her nights—trying to help people. She thought of the elderly woman who lived alone and had a heart attack. Claire had held her hand the whole way to the hospital while keeping an oxygen mask in place with the other.

The woman had lived, and Claire later received a call from her grateful daughter, who lived in Texas. "Mom insisted that I thank the red-headed angel that helped her that day," the daughter said.

Claire shook her head. "I didn't really do anything special. It was just my job—"

The daughter cut her off. "No, it was more than that. Mom said she could feel time slowing down for her when you held her hand. It was like you were protecting her, holding her in a safe, special bubble until you got to the hospital."

Claire was speechless, unsure of how to respond.

"Regardless," the daughter said, "whatever you did, I think you have a healing touch. Thank you for saving my mother."

Claire had mumbled some response, her words lost to her memory the moment they were out of her mouth. But the daughter's gratitude had shone through in her voice, and that stayed with Claire for a long time.

And when things were really difficult and her days were truly dark, Claire remembered the man in the hard hat and high-vis vest at the scene of her first Vengeance encounter on her very first day of work as an EMT. "That's what I'm talking about," the man had shouted. "New York City's emergency personnel—the *real* superheroes around here!" Claire had been embarrassed at the time, but whenever she felt discouraged or like she couldn't take another day of endless calls and needless injuries, she thought of that man and his genuine admiration. He hadn't even glanced at Silver Fist—at Jack. His applause was all for Claire.

Turning her gaze back to Jack, Claire chose her next words carefully. "I do see a lot that I wish I didn't: pain, suffering, loss. But those things would still happen whether I was there to witness them or not. Being there, I know I can make a difference and help people."

"But even if you weren't there, someone else would be," Jack argued. "Even if Claire Green had ended up being an—oh, I don't know... a computer programmer—even if you had ended up being a computer programmer and not an EMT, someone else would be there to fill your shoes and be an EMT." His face was strangely intense, and Claire wondered what this conversation was actually about for him.

"That's true. But it's not about doing something that no one else can do. It's about being passionate about what I do. I never got to be a Superhero—" Jack opened his mouth to respond, but Claire held up a hand to stop him. "I never got to be a Superhero, but I can still help people. I can save lives. I just do it with Narcan or a defibrillator instead of Superpowers. And even on the worst days, I like knowing that I'm making a difference. I don't think I would want a job in which I wasn't. It would just feel like going through the motions."

Jack nodded, and he turned back to cleaning and treating the wound on her big toe without a response. His silence felt heavy, as if her words had sent him off down a trail of thought that Claire didn't dare interrupt.

He didn't speak again as he bandaged her big toe and then turned to her other ankle. Claire's headache had receded to the point where she wasn't sure if it was still there at all; maybe the pounding she felt was just the distant bass beat coming up from a few floors below. In the comfort of the moment, her drowsiness crept in, and she leaned back against the futon, careful to keep her head tipped to the side so the bloody wound on the back of her head didn't come into contact with the mattress. Her eyelids fluttered closed, and she sighed at the sensation of Jack gently caressing her ankle.

Claire must have drifted off briefly because she startled awake when Jack said, "Okay, all done. Let's take a look at your head, and then, I can tuck you into bed and let you get some sleep."

She looked around, blinking. "Right. Thanks." She sat up and swiveled away from him so he could get a good look at the back of her head.

His fingers gently parted her hair, and Claire fought the moan that threatened to escape her lips at the sensation of his hands in her hair. She closed her eyes, greedily drinking in the moment. It had been a long time since someone played with or caressed or even just touched her hair other than her and her hairstylist—and she wasn't exactly getting regular haircuts.

"It doesn't look nearly as bad now that you've washed most of the blood out," Jack said, "but I'll still treat it."

His hands left her hair for a moment, but before Claire could mourn their loss, the stinging sensation of harsh, strong antibiotic against her raw flesh replaced them. Claire bit her lip, then asked, "So, what's next? Are the other Superheroes rushing in to capture Vengeance? Are you going to go join them?"

Jack's voice was calm and focused, like he was giving a mission briefing: "As I'm sure you already figured out, I gave Vengeance false access codes to The Elite Five's base, so he's going to be on a rampage for a while looking for me—and you. I'm under orders to lay low for a while and keep you safe. Once I've been given the all-clear, I'll escort you to the hospital so they can check you out. I'm sure the police will want to take your statement, and the IAS will eventually want to debrief you about everything you saw and heard. But for now, our role in this is done."

Claire was disappointed in spite of herself. With all of Jack's talk about teams and missions, she'd suspected this wouldn't be something that Silver Fist was expected to handle on his own. She also knew her role in this story was probably done. Still, part of her had secretly hoped to see Jack on the news later, escorting Vengeance into a Super-enhanced containment cell. She imagined that the news was already spinning tales of Vengeance being Silver Fist's archnemesis, complete with vows of revenge.

Oh god, there's gonna be a Superhero biopic about us, Claire thought sleepily. *I wonder who's going to play me. Do I get to make any suggestions? And will they go more for the love interest/damsel-in-distress route or the selfless civilian sidekick?*

Jack gently pressed a gauze bandage to the back of her head and then began winding a cloth dressing around her head like a bandana to hold it in place. "What did you mean earlier about 'going through the motions'?" he asked.

The suddenness of the question woke Claire up again slightly as she struggled to piece together what he was actually asking. She cast her mind back to that part of their conversation. "Umm, I guess I just meant that I don't want a job that I just do in order to pay the bills. A job like that would lack purpose for me. I'd be doing it because I had to or because I was expected to, not because I actually wanted to."

Jack chuckled. "You've never been big on fulfilling other peoples' expectations."

"And why should I?" Claire asked, grinning. "I've always been the shortest and the smallest. Everyone always expected me to back down, wimp out, and give up. If I did—if I was what everyone always expected me to be—I'd be living their life, not mine. Sure, that's resulted in more than a few mistakes on my part," she winced internally as she recalled what was possibly her greatest mistake ever—walking away from Jack due to a combination of a bad temper and some misplaced sense of pride—but she pushed it down and continued, "but at least I know I'm living my life for me, on my terms."

Jack was silent for a long moment as he finished smoothing the bandage around her head. Then, his hands drifted away, leaving her feeling colder than she had been before. Claire risked peeking over her shoulder at Jack and saw him sitting there, just staring down at his hands in his lap. His shoulders were hunched, as if he were carrying some heavy burden or fighting off harsh blows that wouldn't stop landing.

Finally, he looked up and met her eyes. "Claire Green, you're a wise woman. I only hope I can be as wise as you some day."

Claire smiled and turned to fully face him. "Nah, I've got plenty of flaws, too. I've still got a terrible temper, am impatient, and can't cook to save my life."

Jack's mouth widened into a matching smile. "As I recall, you make a pretty mean mac and cheese."

"Oh, please," Claire scoffed. "Stuff that comes in a box doesn't count as 'cooking.'"

"Maybe," he said, his eyes still locked on hers.

"Maybe…" she echoed, letting the word trail off.

Neither of them looked away. Neither of them moved. Jack's eyes were blue pools that Claire felt herself falling into. Her heart pounded in her chest. They were close enough that she could feel his warm breath on her cheek. She licked her chapped lips and, without even thinking about it, subtly tipped her chin up, toward him.

Jack leaned forward ever so slightly, the movement so tiny she could have imagined it. His eyes drifted to her parted lips.

But then, his face seemed to freeze. The light went out of his eyes, and he drew back, putting space between them again. "You should get some rest," he said, standing up and starting to gather his first aid supplies. "It's been a long day."

Claire nodded mutely. *What's going on here? Did I just imagine us having a moment?* "I am pretty tired," she confessed. *He's running so hot and cold, I don't know how to read him.*

Jack kept his back to her as he packed away the med kit. "You can fold out the futon into a bed. It's not the comfiest in the world, but it'll do in a pinch. I need to shower."

He rummaged through the wardrobe and chest of drawers for some clothes of his own, then headed to the bathroom without a backward glance. When the door closed behind him, Claire felt more alone—and more confused—than she had in a long time.

What the fuck just happened?

Chapter 10

Jack steeled himself before opening the bathroom door. Claire was just a few feet away in the only bed in this small room—the same bed he was about to climb into. *She's exhausted. She's possibly concussed. She might not even feel anything for me anymore,* he told himself. *Nothing is going to happen. We're two adults forced together by extraordinary circumstances. The professional thing to do is just lie down, pretend she's not even there, and go to sleep.*

Easier said than done.

Jack took a deep breath and slowly opened the door.

The room was dark, but the harsh light spilling out of the bathroom revealed that Claire had folded down the futon into a bed. The small lump curled up on the side of the bed closest to the wall didn't stir at the onslaught of bright light. A mass of bright-red hair stuck out of the blue comforter, splayed across the pillow, and made his heart leap and then clench. Jack turned off the light, plunging the room back into darkness. *Sometimes, it's better to not see what you're walking into.*

He'd left his soiled Superhero suit on the floor of the bathroom, right beside Claire's pile of bloody clothing. He didn't want to deal with any of that right now. The sight of her blood slowly drying and crusting on the floor was more than enough for one night. It was well past midnight, he'd been up since 6:30 in the morning, and they would have plenty of time to clean up tomorrow before he took Claire to the hospital. Maybe they could stop and get a cup of coffee on the way. Maybe, once she was feeling better, they could talk. Maybe—

Jack shut down that train of thought before it could go anywhere. *No maybes right now. You're chasing ghosts. Let it go. Get some sleep.*

He blindly padded across the room toward the bed, his bare feet making no sound on the wood floor. The black sweatpants and cheap white 'I love New York' T-shirt he'd grabbed earlier were a little short for him, but that was fine. He was going to lie down, sleep, and not think about the woman just a few inches away.

Liar.

Claire's breathing was slow and even, and she did not stir as he lowered himself onto the futon beside her. She lay facing the wall, her back to him. Despite that, Jack held his breath as he slowly, *slowly* lay down on his back beside her, stretching his long torso out on the admittedly too-short futon mattress. The mattress was a bit firm for his taste, but the pillow was delightfully cool and fluffy, and he rolled his head back and forth on it, trying to find just the right spot.

Jack pulled the warm comforter away from Claire just enough to slip it over himself. He wasn't prepared for the heat of her body suddenly so close to his. They weren't even touching, but Jack felt like he was on fire from within and without.

The last time he'd shared a bed with Claire, they were eighteen years old, and it was the night of their senior prom. They had both told their parents that they were going to a friend's party after the dance, and the friend had agreed to cover for them while they actually spent the night at Claire's family's cabin on the Cedar River. Jack's older brother had purchased a bottle of wine for them, and Jack himself had bought a huge box of white pillar candles and fake rose petals at the craft store. He'd done his best to create a sexy, romantic ambiance, but looking back at his adolescent efforts now, as a thirty-year-old man, he couldn't help but laugh. *That poor kid had no idea what he was doing,* Jack thought with a grin in the darkness. *He was trying so hard!* As the deep bass beat from the strip club below slightly changed tempos, he mentally amended, *Of course, it's not like adult me is batting a thousand right now.*

The heat pouring off Claire's body kept his heart racing. He longed to reach out and touch her. To hold her. But he could think of a thousand reasons why that was the worst idea in the world. His fingers itched with the effort of holding back.

With a deep sigh, Jack rolled onto his side, facing away from her. He could still feel her warmth on his back, but the temptation to take her in his arms was noticeably smaller and much easier to fight. He focused on his breath, drawing it in slowly, holding it for a beat, and then slowly releasing it.

In the comfortable, safe darkness of the small room, his heart rate gradually slowed, and his breathing soon matched Claire's. *This is nice*, he thought as his mind settled into a peaceful haze. *I could get used to this.*

After that, he slept, and he did not dream. It was a deep sleep the likes of which Jack hadn't experienced in years. There was no tossing and turning to find a comfortable position, no painful muscle aches or cramps startling him awake in the wee hours, no urgent calls from work or nightmares to interrupt his slumber.

Jack woke sometime later, warmer and more comfortable than he had been in the morning in what felt like ages. He snuggled closer to the source of the warmth behind him, sighing. An arm snaked over his waist, and a delicate hand came to rest against his chest, pulling him closer. A pair of small breasts pressed against his back. He froze. He was in a strange bed with a strange woman. A very warm, well-built woman who smelled incredibly enticing.

For a moment, Jack mentally floundered, trying to remember where he was and who he'd ended up in bed with. He wasn't the type to go out drinking and partying and then go home with a faceless stranger for a night of largely forgettable sex. That was more Giada's thing.

At the thought, Jack froze in horror, wondering if he'd somehow ended up in bed with Giada. His mind was a fuzzy blur, but he knew he'd spoken to her yesterday... right?

Jack recognized that the world saw Giada as highly desirable, but to him, she had never been more than a slightly exasperating older sister with a penchant for giving him a hard time and an occasionally unnerving intelligence that took in far more than she let on. She brought him expensive coffee, teased him about his love life—or lack thereof—and offered to fix him up with her so-not-his-type friends. When one of her epic romances turned sour—as they always did—she would cry on his shoulder and swear off men or women, depending on the identity of the person involved, and he would comfort her with a tub of ice cream and her favorite documentary about the development of the first analogue flight simulator back in the 1920s.

His momentary panic awoke him fully, though, and the previous day's events rushed back: the bank robbery, Vengeance, his capture and escape, Claire. Claire, who now lay pressed fully against his back, one arm wrapped around him, spooning him.

Feeling her curves fit against his body made him very glad that he was still facing away from her; otherwise, he wouldn't be able to hide the evidence of just how much he enjoyed this. He reached down and adjusted himself in his sweatpants, then settled back and allowed himself to bask in the moment.

Her breath was gentle against his ear, still coming in a slow, even rhythm. Her knees were tucked up behind him, and he could feel her whole body pressed against his. He wasn't surprised by how firm and muscular she felt; she had a physically demanding job, and knowing Claire, she probably still trained in some sport or martial art regularly. What did surprise him, though, was the softness of her skin when he dared to raise a single finger and run it down the length of her forearm that clutched his chest.

Stop it, stop it, stop it, a part of him chanted, causing his fingers to freeze just before they reached the bandage covering her wrist. *This isn't the time or the place. You barely know this woman anymore. You're only going to get your heart broken. Again.*

Before he could retract his hand, Claire stretched behind him, pressing her curves even closer to him. She murmured something, but he couldn't quite tell what it was.

Oh god, what if she's married? The thought sent ice water coursing through his veins, killing his growing erection. *Am I in bed with another man's wife?*

At that moment, Claire's breathing changed, and she yawned, stretching her legs out straight. She pointed her toes, and they brushed against his calves. Jack froze, unsure whether he should pretend to still be asleep and let her extract herself from their embrace, or if he should just live with the potential embarrassment.

"Fancy meeting you here," Claire chuckled from behind him, slowly retracting her arm from around him and rolling away. Her voice was thick with sleep, but not blame, anger, or confusion. "Sorry about that."

"No apologies necessary," he said, rolling onto his back. He stared up into the darkness above them. He had no idea what time it was. Without a digital clock or light coming in through windows to tell them the time, they could have slept for ten hours or ten minutes. He suspected it was somewhere in the middle of that, given how well-rested he felt and the lack of an all-clear phone call from Professor Optimo. Considering

Claire's easy manner, he added, "I'll be honest: that's the best sleep I've had in years.""Same here," she said. Her fingers brushed against his under the covers.

His hard-on surged back to life, and he felt like a horny teenager to be getting so aroused by such a small, insignificant touch. He was glad she couldn't see his face, because he was sure it would give him away. *It was an accident*, he told himself. *She didn't mean anything by it.*

Claire didn't pull her hand away at the contact, though, and when Jack didn't, either, her fingers closed around his.

Jack swallowed hard. A pleasurable warmth kindled in the pit of his stomach, and his heart began to beat faster. Without any conscious decision on his part, his fingers began to move, caressing her palm and the inside curve of her thumb.

Claire purred, a soft, low sound deep in her throat that seemed to be an encouragement.

Is this really happening? Jack wondered. *Or am I still asleep and dreaming?* He felt like he was alert and awake, but the situation just seemed too impossible, too much like something out of a dream for him to fully trust it.

Claire slowly drew her hand out of his. Before he could feel bereft at the lost contact, though, she ghosted her fingers along his forearm, barely touching him, yet brushing the hairs in her path.

Jack shivered and swallowed again. Tingles danced down his spine. "Claire?" he said, though he had no idea what he was asking by saying her name.

"Yes?" she responded, her voice low and husky in the darkness.

His voice dropped to a whisper. "I... I missed you." The unexpected confession shook him even as the words left his lips. He mentally kicked himself.

Claire's response was immediate: "I missed you, too." Her fingers left his arm, and she rolled onto her side, facing him. Her small breasts pressed against his upper arm. "I'm glad I found you again."

Jack wished he could see her in the darkness. He rolled onto his side as well, carefully angling his lower half away from her. They were close enough that her breath caressed his face, and he didn't need Claire to know how aroused he was. He parted his lips as if to speak, but no words came out. He licked his lips, stalling for time. *What am I doing?*

"Jack."

The one word, uttered softly from both inches away and across the vastness of time and space, jolted him out of whatever statis field had held him. He raised his free arm, found Claire's face in the darkness, and cupped her cheek. Her slight inhalation of breath made him chuckle deep and low in his throat. She pressed her face more firmly against his palm.

Jack leaned forward, slowly, tentatively. The night hid her expression, but he could feel her breathing become slow and deep with excitement. Feeling daring, he let his thumb dip down to tenderly caress her chapped lips. She pressed a soft kiss to it. Then, her lips parted ever so slightly, and her tongue slipped out between them to graze his thumb.

The effect was immediate. Jack groaned softly, and his hard-on raged even more insistently. Now, it was Claire's turn to chuckle.

He drew his fingers gently down her throat, sending a noticeable shiver through her. At some point during the night, the collar of her T-shirt had dipped low. Now, Jack's fingers ran lightly along her collarbone. Claire shivered again at the contact. This particular spot had always been very sensitive—a fact he'd discovered when they were fifteen and making out in his basement after Homecoming. Without thinking, he ducked his head and pressed his lips to the hollow of her collarbone. Claire's reaction—a half-purr, half-moan—wiped away any remaining thought or hesitation in his mind.

His tongue darted out, and he licked that sweet spot that made her tremble in his arms. Her free arm snaked up and tangled in his hair, pressing him down and holding him in place against her. He licked and sucked that one tiny patch of flesh, then slowly—agonizingly slowly, he hoped—kissed his way back up her neck to her jaw.

"Jack," she moaned in the darkness, "I want you."

That was apparently all it took to release the last of his restraint. His lips crashed against Claire's, and she met him with equal fervor. She parted her lips for him, her tongue moving to tangle with his. His free hand ran up and down her side, tracing her curves, while hers wrapped around his waist, pulling him in, holding him close.

They tangled in the darkness, all lips and tongues and hands touching, tasting, feeling, trying to re-familiarize themselves with a body they had once known so very well. Claire smelled of the same soap and shampoo Jack had used, but there was something else, something that reminded him of warm, sunny days. He pressed his hard length against her, and she arched into him, purring in the back of her throat.

"I need to feel you," Jack heard himself say before the thought fully formed in his mind.

Claire pushed herself up and knelt beside him. Jack had just enough time to panic and worry that he'd said the wrong thing. But then, she found his hand in the darkness and pulled him up to also kneel on the bed next to her. She guided his hands to grasp the bottom edge of her T-shirt and then covered them with her own. Without speaking, they both drew her shirt up and over her head, Jack's hands following the soft curves of her body. He flung the shirt into the void. The world outside their bed no longer existed. The darkness was a cloak, keeping reality at bay.

Claire's hands were on his again in an instant, guiding them to the hem of her tank top. They repeated the process, revealing bare skin that burned Jack and set his entire being on fire as his fingers grazed the length of her ribcage. He also discarded that piece of cloth into the nothingness beyond the bed.

And then, his mouth was on Claire's, and his hands were on her breasts, and she was moaning into his mouth and clutching at his back, and time lost all meaning. They rolled together in the sheets, limbs and flesh meeting and mingling as they shed the rest of their clothes. She tasted so familiar, yet different. Her gasps of pleasure as he entered her were like coming home after years away and recognizing everything, yet noticing a new coat of paint on the neighbor's house. Her body, her curves, her flesh were a map he could follow in the dark from memory alone. He didn't need to see to know what gave her pleasure. Past, present, and future crashed into one another as they moved together in the darkness. When she came and cried out his name, Jack could no longer tell where or when they were. They were teenagers having sex for the first time and adults rediscovering each other again. They were both at once, yet neither. Claire's voice, her moans, echoed across the years and sent him over the edge to his own release.

***

Afterward, they lay tangled together, sweaty, sated, and sleepy. Claire curled against him, her head resting on his chest, her fingers idly playing with his scant chest hair. Jack held her loosely, his fingers mindlessly caressing her spine. He was desperately trying to hold the wider world at bay and maintain this small bubble that contained just the two of them, even if just for a little while longer. Alas, even Super-strength wasn't strong enough for that. Reality was beckoning, clawing its way back into his consciousness whether he wanted it to or not.

He needed to ask something, say something, but he wasn't sure what. His earlier fears that Claire had moved on and found someone else had been allayed—mostly—by their lovemaking, but others lingered. Possible questions danced through his mind, but they all seemed wrong for the moment. *Do you still have feelings for me? Do I still have feelings for you? Do you forgive me? Do I forgive you?*

As Claire's fingers danced across his bare chest, Jack realized that he had to be the one to answer two of those questions.

The first, whether he still had feelings for Claire, seemed clear enough. Yes, definitely. All it took was the sight of her face on a New York City street to discombobulate him and throw him off his game. Even Giada noticed it, calling him out on his "crush." But the second question, whether he had forgiven her for how things ended between them years ago, was less certain. She had hurt him. She had never really apologized. She had walked away. That pain had festered for over a decade, and while it had dulled with time, it was still there.

"You may trust this woman with your life," Professor Optimo had said, *"but that doesn't mean you can or should trust her with your heart."*

The memory of his mentor's advice calmed and cooled Jack. He gently rolled her off of him, and his whole body suddenly felt colder, the space between them on the futon stretching to impossible distances.

Jack sat up and scrubbed his eyes with the heels of his hands. He took a deep breath in through his nose, releasing it through his mouth. And another. And another. He needed to find the words to convey how he felt and where he stood with her, especially after what had just happened between them. "Claire—"

At that moment, his burner cell phone began to ring, its LED screen casting a bright glow onto the wall nearby. The all-clear call. Their reprieve together in this little hidden sanctuary had come to an end. It was time to return to the real world. Jack was both relieved and disappointed.

He sighed, stood up, and walked toward the mini-fridge, where he'd left the phone. Wiping any trace of frustration or regret from his voice, he answered the call, fully expecting to hear Professor Optimo's tired yet triumphant voice on the other end.

Instead, he heard Andrew, one of the New York IAS logistics agents, blurt out, "We have a problem."

All thoughts of Claire and broken hearts fled from his mind in an instant. His posture shifted slightly as he came to attention, ready to listen and strategize. "Go ahead."

Andrew wasn't prone to panic, but his tone was dangerously close to that emotion as he explained, "Vengeance has taken down the entire team we sent in to deal with him, including Professor Optimo. Reports from on the ground suggest that his magic power is considerably stronger than anticipated. Our people managed to retreat, but there are significant injuries. Another team is en route, but you're closer. I know you're on protection duty, but we need you to go in on surveillance instead. Do not engage, but keep an eye on Vengeance until more people get there."

"Understood," Jack said. "And the civilian?"

"Alfredo is en route to your location. He can look after her," Andrew said.

Jack nodded, feeling the vice that had started to tighten around his chest release at least a little. Claire would be in good hands with Alfredo. "Understood. I'll move out shortly."

He ended the call and stood there for a moment, looking down at the phone in his hands. It read 6:38 a.m. They'd slept for about six hours. Well, they'd been in bed for six hours. They definitely hadn't slept the whole time. It wasn't much, but it would have to do.

"Is there a problem?" Claire asked from behind him, drawing Jack back into the present moment.

"Yeah," Jack breathed, striding toward the bathroom, "a big fucking problem."

He turned on the bathroom light, blinding them both, and raised a hand to shield his eyes. When he was able to open them slightly, he saw Claire reflected in the bathroom mirror, squinting and turning her head away slightly. The bandage had slipped off her head at some point, and her hair stuck out at odd angles. Her lips looked red and bruised from his attentions, and a hickey was beginning to form on her collarbone. The sheet lay pooled around her waist, revealing her small, pert breasts and taunt nipples. Breasts that he had cupped worshipfully not that long ago. Nipples that he had licked and sucked, eliciting gasps of pleasure. At the sight of the disheveled woman he had just loved so thoroughly, Jack's professional façade melted. "Sorry," he said softly. "I should have warned you about the light."

He forcefully dragged his mind away from his groin and back to the more pressing matter at hand. As he rummaged through the assorted clothing for something to wear, he briefly explained Andrew's instructions. He didn't mention the undercurrent of panic at HQ that accompanied these new orders, but he didn't think he needed to. Claire was smart, and she knew enough about Superheroes to be able to figure out that the situation was dire. More dire than it had been last night.

"And what about me?" she asked. Her tone was clipped and professional, yet Jack could detect the undercurrent of sadness and worry within it. "Do I stay here?"

Jack turned away from the chest of drawers to look at Claire. She sat on the futon, her feet on the floor, the sheet drawn up to cover her breasts. She was absently rubbing the bandage on her left wrist. Her eyes were fixed on him, but they were closed off, revealing nothing.

I'm about to go fight another battle—or at least go on another mission—that she wants to fight for herself, he realized. The thought hit him like a Supervillain's punch to the gut. The younger version of Claire would probably have argued with him, insisting on coming with him, insisting she could help. Yet this older, more mature Claire just sat there staring at him, her eyes clouded and her posture rigid. *She really has grown up,* he thought, and he found himself admiring her even more for it.

Jack took a step forward and sat down beside her. "No. Alfredo is on his way. You probably know him better as the Brooklyn Boulder."

Her eyes widened at that. "The same Brooklyn Boulder who took down the famous vampire gang, the Necrosis Army, in the early 1970s?" she asked eagerly.

Leave it to Claire to know her Superhero history. He nodded. "One and the same. He's retired now, but he still helps out when we need him, often as a civilian advocate and bodyguard. He'll take you to the hospital and stay with you the entire time. He won't leave your side until we're sure Vengeance has been captured and you're safe. You can trust him. He'll take good care of you."

She nodded but didn't say anything. Her tense, closed-off body language was such a stark contrast to the uninhibited passion she'd shown less than an hour earlier that Jack ached with longing. He wanted nothing more than to toss his orders out the window, turn off the lights, crawl back into bed with Claire, and get lost in her again, pretending the outside world did not exist. But he knew that wasn't possible. More importantly, Claire wouldn't allow it. With her, duty always came first.

Jack lingered beside her for a moment, anticipating more questions, but when she remained silent, he got up again and started assembling an outfit. Surveillance meant civilian clothes would be fine, which was good because his Superhero uniform was still dirty and covered in blood. Plus, he hadn't gotten his mask back, and he didn't exactly want to run around Staten Island dressed as Silver Fist, with his face bare and on display for everyone to see.

"Jack," Claire said from behind him.

Jack turned around, clutching two different hoodies, one in each hand. Claire stood before him completely naked, her hands clenched into fists at her sides, a grim and determined expression on her face. Her chest heaved slightly, giving him a clue about the emotion likely churning behind her otherwise stony expression. *Ah, here it comes*, he thought, deflating slightly. *She's going to make her case for coming with me.* He steeled himself to turn her down.

"Promise me that I'll see you again," she said.

Jack opened and closed his mouth a few times. He realized that he probably looked like a fish and closed his mouth with a snap. This wasn't what he was expecting, and he had no idea how to respond.

Claire continued, "Promise me that after I leave here, I'll see you again. In person. As Jack Elliott, not Silver Fist. At a coffee shop or a bar or something, not at a crime scene. Promise not to disappear on me."

She wants to see me again. As me. Maybe...

When Jack didn't respond, Claire took a step forward, her eyes becoming desperate. "I've made mistakes. Lots of mistakes. My biggest was you. I know it's been twelve years, and I realize that I don't fully know who you are now, but... I'd like the chance to get to know the person you've become. If you want, that is..." she trailed off, all her bravado melting away. She looked remarkably like the fourteen-year-old girl who suddenly seemed nervous and uncertain the first time he'd asked if he could kiss her.

It's not an apology for the past, he observed, *but it's a start. Maybe the apology can come later, once we're out of this dire situation and can sit down and talk like normal people.*

Still, another concern lingered, and he had to address it. "I have one question for you," Jack said cautiously, taking a step forward. "You aren't currently involved with anyone, are you? I mean, I hope I didn't just make love to another man's wife."

A grin spread across Claire's face. She placed a hand on her bare hip and cocked it to the side suggestively. "I'm as single as the day is long. And you?"

Jack tried—and failed—to fight the smile blooming on his own face. "Painfully single. Embarrassingly single. Giada makes fun of how single I am and tries to fix me up with her friends."

At that, Claire let out breathy laugh. She smacked both palms to her forehead. "Oh god, I'm such an idiot!" At Jack's questioning expression, she explained, her cheeks heating to a bright red color, "I was worried that Giada was your wife or girlfriend or something!"

Jack just stared at her for a second, confused and bemused. *How on earth did she get that idea?* Then, he burst out laughing. Claire must have caught onto his hilarity because she started laughing as well. "Me... and Giada?" he wheezed. "Oh Claire, that's a good one!"

They both gave into their laughter for a few minutes, and when it subsided, they wiped away the tears gathering at the corners of their eyes.

Jack felt lighter than he had in ages. He still didn't fully trust Claire with his heart again, but he was willing to at least see where this whole *thing* between them might go. Perhaps it was time to, as Claire had put it, stop going through the motions of life and actually live it. "Okay, it's a date," he said. "Once this is all over, and Vengeance is behind bars, and you're feeling better, let's meet up at Moonbucks and talk. *Really* talk."

Claire smiled and nodded, her eyes still a little wet from her embarrassed laughter. "It's a date," she agreed.

Jack's stomach fluttered just like it had freshman year when Claire agreed to be his girlfriend. Somehow, that long-ago September day in Iowa felt both like it was yesterday and like it was a million years ago. He didn't think he could return to that place of innocence, but he liked this new place he was in, too.

A date, he thought, turning away to get dressed. When he stepped into the bathroom and closed the door behind him, the face reflected back at him in the mirror wore the dopiest smile.

***

Fifteen minutes later, Jack swung the door of the wardrobe open into Regina's office. Claire was right behind him, and they were both bundled up in warm civilian garb.

It was nearly seven a.m., and the club was closed. Only Regina remained, doing her bookkeeping for the previous night. She still wore her suit, but her jacket was slung across the back of her chair, and she looked like she was ready to fall asleep at her desk. She startled and dropped her pen when the pair stepped out of the closet. "You're up early, given how late you got in. How did you sleep?" she asked without getting up.

"Great, all things considered," Claire said, smoothing the front of her slightly oversized navy blue trench coat. She'd had to roll up the cuffs so they wouldn't cover her hands, but based on the nonchalant way she'd done so, Jack assumed this was still normal for her.

"Mmmm hmmm..." Regina said suggestively.

Jack eyed her and didn't like the knowing smirk that was slowly spreading across her face. She arched an eyebrow at him, and his own face heated. "Knock it off, Gina. We have a situation."

At that, Regina became all business. She held up a hand to stop him from saying more. "I don't want to know about it. The less I know, the less danger to me and mine."

Jack nodded. She was right. Regina was a vital asset to the New York Superheroes, and a large part of what made her so vital was the fact that she limited her involvement with them to simply hiding them when they needed it. If she were to get in any deeper, it could put her entire operation—and the benefits they reaped from it—at risk. With that in mind, he simply said, "I need to go. Alfredo will be here soon to take Claire back to Manhattan. Don't let her leave until you see and speak with him, and don't let her leave with anyone but him. Understood?"

"Of course," Regina said, raising her palms in the air in a casual gesture of surrender. "I'll keep your girlfriend safe for you. Don't worry!"

Jack made a choking noise in his throat, but he was distracted by the feeling of Claire's small hand in his, tugging him past Regina's desk and out into the hallway. Regina's chuckle followed them until it was cut off by the click of the door closing behind them.

Once they were alone, Claire laughed. "I haven't seen you turn that red over me being called your 'girlfriend' since we were fourteen!"

He sniffed and raised his nose in the air. "Regina just likes to tease me."

"It sounds like you're surrounded by strong women who like to tease you," Claire countered. "This Giada person... Regina... me..." She trailed off, letting the implication hang between them.

Jack swallowed, unsure how to respond. Back out in the harsh light of day, their interlude upstairs felt like a dream. He could still taste Claire on his lips, but he was also conscious that it hadn't even been twenty-four hours since she came back into his life. He was slightly dazed by the whole thing. *Or maybe I'm just too tired to process anything*, he thought. Playing it safe, he took a step toward her and tucked her red scarf around her neck.

"So... can I get your number?" he asked as casually as he dared. "You know... so we can set up that coffee date?"

Claire's expression morphed from teasing to delighted, and Jack found that he was charmed by the way her red scarf set off her blazing-red hair. She was still pale, there were dark circles under her eyes, and her entire cheek was covered by a flesh-tone Band-Aid that was actually several shades darker than her naturally fair skin, but she looked warm and bundled up in her borrowed clothes. He could picture her grasping a steaming cardboard cup of hot coffee between her hands, taking little sips, and smiling up at him in appreciation. It was a mental image cultivated from countless rom-coms set in New York in the winter, and Jack realized with a start that he was eager to bring those rom-com scenes—ice-skating at Rockefeller Center, admiring all the holiday window displays in the shops along Fifth Avenue, sipping hot chocolate in a tiny café while snow swirled outside—to life with her.

Claire opened her mouth to reply, then paused and gave him a bemused look. "You don't have your own phone with you, do you? You can't exactly plug my number into a burner phone, you know."

Jack wanted to kick himself. She was right. His personal phone was back in his locker at IAS headquarters. He didn't want to risk writing it down on a scrap of paper and losing it, and given the dangerous situation he was heading into, writing it in ink on his flesh seemed even more foolhardy.

Claire laughed at what he could only assume was a look of frustration on his face. She reached up, tugged at the lapels of his nondescript black peacoat, and adjusted his own matching red scarf. "No worries. Just look me up on Facespace. Look for the 'Claire Green' who lives in Manhattan and is dressed as a sexy cartoon chipmunk. You can't miss me."

Jack laughed and filed that information away. "Aren't you worried I'll disappear and not contact you?"

"Nah," she said. Her hands lingered on his chest. "I trust you. Just... be careful, okay?"

"I will. I promise."

Acting on instinct, Jack wrapped his arms around her. His movement was so fast that Claire squeaked in surprise. He pulled her toward him, mindful of his Super-strength and being careful not to crush her. He buried his nose in the hair on the top of her head, inhaling briefly. Claire's arms drifted up to wrap around his waist as well, and Jack allowed his eyes to flutter shut and enjoy this stolen moment with Claire in his arms. Visions of the two of them entwined in bed danced through his mind, and Jack found himself looking forward to repeating the experience—but this time, with the lights on so he could see her. She squeezed him slightly, and he squeezed back.

And then, Jack pulled away and was out the door before he lost all willpower. He didn't dare look back or say another word. If he did, he wasn't sure he'd have the strength to leave.

The early morning sunlight was weak, but it still stung his eyes after the dimness of their hidden nest and Regina's office. His breath was visible in the chilly air, and the cold stung his nostrils. Jack pulled the hood of his black hoodie over his head to help keep him warm and shoved his hands in his coat pockets.

It's game time, he told himself as he turned and started walking back toward the warehouse he'd escaped from last night. He pushed all thoughts of Claire out of his mind. He needed to focus on Vengeance and his mission.

After all, he and Claire would have all the time in the world. Later.

Chapter 11

Claire felt unexpectedly bereft as she watched Jack practically fling himself out the door. Her arms hung limply at her sides, the sensation of his firm, muscular body beneath her hands still lingering. She couldn't erase the memory of the glimpse she'd gotten of his face as he practically ran away from her: an expression of pain and adoration mixed into one.

Regina clicked her tongue behind Claire, drawing the shorter woman out of her reverie. "That one," Regina said, nodding toward the door Jack had just vanished through, "has got it bad." Turning to look at Claire, she added, "Come on. I just brewed some fresh coffee."

The two women enjoyed their coffee in companionable silence in Regina's office. The coffee was richer and darker than what Claire usually drank, but it woke her up and helped her synapses start firing again. She desperately wanted to question Regina about New York's Superheroes, but judging by her exchange with Jack earlier, the club owner evidently operated by her own code of silence. Instead, Claire settled for looking around the office. She noticed that all the mugs sitting on a shelf beside Regina's coffee maker were various shades of pink, and she laughed when Regina handed her hers. It was hot pink and featured the outline of a cat around the words, "Show me your kitties."

Claire was about to comment on the mug when a bear of a man—as tall as Jack, but much, much wider—all but stomped into the office without knocking. He doffed his blue tweed flat cap, revealing a bald head that shone brilliantly even beneath the dim lights in Regina's office. "The coyote howls at night," he said, his grey eyes bright and focused.

"But the lion roars alone," Regina answered evenly, not rising from her seat at her desk. She sipped her coffee and looked up at the man expectantly.

"Nonetheless, the deer flees from them both," he answered in a heavy New York accent.

Claire couldn't quite believe that they were using this kind of old-fashioned passcode. Surely, they would have high-tech security systems or digital wallets that bore their credentials... right?

"And runs straight into my arms," Regina finished. "It's good to see you, Alfredo. You should come out to one of my clubs some time and see me."

Alfredo smiled and stepped farther into the room. "You know my old lady wouldn't like that, Gina. She's annoyed as it is that I was called out early in the morning to escort a lovely young lady named Claire"—here, he looked at Claire and waggled his bushy eyebrows comedically—"around the city for a few hours." He eyed Claire's mug and asked, "Say, is there more of that coffee? I could use a cup of joe before we get back on the road."

Regina poured another cup of coffee into a pastel-pink mug, and she and Alfredo spent a few minutes chatting about the state of the local roads while he drank the brew down as quickly as he could.

Claire liked the look of this huge man, with his warm manner and animated facial expressions. She tried to picture him as the Brooklyn Boulder, his skin hard and grey and crackled like the surface of the moon. He still had the huge muscles and thick torso of a lifelong bodybuilder, but the laugh lines around his eyes and the thick gold band around his left ring finger spoke of a life that involved far more than physical training and punching bad guys.

Alfredo threw back the last swallow of his coffee, put his mug down on Regina's desk, and announced, "Okay, ladies, we should hit the road. Miss Claire here has an appointment with the ER, as I understand."

Claire soon found herself in the front seat of a spotlessly clean, though rather old and worn, silver sedan. She couldn't understand how Alfredo fit inside his tiny car, but he folded himself behind the driver's seat without any problems. To her surprise, 1990s ska-punk music blared from the radio when he started the vehicle, and he immediately reached out to lower the volume. "Sorry about that," he said with a grin. "I really like the trumpets."

Claire grinned back. "No worries. I actually like it, too."

Alfredo brought the volume back up a little, and they cruised away from the strip club accompanied by a hard, driving beat and brassy, sassy trumpet riffs.

As they headed out of this neighborhood and started making their way back to Manhattan, Claire finally allowed her mind to drift back to her normal life and everything—and everyone—that awaited her there. Everyone would be worried about her: her parents back in Iowa, Ramona here in the city, her coworkers. Her and Silver Fist's abduction had certainly been all over the news. Claire would have to call everyone and let them know she was okay. Her inbox would be filled with messages. Her social media pages would be blowing up. And her blog—oh god, her blog! For a moment, Claire thrilled at the amount of traffic her blog was probably getting.

But then, her thoughts drifted to more practical matters, and her excitement cooled. She'd have to make a statement to the police, and that meant having to be careful about not revealing Jack's true identity. The police and Superheroes often worked together, but they also had an adversarial relationship at times. Claire didn't want to complicate an already-tense situation.

There was also her looming debriefing with the IAS. She wasn't nervous about that; if anything, she was excited. But it was another task to complete.

And then, there was the fact that she was still uncertain about exactly what had happened in her apartment yesterday when she appeared to lose time and woke up to find that she had somehow defeated Zoe and Sucker-Punch without even realizing it. *Was it really only yesterday morning?* Claire wondered in shock. It hadn't even been twenty-four hours yet, but it felt like years since her biggest concern was just going home after a long shift and going to bed.

As they approached the waterfront, Claire gazed out the window, watching New Jersey grow closer and closer, while Manhattan's skyscrapers appeared on the horizon in the distance. A movement out of the corner of her eye drew Claire's attention and then snapped her out of her thoughts about her pre-Vengeance life.

About three blocks away, a tall man in a dark suit marched into a large industrial boathouse. Several people followed him, including two men dragging a large, limp male body behind them. A red scarf dangled from the unconscious man's neck.

Ice ran through Claire's veins, and she sucked in a harsh breath. She knew that scarf. She had just handled it less than an hour ago. It exactly matched her own. "Stop the car!" she ordered, shooting a hand out in front of Alfredo.

He slammed on the brakes so hard that Claire worried the airbags would deploy. "What? What do you see?" Alfredo demanded, but Claire was already opening her door and running after the men who had vanished into the boathouse.

"I spotted Vengeance! They have Jack!" she called behind her. "Let the IAS know!" She glanced back just long enough to see Alfredo nod and pull out his cell phone.

Claire's mind was already racing through possibilities and plans. Vengeance had recaptured Jack. Whether it was a trap or an accident, something awful had happened, and less than an hour after he'd promised he would be careful, he'd been captured by a Supervillain. Claire bit her lip as she ran, her breaths coming out as visible puffs in the cold morning air. She was fully aware that she was now running back *toward* the very criminal she had escaped from the night before and whom she suspected was perfectly capable of following through on his threat to kill her just to teach Jack a lesson. *Well, I just won't let that happen, then*, she thought tartly.

Claire skidded to a halt at the open sliding corrugated-metal door that was wide and tall enough to drive two semi-trucks in side by side. Most of the shed-like structure extended out over the Kill Van Kull, the tidal strait that separated Staten Island from Bayonne, New Jersey. The open doors at the far end of the structure led directly into the Kill. The covered artificial bay was surrounded on three sides by a high concrete 'U,' which was packed with enough pallets of unmarked cardboard boxes to provide cover for an interloper like Claire. Several old motors the size of a car were suspended from metal racks. A sixteen-foot ladder leaned against the wall beside the door. The amount of dust and cobwebs everywhere suggested that this wasn't exactly a high-traffic area.

As Claire poked her head in, she wrinkled her nose at the acrid scent of diesel fuel and the fishy smell of the Kill. But that's not what truly held Claire's attention. Floating in the middle of the boathouse's bay was an old, rusty submarine that looked like it couldn't hold more than twenty people. From what she could see of the exterior, Claire was concerned about its structural integrity. That thing looked like it had last been used during the Korean War, and it didn't appear to be well-cared-for.

Vengeance didn't seem to share her worries, though. He boldly strode across a wide gangway to the sub, and his followers dragged Jack along in his wake. One of them lost his grip and almost dropped Jack head-down on the sharp metal grate surface of the gangway, but he recovered quickly. Claire let out a breath she didn't realize she was holding as they continued into the sub.

Claire ducked back out of sight and crouched down behind a rusty oil drum, thinking hard. Jack had rushed over here because he was the closest Superhero, and the IAS needed someone to keep an eye on Vengeance. Others were on the way, but if Vengeance disappeared beneath the surface of the water in this submarine before they got here—which appeared to be his plan—it wouldn't matter. Time was of the essence. If the Superheroes needed eyes and ears on Vengeance, Claire and Alfredo were the most obvious candidates to do just that.

Green, this guy wants to kill you, the more practical voice in her head reminded her. *You don't have Superpowers. Alfredo is retired. You don't know where they're going or why. Once you get onboard that sub, you don't even know if you'll be able to contact the IAS and let them know what Vengeance is doing. You are well and truly out of your depth.*

But they had Jack. And in the face of that fact, everything else was inconsequential.

Claire glanced back toward Alfredo's car. He had gotten out and was now speaking animatedly into his phone, his gestures large and angry. With his free hand, he pointed toward the ground in a sharp, stabbing motion several times. When he noticed her watching him, he pointed directly at her and then at the ground beside him, the universal signal for "Get your ass over here now." Before he could do more than that, though, he was distracted by something the person he was talking to said. He turned away and threw his free arm up in the air in frustration.

At that moment, the sub's ancient diesel engines sputtered to life with a dull roar.

Shit waffles, Claire thought, panic spreading through her. *I'm running out of time. I can't wait for him to sort this out.* She looked back once more and saw that her temporary protector's back was still turned to her. *Sorry, Alfredo. I'm sure you're going to get in trouble for this.*

Claire took three slow, deep breaths to steady herself, then stood up and peered around the corner back into the boathouse. No one was around, but the sub's hatch was propped open. It was now or never. She darted in, keeping to the shadows behind the pallets. If she was lucky, there might be a second hatch or another way in, but she couldn't see anything from afar. She would have to get closer.

Claire crossed the metal grate gangway and climbed up onto the top of the sub. That's when she saw it: a larger hatch that looked like it was intended for loading equipment toward the aft of the sub. Her heart raced with joy, and she hurried over, walking as quietly as she could and crouching low for fear of being seen or heard. Unfortunately, this other hatch was rusted in place. Try as Claire might, it wouldn't budge, and all she got for her trouble was flakes of rust coming off on her palms and scraped, bloodied knuckles.

While Claire had been studying the sub from behind her cover of boxes, she'd noticed a large access panel just above the waterline on the port side of the sub that appeared to have handle releases. Now, it seemed like her last, best hope. *Perhaps I could get the panel off and find a way inside?*

Claire slid over to the port side of the ship and lay flat on the deck on her belly. Her fingers could just barely reach the edge of the panel. *Thanks, short arms,* she thought for what seemed like the millionth time in her life. She wiggled farther over the edge, letting her head and shoulders swing free. It was only about a five-foot drop into the water below, but she knew that water would be filthy and cold. She reached for the panel's handle release, but her fingers just brushed it. *Now would be a really great time to suddenly develop the Superpower to stretch my limbs at will,* she thought, reaching with all her might.

Her fingertips just curled around the edge of the handle. Before she could celebrate, though, cold, rough hands closed around her bandaged ankles, sending a jolt of pain through her. Claire yelped as she was dragged backward, away from the edge of the submarine. Her body was raked across the sub's harsh, rust-covered surface, and one of the bandages around her wrist caught on a sharp bit of corroded metal, unraveling itself as she was pulled away.

"What do we have here?" a voice thundered behind her, and Claire twisted around to see who had grabbed her. It was Sucker-Punch, the goon who had invaded her apartment yesterday morning and whom she had apparently taken down without any memory of doing so. He now sported an impressively dark black eye, and his jaw seemed bruised and swollen. And he did not look pleased to see her again.

"Fancy meeting you here," Claire said with a smile before kicking out at him with all her might. That must have surprised him because he released his grip on one of her legs, and she kicked upward at his genitals, landing a solid hit. That was all it took. He released Claire entirely and bent over double, clutching his sensitive manhood. His face and shaved head turned grey, his eyes bugged out, and he exhaled in a sharp wheeze.

Claire scrambled up and raced toward the hatch. The engines were growing louder; the sub vibrated beneath her feet now. She had to take the chance. Sucker-Punch tried to call out after her, but he couldn't manage more than a squeaking gasp.

Claire climbed up the ladder to the hatch and peered down into it. She had no idea where it led, but she didn't see or hear anyone immediately below, so she swung her legs over the lip and started climbing down.

The inside of the hatchway was illuminated by red work lights, many of which appeared to have burnt out over the decades. It smelled strongly of oil, diesel, and cigarette smoke, which turned Claire's stomach. The ladder ran down through the tight space for about eight feet before it entered the brightly lit room below.

Claire hesitated. Just because she didn't see or hear anyone below didn't mean that there wasn't a guard stationed just out of sight, ready to take her prisoner again. But she couldn't stay here. Sucker-Punch would be climbing down the ladder after her any second now.

As her panic mounted, Claire glanced around and spotted something that looked very promising: an access tube, probably intended for repairs. And it was small. Very small. Claire wriggled into the tube. She fit, but only just. If this had indeed been designed as an access tube, it must have been meant for the very smallest of sailors. Or perhaps it wasn't an access tube after all. In that moment, it didn't matter to Claire. It was a solid, round metal tube that she could get through and that supported her weight. She started army-crawling, trying to get away from the sub's entrance as quickly as possible.

The tube became dark as soon as Claire got a few feet away from the opening, so she had to slow down. Her bulky coat, scarf, and hat made crawling cumbersome and uncomfortable, and her injured wrists hurt, especially the one that had come unbandaged and was now exposed to the air, but she kept going, slowly advancing one crawl at a time. It was hot and stuffy in the tube, and the vibration from the engine rattled her teeth. She tried to move silently so the submarine's other occupants wouldn't hear her, though the engine was loud enough to give her some cover. Plus, she was fairly sure no one onboard would be able to follow her down here. Claire herself couldn't even turn around in this tight space, and Vengeance seemed to favor the large and muscular. *Alfredo would never have fit in here. Maybe being small is an asset after all*, Claire thought for the first time in her life.

A few moments later, Claire heard someone descending the ladder behind her, and she froze. She couldn't see anything, and she waited in dread for Sucker-Punch to grab her ankles again and yank her backward out of the tube. He descended the ladder slowly, so slowly. Claire could practically feel his eyes on her rear end, but she resisted the urge to pull her feet close in behind her. She didn't want the movement to catch his eye. She held her breath and waited, listening to her heart pound against her ribs.

Sucker-Punch continued on down. She didn't hear him raise any kind of alarm. *But he saw me come down here, right? He must know I'm on the sub. Why isn't he alerting the others?* Claire's thoughts flashed back to those two guards in the warehouse the night before. They had seemed strangely anxious to recapture her. *Could it be they're more scared of Vengeance's anger over failure than anything else?* The thought unnerved her.

Claire waited a few more seconds to make sure he was truly gone, then continued on. There was a dim light up ahead, and as she approached, she saw that it was coming from another tunnel that connected on the right. The light was dim, but Claire could see that the tube ended in a large fan ahead of her. *So that's what this tube is: an air filtration system. I'm in the air vents!*

Claire stifled a giggle. Action movies were full of heroes crawling around in the air vents, and she had endured more than a little teasing over the years about the fact that she was one of the few people who could accurately, realistically do that. Even Jack had joked about it when they watched *Mission Impossible* once at his house as teenagers. And now, here she was, actually crawling through the air vents of a decrepit submarine to rescue him.

Since there was no going back, Claire turned to the right and headed toward the light. She quickly realized that the illumination came from a grate in the floor just head of her near the fan. And she could hear voices through it.

At the grate, Claire lay flat on her belly and peered down into what looked like a command center filled with Vengeance and his crew. Claire shrank back into the shadows. Vengeance sat in the captain's chair, looking grand and giving orders with a self-satisfied smirk on his face. The lighting wasn't the best, but she could see that his minions were running checks on various systems, most of which appeared to be controlled with analogue switches and knobs, rather than computers. To her horror, she realized that they were all carrying guns, and ammunition, boxes of explosives, and detonators filled the room. Whatever they were doing, it was on a large scale.

As Claire looked around, she recognized Zoe from her apartment. She hadn't seen the beautiful raven-haired henchman since then and wondered if she was actually a part of Vengeance's organization or just a hired hand brought in to handle Claire's abduction. Now, seeing her study a tablet closely while other goons kept busy around her, Claire concluded that Zoe was definitely a part of Vengeance's team. Possibly even a chief lieutenant, based on how the other henchmen kept as wide a berth around her as they could in such a small space.

Sucker-Punch was down there as well, carefully peering around the room, studying everything. His gaze swept up toward the ceiling—and Claire. She held her breath, but his eyes moved across her as though she wasn't even there. *He doesn't want his boss to find out that he spotted and then lost an intruder,* Claire realized. *That's why he hasn't raised the alarm. He'd rather "find" me and claim the glory than admit that he screwed up and face punishment.*

Sucker-Punch moved away, continuing his surreptitious search, and that's when Claire spotted Jack. He sat on a thinly padded metal bench, slumped against the bulkhead behind him—out of the way, yet close at hand, should they need him. He was again bound and held in place by the same bright-blue glow that had restrained him last night. Her eyes were drawn to a point of bright light on his chest, and she realized that some kind of amulet was affixed there. This was the source of the light that rippled and danced around his unconscious form. A jagged crack ran through the stone at the center of the amulet, and Claire wondered if it had anything to do with how he'd escaped the night before. He appeared to be uninjured, but he was unconscious. He sat slumped over in his shapeless black wool coat, hoodie sweatshirt, and jeans, his feet in their Timberland boots kicked out gracelessly. His red scarf dangled around his neck, almost ready to fall off.

Activity picked up in the command center, and Claire's eyes moved back to Vengeance. There was a loud bang, followed by a grating sound. A moment later, one final crew member appeared, and those manning the various stations went into action, pressing ancient buttons and turning half-rusted knobs.

Several different whirring, humming sounds echoed all around Claire, and a deafening roar raced down the air duct behind her. A cloud of dust enveloped her, and Claire was terrified a coughing fit would give away her location. She closed her eyes and covered her mouth and nose, focusing on her breathing with all her might. A few tiny, involuntary coughs escaped, but all the noise around her more than covered them.

The clanking, grinding whir of metal surrounded her, and for a moment, Claire was afraid the air duct would collapse under her weight. Then, there was a jarring jolt to the side. *We're moving*, she realized. *All that commotion was us getting under way.*

There was a second jolt, harder than the first. It forced Jack back in his seat, and his head slammed hard into the bulkhead. Claire winced in silent sympathy. *Maybe now we'll both have concussions*, she thought.

Jack groaned, and his eyes popped open. His arm muscles twitched, as if he were trying to raise his hand to caress his aching head, but he didn't move. He was once again held immobile.

"Oh, so sorry about the jolt," Vengeance said as he turned toward his prisoner. "I suppose I should have warned you to grab onto something." He laughed, mocking Jack's bound state, and his entire crew laughed as well, as though on command. Only Zoe didn't join in. She looked annoyed or bored and even dared to roll her eyes.

The submarine began to move, and Claire settled down to wait out the ride here, unnoticed. Sucker-Punch had vanished from sight, probably still quietly looking for her so he wouldn't get in trouble. Claire knew she'd have to deal with him later, but for the moment, she felt secure in her cramped, Claire-sized space. She could keep an eye on Jack and Vengeance and know exactly what was going on in the command center.

The IAS needed surveillance on Vengeance. It doesn't get much better than this, she thought. *Of course, I don't exactly know where we're going or have any way to contact them and relay any intel I gather.*

At least Jack appeared to be okay. He hadn't responded to Vengeance's taunt, but his eyes were alert, and his ears seemed to be trained on the crewmembers' murmured conversations. His powerful arms struggled against his magical bonds, but it did no good. He was held fast.

The sub descended, and Claire's ears popped gently. She had no indication of where they were going—no display screens to study or whispered coordinates to overhear. *I guess I'll find out soon enough.*

In the meantime, she studied the crew. Claire counted fifteen crew members, plus Vengeance and Zoe. That was a lot to get past. Plus, Vengeance had the ability to fold space. But Claire just had to destroy or damage the amulet on Jack's chest. Presumably, this would break whatever binding spell held him in place, and then, he'd be able to take them all on with his Super-strength.

But what if he can't?

The sudden thought troubled her, but it was a very real consideration. Vengeance had captured him twice now, at least the first time with ease. Plus, he had somehow defeated an entire task force of Superheroes, including the veteran Professor Optimo. Even his own crew appeared to be afraid of him, terrified to admit failure. What was the source of *his* power?

For the first time, Claire turned her full attention onto the man who claimed to be a wizard and studied him.

Vengeance didn't have a staff or a wand or an amulet—other than the one on Jack—or any of the other showy, theatrical items magic users often relied on. Most Superheroes and Supervillains who claimed to use magic actually had powers that could be explained by science. And yet, based on what Claire had read online, even after eight years under observation, Vengeance and the source of his "magic" were still a mystery.

Jack had been able to knock him out with a single punch eight years ago—with a little help from the one and only Claire Green, of course. What had changed? What had enabled Vengeance to go from defeated minor Supervillain to major player, taking down some of the best Superheroes in the world?

Claire looked at him and didn't see anything special: a late-middle-aged man with white hair and a white beard, an obviously fake British accent, and a taste for the overly dramatic. *I'm missing something. Something important.*

She cast her mind back to all the Superhero fan blogs she had read over the years, especially those from the time of Vengeance's capture. Quite a few had discussed and analyzed his powers and motives, which remained shadowy to this day. He clearly had an axe to grind with Superheroes, but why? And why this interest in The Elite Five and their base?

Before Claire could follow that thought any further, activity picked up in the command center below, and the clanking and grinding noises rushed over her again. Whatever their destination was, they had apparently reached it.

In his seat in the middle of the room, Vengeance's face twisted into a pleased smirk. He inhaled deeply, as if tasting his triumph in the stale, musty air that rushed over and past Claire in her hiding spot.

She glanced back at Jack. His face was an unreadable mask, and for a moment, it again occurred to Claire that she didn't know this man. Not really. Not anymore. He had been her first love as a teenager, and she could still taste the salt of his sweat on her tongue now, but in this moment, he was a stranger to her. Here, he was firmly ensconced in *his* world, and the face he wore was that of a stoic Superhero. The man who blushed and stammered as they said goodbye in the hallway outside Regina's office was long gone; in his place was the kind of hero that Claire idolized, yet still felt was so far beyond her, she could never bridge that gap.

That thought, coupled with Jack's icy-cold blue eyes, frightened Claire and sent her mentally and emotionally stumbling back for a moment. She closed her eyes and tried to conjure the image of his bright-red face when Regina had called Claire his "girlfriend." That expression had proved to her that the Jack she'd known—the gentle, quiet, shy Jack he had been long ago—was still there, buried within him. He hid it now in order to do his job, but it was still a part of him. Claire was sure of it.

If we get out of this alive, Claire promised herself, *I'll get to know him again. I'll try to understand the man he is now.* She didn't want to rely on the ghosts of who they had been in a different time, a different world. Jack was, in many ways, a stranger to her now, but Claire wanted the chance to get to know this stranger who wore the face of the man she had once loved.

Her thoughts were interrupted by Zoe looking up from her tablet and announcing, "We're receiving an automated radio transmission from the base."

Vengeance's head snapped around to face Jack. "Silver Fist... no...*Jack*," he purred with a venomous smile.

Jack floated up into the air and toward the Supervillain. Claire stifled a gasp at the sight.

"Now, I will ask you again, Jack: what is the access code for The Elite Five's base?"

Jack said nothing and stared straight ahead, his jaw set defiantly.

"Let's not do this again," Vengeance said with a tired sigh, as if he were dealing with an unruly child. "It's quite pointless. I could threaten you in a variety of ways, none of which will work. But I don't have to do any of that. You see, I have Miss Claire Green locked inside an empty torpedo. At my command, she will be launched from this vessel directly into the walls of The Elite Five's base. I'm sure those are well-armored enough to withstand a single, unarmed torpedo, but I doubt the stray kitten will."

Jack's eyes darted to Vengeance's, his jaw working angrily. His chest visibly heaved, and his arms twitched, as if he were trying to throw himself at the Supervillain.

For his part, Vengeance's bluff was perfect. His gloating smirk and dancing eyes revealed nothing of the bald-faced lie he'd just told.

"Furthermore," he continued, "I know Miss Green's home address and workplace. I possess her list of contacts and have access to her email and social media accounts. I know, for example, that her parents live at 1324 Washington Avenue Southwest in Cedar Rapids, Iowa. I know that her older sister lives in Los Angeles and is an entertainment lawyer. I know that her older brother lives in Chicago and works in the theater as a stage manager. I know that she has two *adorable* nieces." At this, Jack stiffened, and Vengeance leered triumphantly.

Ice ran through Claire's veins. It was one thing to threaten her, but it was another thing entirely to bring her family into this. The roaring in her ears almost drowned out Vengeance's next words. Almost.

"Of course, I'm not an unreasonable man." He leaned into Jack's face, his smile poisonous. Claire shivered. Jack's jaw worked with rage. "As you pointed out last night, Miss Green and her family are all innocent bystanders. None of them have to get hurt. But that's entirely up to you... Jack Elliott, who was tagged in her very first Facespace profile picture. Junior prom, was it? You were a lovely couple," the Villain purred.

Claire's throat closed up, and her heart dropped. She was afraid she was going to throw up. She'd made a royal mess of things, bumbling into matters far above her pay grade. She had posted information about The Elite Five from her great-aunt Lillian that she knew she probably shouldn't be sharing. Which had drawn the attention of a Supervillain. Which had led to her capture and accidentally revealing Jack's name. And now, this same Supervillain with a penchant for revenge against Superheroes knew Jack's full identity as well as hers. If he could put two and two together from that ancient profile picture, he could track down Jack's parents and brother.

Jack's words from that long-ago day in the high school parking lot came back to mock her: *"You can't always do everything yourself... You can't take on the entire world. Not by yourself."* He was right. This whole situation was caused by her thinking she could handle anything and everything. She'd thought she was invulnerable. Sure, she didn't have Superpowers, but she thought being Claire Green was enough. She hadn't thought about the repercussions of posting family secrets on the internet, of going to find Ramona herself, of blurting out Jack's name. And now, Jack's secret identity was blown wide open. And it was all her fault.

It didn't matter that Vengeance was lying about having captured her. What mattered was the information he had about the both of them. That's why Claire knew what Jack would do next, and it almost destroyed her.

"Fine," Jack muttered through gritted teeth. Helpless rage danced in his eyes. He sucked in a breath and then rattled off a long alphanumeric sequence.

Claire didn't have to wait for Zoe's report to know that he wasn't lying this time.

Chapter 12

Claire cradled her head in her hands and silently wept. Her heart felt like it was either going to explode out of her chest or collapse in on itself like a dying star. She wanted to just close her eyes and sleep there in the air vent forever, growing colder and colder until she froze to death and never had to think about any of this ever again.

She had failed. She, Claire Green, had failed at something so spectacularly, it had cost Jack his secret identity and possibly his career as a Superhero. It had put her family and his at risk. He had been forced to betray vital Superhero secrets that could mean all kinds of terrible, evil things, just to protect his loved ones. Even if he could forgive her, Claire didn't know if she'd ever be able to forgive herself.

There in the air vent of a rusty, cobwebbed, seventy-year-old submarine, Claire bid farewell to the bright future that had just begun to dawn. She had felt so much promise, so much hope for rekindling something with Jack when they bid farewell at Regina's place this morning, but now, that future tasted like ashes in her mouth. There was no way he would want to go out for a casual coffee with her and see where things might go between them now that more than a decade had passed since she'd last hurt him. She had inadvertently hurt him again, and this time, it was much, much worse. She had put his family at risk, and she wouldn't blame Jack if he never wanted to lay eyes on her again.

Being a Superhero wasn't like a regular job. Claire had known that since she was a starry-eyed child, but she'd never really appreciated the cost that job had on the people who did it. Putting on a mask or a cape or a Super-suit meant hiding a part of who you were from the world in order to protect yourself. And it also meant that loving a Superhero was to put them—and you—at risk.

As Claire mourned a future that would now never be, she realized that she still loved Jack. She had never stopping loving him, and her heart shattered into a million crystalline shards at the realization. Her arms ached to hold him again, even knowing she probably never would. She longed to rest her head against his firm chest. She wanted to feel his lips against hers. But she wouldn't. It was over before it had begun.

She was a wild card, a liability. If they got out of this alive—and that was still a big *if*—Claire owed it to Jack to stay out of his life and remain far, far away from him.

There would be no coffee dates, no dinner, no dancing, no ice skating at Rockefeller Plaza beneath the massive Christmas tree. There would be no introducing him to Ramona and her friends here in New York, no eventual moving in together, no going home to Iowa for their twenty-year high school reunion as a couple and smiling happily as everyone gushed about how they always knew they were "meant to be." None of it could happen.

Just for a moment, Claire allowed herself to fully live out a future with Jack, imagining all the things they would now never do together: making love, getting married, laughing, arguing, growing old together. And then, when she reached the end, she put it all away in a box and closed the lid. She locked that box in her mind and shoved it in the back of the closet, on the highest shelf imaginable. She had to focus on what was possibly her final mission: rescue Jack and get them out of there alive. That was all.

Claire felt cold and numb and empty. She wept, but she made no noise.

***

When Claire came back out of herself and returned to the world, new, unfamiliar grating and clanking sounds were increasing all around her. For a moment, she feared that the sub had collided with something and was being torn asunder. Then, she realized that the vessel wasn't shaking or vibrating any more than it had before. No, this was most likely something *outside* of the submarine.

Below her, Vengeance gazed through the sub's periscope, captivated by whatever he saw. The crew was busy at their stations, checking their instruments and reading off numbers and data to each other. Zoe was still engrossed in her tablet, her fingers scrolling through and manipulating whatever data she was studying so intently.

Only Jack was still. He sat slumped against the bulkhead, his head hanging down, his shoulders in a posture of defeat. Claire's newfound resolve to remove herself from his life after this almost shattered at the sight. She wanted nothing more than to reach out to him, wrap him in her arms, and protect him. But she held her feelings at bay and looked away from him.

The submarine was surfacing. Claire could feel them rising slowly. When Vengeance let out a cheer of excitement, she knew they must be entering The Elite Five's base. Which was apparently underwater. Somewhere under New York City. *You have to hand it to Supers: they all have a flair for the dramatic,* she thought.

When Vengeance and his crew were satisfied with their new environment, they started to clamber up the ladder leading to the hatch. Climbing was apparently beneath Vengeance's dignity, because he and Jack vanished in a flash, a slight gust of air rushing in to fill the space they had just occupied. The Supervillain had probably transported them both to the docking bay outside.

Within a few minutes, the sub was empty. Even Sucker-Punch had disappeared up the hatchway, still looking uneasy about having lost Claire. It apparently never even occurred to him to look in the air vents.

That was one of the great things about being small: Claire looked at tiny spaces in a completely different way than larger people did. Their minds would dismiss such corners and crevices as impossible to move through and automatically overlook them, but hers didn't.

Of course, she was now faced with the problem of getting out of the air vent, and it wasn't going to be easy. She couldn't turn around, and the grate overlooking the command center was fixed firmly in place, the screws securing it having long-since rusted over. Her only option was to crawl backward on her hands and knees, unable to see what was behind her. She wouldn't be able to tell if someone was waiting for her on the ladder.

I'll just have to take my chances and listen hard. Claire took a deep breath of musty, stale air and started moving, retracing her path.

She lucked out. No one was waiting for her, and Claire emerged into the gloomy red light of the hatchway. She was dusty and dirty, and the Band-Aid covering the gashes on her cheek had vanished at some point, but she was whole and, for the moment at least, undetected.

Balancing on the ladder with one arm, Claire tucked her bright-red scarf into her coat. She pulled her dark-blue slouchy hat from her coat pocket and put it on, then tucked her similarly vibrant red hair into the hat to better hide its color. Her dark coat and hat wouldn't stand out much in the dim light coming down from above, though her pale skin would.

At the top of the ladder, Claire peeked over the side of the hatch. For a moment, she forgot all about the need to move quickly and stay under cover. She simply stood there and stared, her eyes wide, her jaw hanging open, and her head in full view of anyone who may have been looking back toward the submarine.

They were inside a truly enormous natural cavern rising far above the waterline. There were five separate bays clearly intended for vessels of various sizes. All were empty save theirs. The space was lit only by red emergency lights, and it smelled of the ocean and the metallic iron of rust. The sound of water dripping on metal pipes echoed everywhere. The ceiling soared high overhead and vanished into darkness. Along the far wall were five heavy metal doors of different heights. The space felt hollow and empty. It reminded Claire of sneaking into abandoned farmhouses outside of town as a teenager. In both places, she felt the prickle of ghosts on the back of her neck.

Vengeance and his crew were swarming across a rusty metal grate gangway, with Jack floating along behind them, his shoulders slumped. The henchmen all held flashlights and were pointing them around the abandoned space, and the cave echoed with their excited whispers. Even Sucker-Punch, who hung back from the rest of the group and lingered near the sub, gazed around in awe. For his part, Vengeance was clearly excited. He walked with a strut and held his head high like a conquering hero.

They made their way over to the largest of the doors, where Vengeance brought Jack forward. Claire couldn't hear their exchange clearly since the echoing in the chamber distorted and threw around sound, but there was a bit of back-and-forth between the two men.

After a few minutes, another loud *clang* shook the entire space, and the large doors before them slowly slid open revealing a long corridor similarly lit in red emergency lights.

Vengeance took a step forward, preparing to lead the group through, when Sucker-Punch called out, "Boss, I'll stay back and guard the sub."

The Supervillain turned to face him, and Claire ducked back down, realizing she was a bit too visible. She silently cursed herself for momentarily forgetting about Sucker-Punch and the fact that he knew she was here somewhere.

"Why would you need to do that?" Vengeance demanded impatiently. "We have full control of the facility, and I need you to keep an eye on my good friend Jack here." He slapped the immobile Superhero on the back, but Jack barely responded. "He escaped once before, and I need you to make sure he doesn't do that again. Now get over here!"

"But boss—"

"Now, you idiot!" Vengeance roared.

The henchmen around him all took a step back. Even Jack flinched. Only Zoe looked as calm and collected as she had before.

Sucker-Punch's shoulders slumped. He took one last look back toward the hatch—and the hidden Claire—and turned to follow his boss and comrades. For a moment, Claire felt sorry for him. He was definitely going to be in for it when Claire appeared and rescued Jack. Assuming, of course, she even got that far.

The large doors closed behind Vengeance and his crew with another boom, and Claire released a breath she hadn't realized she'd been holding. She waited a beat. Then another. And another before she climbed out of the sub and scampered over to the doors, struggling to remember all that she knew about The Elite Five from Great-aunt Lillian's letters and everything she had read and studied over the years.

The five bays were almost certainly for the five Superheroes' individual vehicles, but beyond that, she knew nothing about their secret base. Great-aunt Lillian had never talked about it in her letters beyond mentioning that they *had* a secret base, and it seemed to be one of the IAS's closely guarded secrets. Judging by all the rust, mildew, and general air of abandonment in the docking bay, they clearly didn't use it anymore. But if that was the case, why was Vengeance so keen on capturing it? And why did an average Superhero like Jack know how to access it?

Claire shook her head to clear away all the questions that threatened to overwhelm her. She couldn't afford to get distracted. Her mission here was Jack, not Vengeance or Superhero history.

Rather than approaching the large door Vengeance and his henchmen had gone through, she went over to the smallest metal door, which was the size of a regular door in a house. Like the others, this one had a keypad beside it. It was lit with a wavering dull green glow. Vengeance must have been haranguing Jack into unlocking all—or at least most—of the base's doors. Claire pressed the open button and inwardly cringed, hoping this one wouldn't make the same loud booming sound the large one had. It didn't, but it wasn't silent, either. She hoped the others—and especially Sucker-Punch, who was probably keeping an eye and an ear out for her—were far enough away by now to not hear it.

This door opened into a fairly nice, posh-looking corridor—most likely leading to The Elite Five's living quarters. Claire entered, and the doors closed behind her, equally noisily.

It was hard to see much in the dim red light, but the carpet was plush underfoot, the walls were decorated with tasteful pre-war paneling, and everything smelled terribly of old, stale cigarette smoke. Claire gagged, unused to the odor, which had been sitting contained in this space for decades. *How could people smoke and still be as fit and active as Superheroes need to be?* she wondered, thinking of her own ragged breathing at the gym as she pushed herself to her limit on the treadmill. *Apparently, things were different back in the 1930s and '40s.*

There were living quarters, a kitchen, a laundry, multiple training and sparring rooms, a huge shooting range, an old-fashioned rock wall, a garage with all kinds of mechanic's tools and devices, a library, and probably countless other rooms Claire never even got to. The whole place was musty and dusty and smelled so strongly of cigarette smoke that she was sure the odor would linger on her for weeks to come. Still, Claire could tell that this had once been a luxurious space. The Radio Flyer had taken on countless endorsement deals in the late 1940s and early 1950s and lent his name and image to products ranging from breakfast cereals to running shoes to the children's toy wagon that still bore his name today. Between that and Flaming Justice being an heiress and former New York City debutante before she got her powers, The Elite Five had plenty of financial resources, and they had apparently used them to outfit their headquarters with everything they needed to both fight crime and live comfortable lives away from prying eyes.

Claire advanced down the corridor and came across a door labelled "Equipment Room" in a decidedly block-like font that practically screamed the 1930s. *This looks promising*, she thought as she ducked inside.

Coming across The Elite Five's equipment room was the greatest stroke of luck Claire had ever experienced in her life. There were all manner of guns and swords and staves. There were utility belts and breathing masks and gloves. There were jetpacks and shields and goggles. For a moment, she was lost in fangirl heaven, running her hands over well-known items, reviewing famous incidents in her head.

"I can't believe it," she mumbled quietly, looking around, her eyes greedy. "I can't believe I'm actually here... and without my phone to take pictures!"

Green, focus! You're here to rescue Jack, not gather material for your blog, her more practical side reminded her.

Yeah, but I don't actually have a plan for that yet.

That's when her eyes landed on a sign that read "Ladies' Dressing Room" in the same blocky font that had been on the door. In a flash, Claire knew what her plan was. Amazed at her own audaciousness, Claire slipped into the dressing room—the same dressing room her illustrious ancestress had once occupied. Goosebumps ran down her arms at the thought.

For a moment, time peeled away, and Claire thought she could actually see the ghosts of the past moving around her. The room was no longer dim and dusty but brilliantly lit and warm. Flaming Justice lounged on a plush red divan in the middle of the room reading *Vogue*. The woman on the cover sported a red hat and dress so vivid, Claire was sure it was real. The Superheroine was wrapped in a pale-pink silk dressing gown, and her blonde hair fell around her shoulders in waves. The walls on either side of the room were lined with tall wardrobes, and at the far end were two dressing tables with lights and mirrors. A floor-length tri-fold mirror separated them. And sitting at one of those dressing tables was a petite woman clothed all in black, her red hair pulled back in a practical, no-nonsense bun.

Great-aunt Lillian.

Claire gasped and took a step forward. She watched as Lillian leaned toward the mirror and carefully applied bright-red lipstick. The face reflected back at her resembled Claire's grandmother's in old photos from when she was young, but with slightly crooked teeth and dimples.

Suddenly, Lillian's eyes met Claire's in the mirror. Claire sucked in a breath. She was afraid to move, terrified of shattering this strange dream. In the mirror, Lillian's reflection held Claire's gaze for a long moment. Then, she slowly nodded once, dipping her chin. "It's alright," Lillian said aloud. "You do what you have to do."

Claire raised a hand toward Lillian, and the spell was broken. In an instant, the room was again dark and cold. The red divan in the middle of the room was covered with a white sheet coated in a thick layer of dust. The lightbulbs that had surrounded the mirrors in front of the two dressing tables were all missing, probably having been removed long ago. The tri-fold mirror was cracked and warped, sending back a distorted image of Claire.

Claire pressed a shaking hand to her forehead and closed her eyes. *Is this the concussion?* she wondered. *Am I losing my mind? Am I just so exhausted that I'm hallucinating?*

Taking a deep breath, she lowered her hand and took another step into the room. *Maybe I just imagined it. I was so overwhelmed by being surrounded by all this history that I just invented the whole thing.*

Claire shook her head to clear it, then strode over to the closest wardrobe on her left and flung it open. Several black bodysuits, masks, gloves, and boots filled the space.

Jackpot!

She tentatively reached out and caressed one of the bodysuits. It felt musty and old, but she didn't care. To Claire, this was like touching one of Marie Antoinette's gowns or one of George Washington's wigs—and then contemplating trying it on. It felt like sacrilege, like she would sully the garment just by touching it.

"She said it was okay," Claire whispered aloud, purposefully ignoring the madness of believing that the vision she'd just had was real. She pulled out the bodysuit and held it up to examine it.

Great-aunt Lillian, better known to the world as The Shadow, was petite even by the standards of her time. In fact, she was under five feet tall, had a small frame, and weighed about a hundred pounds—only slightly smaller than Claire, who trained hard to put on as much muscle as her metabolism would allow. But that also meant there was a good chance Claire might be able to fit into The Shadow's costume and assume the mantle of one of the very first Superheroes.

Claire stripped out of her borrowed clothing from Regina's place and reverently pulled on the all-black bodysuit and gloves. The bodysuit was a bit tight through the hips and thighs, but she had no problem zipping it up. The Shadow's original black boots were definitely out of the question for Claire—they were at least a full size too small, if not smaller—so she stuck with her borrowed combat boots. She tied her long hair into a bun just like the one she'd seen on Lillian in the vision and pulled on the hood-like mask that covered her entire head, leaving room only for her eyes and mouth. To her relief, the scent of cigarette smoke didn't cling to the outfit as much as she'd feared it would. *Maybe Lillian didn't smoke—or at least didn't smoke in costume,* she thought.

That done, she examined her appearance in the cracked mirror. Even under the dim red light, Claire was unsettled by the result. She had seen enough old photos of The Elite Five to feel like The Shadow was staring back at her. She slowly raised her hand to her lips and was relieved when the reflection did the same.

Of course you look like her, numbnuts, Claire thought. *She was Grandma's sister, and Grandma always said we looked a lot alike.*

Claire turned to the side slightly, striking a pose. The Shadow's garments were made of some kind of light-absorbing fabric that allowed her to blend into the shadows, hence the original Superhero's name. It would now help Claire move around undetected.

Back out in the main equipment room, she grabbed a utility belt, a grappling hook, a magnetic screwdriver set, a serrated knife, a magical-containment-field gun, and one of Ray Gun's fanciful-looking pistols. She eyed Radio Flyer's jetpack longingly, but knew that operating an eighty-year-old jetpack that hadn't been touched in almost seventy years probably wasn't the best idea. With that, she headed out the door.

Claire was not a Superhero. She didn't have powers. But she was going to rescue Jack and kick some Supervillain ass, all the same. After all, it's what she'd been training for her whole life.

***

As The Shadow 2.0, Claire melted into the dark corners of The Elite Five's headquarters. *If I were a Supervillain, where would I go?* she silently asked the empty corridors. They didn't respond. *Probably up, right? Maybe?*

Rather than taking the lifts, which were old and loud, she found what looked like the fire escape stairs. One wall was the naked cave face, and the rest was a solid block of concrete walls and stairs. Claire sighed, pushed through her bone-deep exhaustion, and started climbing. After less than six hours of sleep—following the busiest, most chaotic day of her life—she knew that only her adrenaline was carrying her at this point. She would almost certainly crash as soon as this current emergency was over. She could almost feel the hormone racing through her, like a bolt of silver lightning dancing in her veins. *If only*

I could stop time and take a nap. Then I'd be sharp and ready for anything.

It was a pleasure to wear and move in The Shadow's suit. It wasn't made of modern spandex, but was still soft, breathable, and flexible. It allowed for great freedom of movement and was quite comfortable. It didn't chafe Claire's wounded wrists and ankles, and the fabric didn't make a sound when it brushed against itself. Whoever had designed The Shadow's suit all those years ago knew what they were doing.

The stairs ended at a door marked "Command Center 2." It was a regular metal office door, and Claire pressed her ear to it. The hum of computer equipment drowned out any voices that may have emanated from within. It didn't really matter anyway, since she could barely hear anything over the pounding of her heart. She slowly eased the door open, careful to avoid any creaking, and slipped inside.

The command center was a huge room, and unlike the rest of the facility, it was not running on emergency lighting. Claire had been expecting it to be filled with mid-1940s-era communication technology and devices and was instead shocked to see that it was equipped with state-of-the-art computers, viewscreens, and tracking systems. It looked like the control room at NASA. And it was filled with Vengeance's lackeys, including Zoe.

Claire's decision to enter where she did was apparently the correct one. "Command Center 2" was, in fact, a balcony that wrapped all the way around the command center, looking down on it from one story above. While it may have had a function when it was first built back in the 1940s, it was now a storage area for technology from the past seventy years. Ancient computers the size of vending machines, old tape recorders, film projectors, and speakers were left up there to gather dust. Claire was able to glide past them like her suit's namesake and crouch between two massive computers that had been built in the 1950s.

Vengeance's crew were familiarizing themselves with the various stations scattered around the room. The Supervillain himself was studying a computer screen over Zoe's shoulder. And above them all, Jack floated in midair, held aloft by the magical glow emanating from the amulet on his chest. He was almost eye-level with Claire in her crouched position, and he looked tired and defeated. His eyes were dull, his skin was ashen, and his posture reminded Claire of an abandoned, lonesome rag doll.

At the sight of him, a black hole formed anew in Claire's chest, sucking in and devouring all her excitement of the past twenty minutes. Her heart felt like it was going to collapse in on itself again, a dying star on the verge of complete annihilation. This would be the last time she ever saw Jack—if they lived through the next hour or so, of course. She knew she was strong enough to rescue him. She didn't know if she was strong enough to survive saying goodbye, yet she knew it had to be done. Her whole core vibrated with pain, and she slumped forward. She fought back tears that she wouldn't be able to wipe away in her costume. *This isn't the time! Focus, Green. You have plenty of time to feel sorry for yourself later. What would a* real *Superhero do right now?* Claire asked herself.

That seemed to do the trick. She took a deep, shaky breath and shoved all self-pitying thoughts away into a box to examine later. For now, she had a job to do. She lifted her head and examined her surroundings for options. Her initial rescue plan hadn't extended beyond finding Jack.

The ceiling was domed above the center of the room, arcing up another story above the second level. Claire was suddenly thankful for the foresight that led her to grab the grappling hook. Still, she wasn't sure about the angles and lengths involved. She had never done what she was about to do. *Guess I'll just have to wing it.*

Claire glided over to the stairs closest to her. There was another set of stairs opposite her on the balcony's far wall. She took several calming breaths, closed her eyes, and visualized her next moves, just as she had always visualized her routines before going up to perform them at a gymnastics meet as a teenager. It didn't matter that she'd been out of gymnastics for twelve years. This was what all that training had been leading to. This way *why* she'd done gymnastics. *You can do this*, Claire told herself. *It's all a matter of timing.*

When Claire stepped out of the shadows, she wasn't thinking about Jack, or her great-aunt Lillian, The Shadow, or her own lifelong goal to be exactly where she was now. Her mind had locked into the focused state she entered at work when she was on an emergency call. All she could see was the next step, and then the next step, and then the next. That's how lives were saved. And that's how she was going to save Jack's life now.

Chapter 13

Jack was numb to everything going on around him. There was movement, noise, light, but it was all meaningless to him. He'd failed as a Superhero. A Supervillain had ferreted out his identity. His family was in danger. Claire was still being held hostage somewhere on the submarine. He'd betrayed IAS secrets. And worst of all, the first emotion he'd felt when Vengeance uttered his full name, revealing that he knew who Jack really was, was *relief*.

With his secret identity known among the Supervillain community, Jack couldn't continue to work as Silver Fist. He'd have to retire that identity and either create a new one or step back from his role as a Superhero and do something else with his life and his abilities. He was horrified to discover just how seductive the latter sounded.

In that moment, a whole new world, a new life had unveiled itself before Jack's very eyes. He felt freer than he had in a long time. He could go back to school. He could find a role that held meaning and purpose for him. He could, as Claire had put it, "stop going through the motions" and doing what he was expected to do.

It was that realization, that feeling of freedom, that had left him feeling so numb.

Being a Superhero was supposed to be the highest calling one could have. Every day, he got to serve the people of New York, doing things that most people couldn't do to keep them safe. Claire would have sold her left big toe to have what he had and do what he did, yet he was eager to throw it all away. Everything about being a Superhero—the costumes, the fame, the physicality, the fact that he was more associated with his fists and his strength than any of his other abilities—left him feeling cold. *What kind of hero thinks that way?* he thought mournfully, barely noticing his brightly lit surroundings. *A failure of a hero, that's who.*

A soft *thwack* noise above drew Jack's attention out of himself. He looked up toward the sound just in time to be pelted with a soft rain of plaster and paint. He coughed and squinted, wishing he could raise his hands to wipe his eyes.

Below him, Vengeance's goons began to shout, their voices echoing around the large command center that Jack's brain had only barely registered through his haze of self-pity.

"Holy shit, it's The Shadow!" a male voice exclaimed.

That got Jack's attention. He blinked furiously, trying to clear the dry plaster particles from his eyes.

"She's dead, idiot. It's just someone dressed like The Shadow," countered another voice.

"Stop her!" Vengeance screamed.

Suddenly, an all-black shadow raced toward Jack, even though he was suspended in midair. He had no time to process what he was seeing, no time to prepare for what might happen next. The black-clad figure crashed into him and wrapped its small arms around his waist. This person, whoever they were, was apparently swinging from some kind of grappling hook lodged in the ceiling because their momentum carried Jack forward, and together, they swung toward the balcony on the other side of the room. The air rushed past him, bullets flew by from below, and the exhilaration of uncontrolled flight set his blood racing. The shouts of panic from below seemed strangely distant.

The pair landed on the balcony with ease. Unable to control his body or break his fall, Jack crashed onto the floor on his back, while his shadowy rescuer landed on their feet, not even stumbling. In one smooth motion, they grabbed the knife from their utility belt and slammed its butt down on the amulet with all their might. It shattered, and the glowing blue field that held Jack immobile vanished. He scrambled to his feet and wiped his eyes to clear them of the last debris.

When he opened them again, it was to see a henchman racing toward them from the closest staircase. Jack's arm immediately shot out over his rescuer's head, punching their assailant so hard, he went flying backward off the balcony and down onto his comrades.

A small hand closed around his, and Jack looked back at the petite woman who was already tugging him toward a door marked 'Fire Exit.'

She glanced back just long enough to give him a grin, and for a moment, Jack thought he was seeing things. It was Claire. Claire, who was supposed to be trapped inside a torpedo on a dangerously old submarine. She was dressed like The Shadow from the 1930s and 1940s, but he'd know those sparkling eyes and devilish smile anywhere. Once again, she'd managed to escape on her own. And this time, she really had come to rescue him. His heart swelled at the thought. *I'd willingly be captured a thousand times over just to see her come flying in to save me and then smile at me like that.*

"Come with me if you want to live," she said in a faux deep voice, dragging him along in her wake as she raced around outdated computer equipment.

Jack chuckled and followed her, his heart racing faster than he thought it ought. Vengeance's henchmen were just behind him, and Jack reached out to knock over boxes and old computer monitors as he ran, hoping to slow them down in their pursuit. Not sure what Claire's plan was next, he grabbed the metal frame of a chair that lacked its seat and back cushions. If nothing else, he might be able to use it as a weapon.

Claire wrenched the fire exit door open, and Jack raced through it right after her. As soon as he cleared the door, he slammed it shut and braced the chair under the handle. It probably wouldn't do much, but at least it would slow their pursuers a bit.

"Claire, what the hell are you doing here? How did you escape?" he demanded as he turned from the door. "Also, a *Terminator* reference? Really?"

Claire turned to him and grinned. "Would you have preferred, 'I'm Luke Skywalker. I'm here to rescue you'?" she shot back as she started to run down the stairs. "And I didn't escape. Vengeance didn't capture me. When I saw that he had you, I stowed away aboard his submarine. He never even knew I was there."

Jack's mind raced even faster than his feet. His hand shot out, grabbed Claire's, and dragged her to a halt before she could get too far ahead. "Is Alfredo with you?"

Claire had the good grace to look embarrassed.

Jack sighed. "We'll talk about this later. But first..." He looked down the open stairwell. The pounding on the door just a few feet behind them was loud enough to drown out his racing heart. Vengeance's goons would come spilling out of the first-floor door—and right into his and Claire's path—any moment now. He turned back to her and asked, "Do you trust me?" He held out his hand, palm upward, with a smile.

"Of course," Claire said, though she looked a bit more nervous than her confident tone suggested.

"Then hold on." Without waiting to give Claire the chance to change her mind, Jack swept her up into his arms. In the seconds before he leapt over the railing into the open stairwell below, he luxuriated in the feeling of Claire's arms automatically locking around his neck. She tucked her face into his neck, her breath tantalizingly warm on his skin. And then, they were falling.

On the way down, Jack was treated to the sight of Vengeance's thugs rushing into the stairwell outside the command center's first floor just as he and Claire flew by, the goons' faces frozen in a moment of shock. Then, they were gone in a blur of concrete stairs. The ground rushed up to meet them from ten stories below, and suddenly, they were at the bottom.

Bullets rained down from above, but Jack was already off and running down cement corridors lined with pipes and electrical wires. He put everything he had into his speed, propelled forward only by the need to get Claire to safety. He ducked around tight corners and took twists and turns through the facility, hoping to lose his pursuers. With any luck, they didn't know about his destination. The whole time, Claire clung to him tightly, one hand around his neck and the other grasping the lapel of his coat with all her might.

He skidded to a stop in front of what appeared to be a bare cement wall at a dead end. A series of colored pipes ran along the left side of the wall from the floor to the ceiling. Jack lowered Claire to her feet, and she looked around in confusion. He reached out, praying he still remembered the correct sequence, and twisted the pipes in place one at a time. First red, then yellow, then black, red again, then blue. There was a grating sound that caused Jack to wince and glance behind him in panic. This hide-out would be useless if Vengeance's goons spotted them going into it. Luckily, there was no one in sight and no sounds of any pursuit nearby. Jack turned back as the bare cement wall swung open, revealing a large room beyond. He stepped inside, and Claire followed without a word.

The room was roughly divided in half. One side was a living space, comfortably furnished with two couches, a kitchenette, and a long wooden table with chairs. The other side of the space was a mini command center, much like the one Vengeance had taken control of upstairs, but on a smaller scale. Bright overhead lights had turned on when the door swung open, and the whir and hum of computers booting up told Jack that the backup systems were coming online.

Once they were both inside, Jack closed and bolted the hatch-like door behind them. Internal locks slammed shut with a clang of finality.

That sound triggered something in Jack. They were safe. Claire was safe. Claire, who had risked everything to come save him, literally flying in in a blaze of glory. She could have left him and gone back to Manhattan. She *should* have gone back to Manhattan. Yet here she was, dressed in a slinky black catsuit that showed off all her curves and standing so close he could feel the heat coming off her body.

Jack didn't plan what happened next. His body moved of its own accord before he even knew what he was doing.

Claire was looking around the room in wonder when Jack grasped her shoulders and spun her around to face him. She opened her mouth in surprise, her eyes wide. Before she could ask him what he was doing, he leaned down, cupped her face in both hands, and pressed a passionate kiss to her lips.

Claire moaned and melted into the kiss. Her arms came up to snake around his neck. Acting on instinct, Jack lowered his own arms to her waist and lifted her, and her legs wrapped around him. She opened her mouth to his, and his tongue darted in to dance and vie with hers. She kissed him hungrily, eagerly, desperately, and Jack returned the sentiment in kind. Her fingers ran along the short hairs at the base of his neck, and he shivered, the sensation traveling down his spine and straight to his groin. Claire must have noticed his reaction because she did it again. And again.

Jack growled low in his throat and took a few steps back, turning to press Claire's back again the cool cement wall. He didn't have any trouble holding her up—Super-strength did have its benefits, as he'd discovered in his various one-night stands and brief relationships over the past few years—but the extra leverage the wall provided made it easier for him to press his full length against her and feel the curves of her body.

He began to trail kisses down the side of her neck—or, at least, down to the top of her Super-suit's high collar—and Claire tipped her head back, allowing him greater access. Her hands roamed along the tops of his shoulders and upper arms, her dainty fingers squeezing and kneading the knotted muscles there. It didn't distract Jack from his mission, though. When he reached the black fabric that covered most of her neck, he switched to the other side of her throat and kissed his way back up to her jaw.

When he got back to her mouth, he kissed her again, but it seemed that some of her ardor had cooled. Claire returned his kiss, but it was sweeter, more delicate. Jack forcibly reined in his passion, trying to match her mood. Their kisses grew lighter and softer until Jack was certain he had himself under control. Then, he pulled back to look in her eyes. She looked back at him with regret and... sadness?

Maybe she's worried about taking advantage of me in case I'm injured. Just like... her... Jack could kick himself. He'd spent all night reminding himself that Claire was possibly concussed and vulnerable, and yet, upon awaking this morning, he'd made fierce love to her. And now, he'd just thrown her up against a wall and practically mauled her. *I'm such an ass...*

He stepped back and gently lowered her to the ground. Once Claire was standing on her own two feet again, he stepped away a respectable distance and cleared his throat. "Sorry," he said, glancing away. He could feel his cheeks turning red. "Apparently, getting rescued from a Supervillain by a smoking-hot Superhero really does it for me."

His humor had the intended effect. Claire laughed and placed her palm on his cheek. When Jack looked back down at her, her expression was warm and open again. "*Never* apologize for kissing me... even though this probably isn't the best time or place."

"Point taken," he said with a sheepish grin. "So, Claire Green, would you care to tell me how exactly you came to be my rescuer? And dressed in such fetching attire, I might add?"

Claire stepped away and pulled off the black hood she still wore. Her hair was tied back in a tight bun, and the bandage had come off her cheek at some point, revealing the two angry red gashes that dominated her cheek. Jack hoped they wouldn't scar. Claire flopped on one of the couches, and Jack sat down beside her—close enough to reach out and touch her if he chose, but not so close that they would accidentally touch. He didn't want his hormones to take over again, especially since he really liked the way her hips swayed in that black costume.

Claire briefly told him the tale of what she dubbed "The Second-Worst Morning Ever." Apparently, "The Worst Morning Ever" had been the previous day, when she came home from a long overnight shift and found Vengeance's henchmen in her apartment. She detailed meeting Alfredo, taking off after Vengeance and his goons, fighting the henchman she referred to as Sucker-Punch, sneaking onto the sub and then around the base, finding The Elite Five's equipment room, and formulating her plan. By the time she was describing her acrobatic feat of swinging out to grab him, Jack was in awe of the woman who sat beside him. *Of the two of us, she should have been the Superhero.*

When she was done, Jack uttered the first words that came to his mind: "Thank you."

Claire looked at him in surprise. "You don't need to thank me. It's the least I can do... after all the trouble I've caused you..." Jack cocked his head to the side in confusion. Before he could ask what she meant or address the sudden look of guilt that flashed across her face, she cast her gaze around somewhat wildly. "So, where are we?" she asked.

"The safe room," Jack explained, filing her guilty reaction away to address later. *Maybe she thinks I'm angry about her not following instructions and heading back to Manhattan. But if she'd done that, I'd still be Vengeance's prisoner.* "This room isn't on any facility maps, so it'll be hard for them to find us. Plus, it serves as a secondary control room." He stood up and walked over to the line of four computers and the large viewscreen hanging above them in the command center portion of the room.

"So, I take it the IAS still uses The Elite Five's base from time to time? This part seems a lot cleaner and much more up-to-date than some other areas I saw. Smells better, too," Claire commented, coming up behind him as he sat down in front of the nearest computer and turned on the screen. "And where exactly is this base, anyway?"

"This whole facility is built into a sea cave deep under Manhattan Island," Jack explained. He could hear her take a breath to say something, but he pressed on. "And yeah, the IAS has been using this facility off and on since the '60s. Not often—it's not all that convenient. A few Supers hid their families down here during the Cuban Missile Crisis. The Freedom Four did actually use this as their regular base of operations during the Reagan administration. And in the '90s, the Weird Sisters cast a spell on the place to hide it from mortal eyes."

"Wait, they did what?" Claire asked from behind him.

Jack turned back to grin at her. "It just makes it even harder to find this place than it used to be," he answered with a twinkle in his eye. "For example, I bet you thought there weren't any sea caves under Manhattan."

"There *aren't*," Claire insisted, her face serious. "There are tunnels and sewers and catacombs and forgotten cellars, but there aren't sea caves. Stop teasing me."

"I'm not. It's part of their spell. Even though the Weird Sisters are all retired and living in Queens now, the spell is still strong and in place," Jack said.

The screen in front of him came to life. Jack shed his coat and scarf and entered his passcode. A few keystrokes later, the feeds from security cameras all over the facility appeared on the large screen above them. It looked like the henchmen had split into teams. Four teams of two had fanned out across the lower level, looking for them. In the main command center, Vengeance, Zoe, and the remaining henchmen were hard at work on the computers. Jack examined the feeds, feeling pleased. *I can work with this*, he thought. "They're nowhere near us. And even if they were, they couldn't get in here."

"Which leaves us trapped," Claire pointed out.

"Only until backup arrives." Jack's mind went to work, and his fingers flew across the keyboard. "For now, the most important thing is to lock them out of the base's systems."

Claire pulled over a chair on wheels from the next work station and sat down beside Jack. She watched him silently for a few minutes, then yawned.

"You can lie down for a bit," he said, tearing his eyes away from the screen to glance at her. She was probably crashing after whatever adrenaline surge had carried her this far.

Claire shook her head and licked her lips. Jack couldn't stop his eyes from following the trail of her tongue across her teeth. He still had the taste of her on his own lips, though he was vaguely disappointed that she didn't taste of the Dr. Pepper lip gloss she had been obsessed with in high school. To him, that flavor always and forever meant *Claire*.

She sat up straighter and asked, "So, what are you doing?"

"This," he said, turning back to his keyboard. He hit a few final keystrokes with a flourish and then pushed himself back from the terminal. "Behold," he said proudly, gesturing to the overhead viewscreen like a used car salesman showing off his wares.

At first, nothing happened. But then, the henchmen in the main command center started to look panicked. Even Zoe's eyebrows furrowed in concern. They hit their keyboards with increasing urgency, risking occasional glances over at Vengeance, who was pacing the room. There was no sound in the security cameras, but Jack could still pinpoint the exact moment the knowledge that something was very wrong reached their boss.

Vengeance stalked over to Zoe and started yelling at her. Soon, the command center was in chaos, with all the henchmen scrambling to figure out what was happening, while Vengeance ran around, shouting at everyone.

Jack didn't even try to stop the grin that spread across his face. *Serves you right.*

"What did you do?" Claire asked, watching in fascination beside him.

"I cut their access to all systems. This is the only place in the whole facility where you can circumvent access to the command center," Jack said proudly. He spun to face her, but her eyes were still fixed on the screen. "I've also sent a message to IAS HQ, letting them know the situation. Now, all we have to do is sit back and wait for backup to arrive." He stretched his arms up and laced his fingers behind his head.

His day had vacillated so wildly between highs and lows that Jack felt like he had whiplash. He'd started his morning waking up in bed beside Claire—and then making love to Claire—glowing with the possibilities of new beginnings.

Then, he'd been recaptured by Vengeance, his identity revealed and his family threatened. And then, Claire had burst onto the scene in typical Claire Green fashion, rescued him, and kissed him in a way that left him dizzy and lightheaded. But now, finally, it was almost over. Help was on the way, and all he had to do was sit back and wait for it. With Claire by his side, dressed in a Superhero costume that was giving him all kinds of ideas.

His thoughts raced ahead as Claire continued to study the viewscreen, nervously chewing on her lower lip. *I can get out of the Superhero game. Maybe work in planning and logistics for the IAS instead. Or enroll in CUNY and take computer classes. Claire and I can go out to dinner and get to know each other again. And I won't receive a call in the middle of dinner about an evil robot or a mad scientist or a Supervillain with a grudge. I can live a normal life and leave the heroics—albeit regular, medical-related heroics—to Claire.*

Jack sat up straight and leaned toward Claire. He wasn't sure what he was about to say, but he knew it had something to do with them, their past, and their future. His heart pounded in his chest. He reached out for her hand, which lay clenched in a fist on her lap.

Before he could touch her, though, Claire blurted out, "How long until the backup team arrives?" Her eyes were fixed on the viewscreen, where Vengeance and his crew were frantically trying to override what Jack had done to lock them out of the system.

Jack withdrew his hand as if she'd slapped it away. He sighed and sank back in his seat. "I don't know. I think it took us about twenty, maybe thirty minutes to get here. The IAS HQ is closer than we were, but they'll also have to reroute a team or two and prep the sub. So, probably another twenty or thirty minutes. Like I said, we don't use this base much because it's not convenient."

Claire turned to him, her eyes wide with concern. "Is the backup team going to be okay?"

At the question, Jack's mind clicked into gear again. He'd been so wrapped up in his own problems and then his own exhilaration that he'd forgotten the reason he was here in the first place, rather than still wrapped up with Claire in bed. Andrew's anxious voice on the phone that morning drifted back to him: *"We have a problem... Vengeance has taken down the entire team we sent in to deal with him... Reports from on the ground suggest that his magic power is considerably stronger than anticipated... significant injuries..."* Jack's spine stiffened, and he glanced back up at the viewscreen again. He could laugh at Vengeance's bumbling efforts from here, but that didn't change the fact that this man was dangerous. "I... don't know," he confessed.

Claire stood up and started pacing. She wrung her hands together as she spoke. "Vengeance is powerful. Far more powerful than he used to be, don't you think?"

Jack nodded. "Eight years ago, he was a nuisance. But from what I've seen in the last twenty-four hours, he's much more than that now."

In the bank, Vengeance had knocked him out cold with some kind of sleep spell. One minute, Jack had been charging at the Supervillain; the next, he'd been dreaming about ducks trying to operate an ATM. But it hadn't been a restful sleep. He'd awoken feeling exhausted and sore. And all of his dreams had been permeated by a sickening green glow.

Then, this morning, Jack had been jogging back toward the warehouse they'd escaped from last night when there was a strange rush of air, as if he'd entered a tunnel. He felt dizzy and stumbled, and when he looked up again, he was standing in front of the warehouse—which he was sure was still five minutes away—surrounded by Vengeance and his squad. There was that green glow again, and then, Jack was unconscious. When he came to, he was inside a decrepit submarine, bound by that magical amulet.

"You know, Vengeance didn't have that amulet eight years ago," Jack pointed out. "Back then, all he could do was manipulate and fold space."

"And electricity magic," Claire shot over her shoulder, still pacing.

"And he could control electricity," Jack agreed. "But where did he get the amulet? Do you recognize it? After all, you're the expert on Superhero history."

Claire threw him a grateful smile but shook her head. "No, I've never seen it before. Maybe he picked it up in one of his bank heists? Or perhaps he met and struck a deal with someone while he was in prison?"

Now it was Jack's turn to shake his head. "Unlikely. Supervillains are generally kept isolated from one another. And the IAS would know about some kind of Binding Amulet."

They both fell silent, pondering. Jack racked his brains, trying to put all the pieces together. He watched Claire pace, the sway of her hips mesmerizing. "Okay, so Vengeance now has a

Binding Amulet. That's new," Jack said, counting the point off on his finger.

"He also has some kind of sleep spell. That's new," Claire added. Jack held up another finger. "I can see how binding would relate to manipulating space. But what about the sleep spell? Maybe it's a new power?" she asked.

Jack considered this. He glanced up at the viewscreen and watched Vengeance shout at his minions for a moment. "Probably not," he decided. "It's rare for Supers to get additional powers after they're Awakened. Usually, what you get is what you get."

"What if..." Claire mused, staring off into the distance, "what if his sleep spell isn't actually a sleep spell?" Jack turned a questioning look at her, and she continued, "What if it's somehow just another kind of spatial manipulation? I read that, in prison, Vengeance was kept in an anti-magic cell especially designed to keep him contained so he *couldn't* warp space and escape. What if he figured out a different kind of spatial warping—one that wouldn't be contained by his cell?"

"But what kind of spatial warping would cause other people to fall asleep?" Jack asked, leaning forward, intrigued by this line of thought.

Claire shook her head, uncertain. "I'm an EMT, not a physicist," she said.

Something in Claire's comment triggered a brainstorm in Jack, and his eyes widened in horror. He leapt to his feet and began pacing as well, following a path perpendicular to Claire's. "Vengeance has always been able to bend and fold space on our human scale," Jack said, thinking aloud. "He can move between places, appearing and disappearing in the blink of an eye, so long as he's been there before and can clearly picture the place he's trying to get to. But he's never been able to work on other scales: he couldn't fold space enough to move across the galaxy or even much beyond our planet. If he could, I'm sure he would've found a way to take control of satellites or the ISS or the moon base or the ship carrying the Mars mission by now."

As he walked, his path crossed Claire's. Their shoulders brushed as they passed each other, but they both continued on, each going in their own directions.

Claire nodded. "That would make sense. Vengeance has a weird axe to grind with Superheroes, and any one of those things could be used to make your lives miserable," she said. "But how does that relate to a sleep spell?"

"In the past, he was never able to work on the microscopic scale, either," Jack said. He reached the far wall and turned to retrace his steps. "What if he figured out a way to do that, and his sleep spell is actually just him folding space on a microscopic-enough level to temporarily short-circuit someone's brain?"

Claire spun around to face him, her eyes wide. "It would probably be a small-enough fold in space that it wouldn't be picked up by the parameters of his cell," she said.

Jack advanced toward her, another thought occurring to him. "What if he's just getting started with this new kind of folding? What if putting people to sleep was just the first and easiest thing for him to do?"

Claire matched his movements, approaching him. "He could kill people by causing strokes and heart attacks and aneurysms."

"He could take control of people's minds."

"And this base offers him a secure facility from which to develop and increase his skills," Claire added. They both came to a stop mere inches away from each other. "Of course, he wasn't expecting to get locked out of the system."

Jack nodded. "Regardless, we have to stop him and warn the others."

Claire looked up at him, her eyes wide and trusting. It was an expression he had missed seeing for so many years. "We need a plan," she said, "and you've always been the best with plans."

Jack felt his heart expand at the look of faith in her eyes. Claire believed in him, and with that belief, he could move mountains. He would do this one last job as a Superhero before hanging up his mask for good. For Claire. Always for Claire.

Chapter 14

The Shadow 2.0 crawled through the air vents of The Elite Five's secret base.

As a kid, Claire had once seen an episode of some weird sci-fi show in which an android tried to express the emotion of "ambivalence." His face had twisted and contorted like a dog licking peanut butter from a spoon, only to discover that it was actually anchovy-Sriracha-flavored peanut butter. Claire had laughed as a kid, but now, the actor's expression returned to her and seemed strangely accurate. She was fairly sure that if she could see her own face right now, it would be making that very same expression.

She should have been having the time of her life. She was as close to being a Superhero as she would ever get. And yet, something deep in the pit of her stomach was churning and crumbling. She felt the waves and tremors of the destruction rippling up through her body.

Stupid, stupid, stupid, she repeated over and over again in her head. She shouldn't have kissed Jack, shouldn't have let him kiss her. She kicked herself for that lapse of judgment as she crawled on her hands knees through the vents. And now, he seemed to be under the impression that they were about to embark on a wonderful, romantic adventure together, while she finally understood just how impossible that was. She was a danger to him, a liability. And she couldn't do that to him. Everything about this was awful. And she resented that fact even more because it was making her miserable when she should have been on top of the world.

Ambivalence is a bitch.

Fortunately, it appeared that the facility's original designers had actually built the air vents around the original Shadow's small proportions. Claire fit through them perfectly, but anyone much taller or broader wouldn't be able to. None of that awkward, painful shuffling she'd done aboard the submarine. For the third time in one day, Claire sent a brief prayer of thanks up to Great-aunt Lillian for having inherited her small stature. *Maybe being short isn't so bad after all.*

Still, the vents were incredibly dusty and filled with cobwebs, and Claire struggled to stifle a sneeze several times. Her nose itched desperately, cobwebs kept collecting across her already-limited field of vision in her mask, and her knees screamed as she crawled. If this was Superhero work, it was a lot more like the Search and Rescue activities her firefighter friends talked about than the heroic drama she'd once imagined. Plus, there was the pain of her heart breaking as it still beat inside her chest.

Ambivalence really is a bitch.

Jack had long-since gone radio silent, as they'd agreed, so Claire could only hope he was okay and carrying out his end of the plan. She simply had to get up to the main command center undetected, which was proving to be easier—and dustier—than she'd expected, and wait for his signal. The maze of air vents and ladder shafts was complicated, but as long as Claire kept going up, she would eventually reach her destination.

At long last, she reached the top of a ladder well and couldn't climb any higher. A stainless steel shaft branched off to her right. At the end of it, a grate set in the floor revealed the brightly lit room below. The hum of computers reached her ears. She had made it to the command center.

Transferring her weight from the ladder to the air vent, Claire crawled the last few feet of her hands-and-knees journey. No matter what lay ahead, her knees were grateful that this portion was over. Thirty years of abuse through gymnastics, karate, MMA, and EMT work had left them far weaker than they had once been.

As Claire approached the grate at the end of the vent, she saw that it was set into the wall about eight feet above the ground and just under the second-story balcony.

"Report, Unit Three!" Vengeance practically screamed into a microphone. It sounded like he was immediately below Claire, and she slowed her pace, barely inching forward so she wouldn't make too much noise. When she was as close as she dared get to the grate, she crouched down on her belly and looked out.

All the henchmen left in the command center sat hunched over their keyboards, their faces clearly showing how unhappy they were with Vengeance screaming at them. Even Zoe looked tense as she studied her ever-present tablet.

Nothing but static came back over the microphone Vengeance had yelled into. Then, a moment later, there was a clicking sound, and a garbled, staticky male voice called out, "This is Unit Two. He's—" Then it cut out.

"What the hell is going on?" the Supervillain demanded. "There are only two of them. How can they have taken out all four teams at once?" In his anger, Vengeance had completely shed his phony British accent.

"Maybe more Superheroes showed up," Zoe muttered under her breath.

Vengeance rounded on her and screamed, "Well, we would be able to tell that if *somebody* hadn't lost control of the base!"

Claire flinched on the other woman's behalf. Zoe didn't appear to react, but Claire could see her hands shaking even from across the room.

Vengeance inhaled sharply, tipping his head back as though sniffing the air. Composing himself, he adopted his usual accent again and said, "I don't need maybes, Zoe. I need you to be useful and get us back into the base's system!"

"I'm working on it," Zoe said, her voice subdued.

Vengeance resumed pacing. Jack's speculation that the Supervillain's ability to fold space and transport himself elsewhere was limited by the fact that he needed to have been there previously and could envision it perfectly seemed to be accurate. With Jack racing all around the base's lower levels at top speed, taking out teams, grabbing their walkie-talkies, and then moving on as quickly as possible, he was confusing any sense Vengeance had of where this threat was. Not long ago, Vengeance had practically been gloating. Now, hopefully, he felt cut off, paranoid, and out of control. With any luck, it would make him jumpy and careless. And based on what Claire was now witnessing, their plan seemed to be working.

Jack's barely disguised voice crackled back over the microphone. "This is Unit Four. He's moving so quickly! We can't—" Static again.

In the air vent above, Claire grinned and suppressed a chuckle. Jack wasn't exactly good at voices, but Silver Fist's well-known refusal to speak in public was now paying off. Vengeance and his crew probably hadn't heard Jack say enough to be able to identify him now.

Vengeance slammed his hand down on the nearest computer console, making everyone jump. "Ernesto, Jim, get out there and find those Superheroes," he ordered.

The only two heavily muscled men left in the command center stared at each other for a moment, their eyes wide.

"Did you hear what I said?" their leader demanded. "Get moving!"

The two men nodded, slowly stood, and headed out the door, their guns at the ready. Claire hoped they would actually value their own safety more than their boss's orders and hightail it out of there, rather than seek out Jack to take him on. They would lose. Claire was tired of seeing strong people bullied into serving a Superpowered monster and getting hurt in the process. She didn't want to take out the pawns; she wanted to free them.

It was now down to three henchmen in the command center, and they were all clearly on Vengeance's tech-support team. Claire highly doubted that the pair she'd mentally dubbed Thick Glasses Girl and Anime Hoodie Guy would pose any kind of serious threat to Jack. Zoe was more of a wild card, but she also seemed to be the most sensible person on Vengeance's team. Jack could easily handle this group.

Claire was highly conscious that much of their plan rested on her and her non-Super ability to take down a powerful Supervillain. Sure, she had been training for this her whole life, but now that she was in this position, her heart thundered in her chest, and her palms were sweaty in her great-aunt's vintage gloves. If she failed, it would be even worse than when she couldn't save someone on a call at work. It could quite possibly mean the end of all Superheroes. It would mean the end of the world as Claire knew it. It would mean the end of Claire.

In the face of that heavy weight, she swallowed the lump forming in her throat. This was no time to be psyching herself out with what-ifs. She took a slow, calming deep breath through her nose and let it out just as slowly through her pursed lips. It didn't slow her racing heart, but it did focus her mind.

A crashing sound out in the hallway drew everyone's attention in the command center, including Claire's. All the henchmen froze in place, likely afraid that Vengeance would order them to investigate. Instead, the Supervillain took matters into his own hands and vanished from sight, folding space to reach the hallway instantaneously. He reappeared a moment later, his face dark with anger. He looked up at the domed ceiling above and shouted, "Where are you?"

Silence.

"Maybe..." Zoe ventured, lowering her tablet as her eyes darted around, "maybe we should withdraw."

Vengeance blinked out of existence and back into it directly in front of Zoe, his face inches from hers, glaring maliciously. "We have come Too! Damn! Far! with this plan to quit now!" he shouted in her face. Once again, his accent vanished as his ire increased. Zoe winced and drew back, but he continued his tirade, "We are almost within reach of our goal, and I will *not* be deterred by two errant Superheroes!"

"One of whom is a ghost," Anime Hoodie Guy muttered under his breath.

Vengeance again blinked in and out of existence, reappearing in front of the unfortunate man. "What did you say?" he growled.

The hapless man looked up at his boss, gulped, and said, "The Shadow—she's been dead for decades, right? It has to be a ghost."

"And it couldn't *possibly* be someone in The Shadow's old costume," Vengeance shot back sarcastically.

"But have you seen the old newsreels?" Thick Glasses Girl asked, coming to her colleague's defense. "If it's someone in a costume, she moves *exactly* like The Shadow."

Shut up, shut up, shut up, Claire willed the pair. They were going to get themselves killed, winding Vengeance up like that. Suddenly, Claire tasted blood and realized she had been biting down on her lip as she watched the scene unfold.

Zoe jumped back into the conversation before Vengeance could get in Thick Glasses Girl's face: "Whoever she is, she's clearly more powerful than we expected. And she and Silver Fist seem like a pretty formidable pair. Maybe we should retreat and reconsider our plan."

Something in Vengeance appeared to snap. He didn't even bother teleporting; he just rushed over to Zoe and lifted her from her chair by her hair. She screamed in pain, and he threw her to the ground viciously.

Claire gasped and almost shoved aside the grate that camouflaged her, plans be damned. From what she had seen, Zoe was probably Vengeance's most capable lieutenant. He needed her more than he realized, but he was treating her like yet another disposable minion. The injustice of it all made her want to throw herself into action.

Zoe hit the ground hard, but she immediately pushed herself away from the Supervillain's reach—even though his reach was, practically speaking, unlimited.

Claire tried to get her racing heart and mind back under control. Zoe could take care of herself for the next few minutes. Claire couldn't afford to throw away the element of surprise. She had to be ready when the time was right.

As Claire watched the scene below her, something about Vengeance finally came into focus in her mind: his temper. When he first rose to prominence as a Supervillain, he had been overly dramatic, yes, but he had always appeared to be in complete control of himself and his emotions. Over the past twenty-four hours, though, he had become increasingly unhinged and ready to fly off the handle at the slightest provocation. It would make him sloppy, yes, but it might also make him more desperate. And dangerous. A man who wasn't thinking straight and thought he had nothing to lose could be the most formidable foe imaginable.

Claire focused on her breathing. She had to be the calm one.

A crash on the second story saved Zoe—and Claire—from seeing just how far Vengeance's temper would carry him. Everyone looked up, and again, the Supervillain popped out of view, likely reappearing on the second story of the command center, out of Claire's field of vision. His voice carried down from above: "Okay, Jack, come on out. We seem to be at an impasse. Let's talk about this." His voice was not in the least bit conciliatory. It was full of venom and danger and no longer carried even a hint of his signature faux accent. Claire swallowed hard.

Down on the first level, Thick Glasses Girl and Anime Hoodie Guy gave a sudden shout as Jack leapt up from behind their workstations. Both of his fists shot out and connected with their jaws with a loud *crack*. The two unfortunate henchmen flew out of their chairs, hitting the wall behind them hard and slumping down to the ground. They didn't move. Claire trusted Jack enough to feel certain that they were only unconscious.

"He's down here!" Zoe shouted, but Jack was already moving toward her.

He leaned across the desk between them, knocking the computer screens over in the process, and grabbed Zoe by the back of her shirt. He dragged her over the desk toward him, and she kicked out, sending another computer monitor crashing to the ground. Struggle as she might, though, Jack's Super-strength would win out.

By the time Vengeance reappeared back on the first level, Jack held Zoe in place against him with one arm. The other trained a gun on her that he had clearly taken off of one of Vengeance's own men. Even dressed in the borrowed civilian clothes from Regina's place, Jack looked every inch a Superhero, from his bold, defiant stance to his hard, cold eyes. "Okay," Jack said to the Supervillain, "here I am. Let's talk."

Vengeance snarled at the pair and shot a bolt of lightning at them from the tip of his pointed finger. Jack easily sidestepped it, pulling his hostage with him. A black scorch mark appeared on the wall just inches from Jack's head. Zoe finally looked exactly as terrified as Claire had suspected she'd been all along. No one defies a Supervillain without some measure of terror in their soul. The other henchmen were still unconscious. Only Jack appeared to be calm and collected. It was time for Claire to make her move. With the fire of nervousness running through her veins, she slowly, slowly lifted the grate covering her hiding place, careful not to let it make a sound.

"You know, *Jack*," Vengeance said icily, emphasizing his real name, "by taking me on like this, you've doomed your little friend, whoever she is. She will not escape us. Not on her own. And then, I will kill both her and Miss Green—who, might I remind you, I still hold prisoner."

Jack smiled coldly. "Oh, I haven't forgotten. But I think you'll find my colleague to be even tougher than you expect. She's one of the IAS's top secret agents, spoken of only in whispers and rumors. She was sent in here to extract me and take you down. And she *never* misses her target," Jack bluffed, laying it on thick. For a moment, even Zoe's eyes widened in concern. Vengeance seemed to hesitate, as if weighing his opponent's words. Jack continued, "Now, surrender. You've lost all your henchmen. I've locked you out of the base's computer system. More Superheroes are on their way. There's no way you can win. Surrender now, and I'll speak at your trial on your behalf."

Claire got the grate all the way open without the slightest indication that Vengeance had noticed. Jack was entirely focused on his nemesis, and Zoe was distracted by the gun Jack was holding to her head. Claire was virtually invisible. She shimmied out of the shaft head-first, tucked, and rolled silently onto the ground and behind the closest workstation. She just had to get within five feet of Vengeance without him noticing her.

The Supervillain's voice was venomous as he spat at Jack, "You will not win."

Claire didn't see what happened next, but Zoe slumped in Jack's arms, her eyes blank and empty. Surprised by the sudden dead weight in his arms, Jack was distracted and looked away from the Supervillain. In a flash, Vengeance's right hand was around Jack's throat. His left hand plucked the gun from Jack's hand, and he shoved Jack back up against the wall. Claire froze. In that moment, their careful plan seemed to collapse, along with her heart in her chest. The black hole was back, and it was threatening to rip her innards to shreds right then and there.

"Did you—did you kill her?" Jack demanded, shocked into inaction.

"That woman was increasingly getting on my nerves, and you seemed to be under the mistaken impression that holding her hostage was an effective bargaining tactic," Vengeance snarled.

Claire's mind tumbled over itself. Ice froze her veins. She had to do something, but Vengeance's hand was around Jack's throat, where only a squeeze could end Jack's—and Claire's—life.

"Now, unlock the facility's computers," Vengeance demanded.

Jack stared back at him defiantly.

"I will not ask a second time."

Jack's fist drove into Vengeance's stomach, and the Supervillain flew backward. Jack took off running, and the spell holding Claire in place shattered. She tucked herself more tightly beneath the desk and peered around the corner.

Jack raced around the command center, vaulting up and down the stairs, changing directions at random. Once Vengeance had staggered to his feet, he did his best to head off Jack, disappearing and reappearing in front of him, trying to grapple him, but Jack was too fast and nimble. Vengeance was a much older man, and Jack was ex-army, physically trained regularly, and had Super-speed. Every time it looked like Vengeance would finally appear just close enough to Jack to grab him, Jack danced away, turning on a dime, ducking low, and generally slipping through Vengeance's fingers.

Clearly growing frustrated, Vengeance paused his pursuit, raised his arms skyward in a victory V, and began chanting something. Claire couldn't make out what he said, but his intent was soon obvious as an electric storm suddenly crashed through the command center. Bolts of lightning struck computer systems all around the room, instantly frying them. Monitors shattered, including the one just above Claire's head. She had to bite her lip to keep from screaming in surprise as glass flew everywhere. Several of the computers began to burn, and fire soon leapt from desks all around the room. The command center smelled equally of ozone and burning plastic.

Jack managed to dodge the lightning bolts, even as they continued to crash down all around him. He weaved and bobbed, ducking and running, always staying one step ahead of both the electric storm and Vengeance, who was again in hot pursuit.

They were playing cat-and-mouse, with Jack racing ahead, setting the terms of their engagement, despite the Supervillain's attempt to change the playing field with his lightning. Vengeance took the bait, disappearing and reappearing all over the place in an effort to get one step ahead of his opponent. Jack was drawing Vengeance all over the room, back and forth, up and down, distracting and disorienting him. And enraging him.

As she watched, Claire realized that Jack was planning to lure Vengeance to within five feet of her so she could deploy the magical-containment-field gun. Getting the timing right would require Super reflexes, which she didn't have. She took a silent deep breath and focused on Jack's movements, trying to track and predict where he would dodge to next. It was all a matter of timing. Just like everything else in her life. *Timing.*

Vengeance was definitely becoming increasingly angry and careless; his face was dark with snarling rage. Meanwhile, Jack's grin seemed calculated to annoy the Supervillain.

And then, it happened: Jack headed straight toward her, and everything dropped into slow motion. A lightning bolt crashed into another computer nearby, its movement slow enough for Claire to track. The monitor shattered slowly, piece by piece, and she watched the individual glass shards spray across the floor like diamonds. Red-hot sparks that resembled fireworks shot from the workstation. Claire's pounding heart grew still. Her hands wrapped around the magical-containment-field gun, her finger drifting to the trigger. The space between her ragged breaths became longer and longer until whole lifetimes passed between them.

Vengeance materialized between Jack and Claire, his back to her. The Supervillain's fingers closed around Jack's throat, and in the same space between breaths, between lifetimes, between the birth and death of stars, Claire raised her anti-magic weapon and fired directly at him. She watched the glowing green ring of energy travel toward Vengeance, inch by painful inch. When it connected with his back, his hand released Jack's throat. Jack crashed to the ground beside the Supervillain.

Time resumed its normal speed. The lightning stopped, as if someone had flipped a switch. Vengeance flailed around, but he couldn't break free of the glowing anti-magic field that contained him. He was trapped within the three-foot by three-foot box that extended seven feet above the ground. He slammed his fists against it and roared in anger.

Claire collapsed forward in a gasping sigh. Equal parts relief and disbelief washed over her. Her heart was still racing from the adrenaline, but now, it was making her lightheaded. She climbed to her feet and faced Vengeance. When he saw her, his eyes grew dark with rage. "You!" he bellowed. "You're no ghost! Who are you?"

Almost giddy with relief, Claire reached back to unclasp the snaps holding The Shadow 2.0's hood in place. She pulled it off, shook her hair out of its bun, and grinned at Vengeance. "What was that about killing me?" she asked. It was the kind of banter real Superheroes indulged in after capturing the bad guy. And she had just captured a really bad guy—she, Claire Green, without Superpowers of any kind. She deserved to bask in this moment.

Vengeance's eyes had gone wide. "You—but you're not—how—you're not a Super. You don't have any powers. How did you—" he stuttered.

Claire was half-laughing with near-hysterical glee. "Never underestimate the power of a very determined woman, Super or not. Right, Jack?" she asked over her shoulder without looking back at him.

Silence.

Vengeance's shock transformed into smug triumph. Claire spun around to see Jack still sprawled on the ground where he had fallen. Her giddiness vanished in an instant, replaced only with a chill in her stomach. She crouched down over him, lightly smacking his cheeks to bring him around. "Wake up, babe," she said.

Vengeance roared with laughter, his head tipped back. Claire looked up at him, that chill turning into icy dread that was already spreading its tentacled fingers through her limbs and mind. "Jack?" she said uneasily, turning back to face him. He didn't respond.

That's when she realized that he wasn't breathing. Somehow, that fact snapped her out of whatever dark place she had been about to fall into and back into her professional mode. She lay her head on his chest to listen for a heartbeat. Nothing. Her heart constricted painfully, but she kept moving, refusing to freeze. This was something she could handle. This was where she really was a hero.

Claire arranged Jack's body flat on the ground, tipped his head back and opened his jaw to clear his airway, and started to administer CPR. She pumped his chest as hard as she could to the tempo of the Bee Gees' "Stayin' Alive," as she had been taught. She breathed into his mouth, filling his lungs with air. She repeated the process again. And again. And again. And the whole time, she didn't, couldn't, allow herself to think of anything more than the simple, familiar tasks of CPR. This was just another patient, and she was on just another call. Anything more than that, and her own heart would have stopped working.

Vengeance roared with laughter behind her as she struggled through the motions of her own heroics. "You still lose, kitten," he said after several cycles of CPR. "I may have lost this round, but it would seem that you've lost everything."

Claire tried to tune him out, but it was getting harder and harder to ignore the reality of what she was doing. Tears slipped from her eyes and moistened Jack's chest before she even realized she was in danger of crying. Her motions became increasingly frantic, her breath came in sharp gasps, and her hands shook. "Come on, babe," she gasped, trying not to sob. "You owe me a date, remember?"

"He's dead. I killed him," the Supervillain taunted behind her.

Claire shook her head, refusing to let his words sink in. "Jack, come on. You have to—" She breathed into his mouth again, no longer able to focus on correct technique or tempo. She pumped his chest desperately, sobbing his name. There was a vice pressing on Claire's own chest, pushing her heart and lungs out of her body entirely and into a parallel dimension. She was shaking all over. She couldn't believe it, wouldn't believe it.

"You stupid bitch," Vengeance sneered. "I reached into his brain and folded a few things in on themselves. He died instantly. There's nothing you can do."

Claire's motions suddenly halted, and she spun to look at the gloating Supervillain safely contained in his cell. He seemed inordinately pleased with himself.

"It was too easy, really. I wish I had figured out how to do it much, much sooner. It would have saved me a lot of trouble. But I just figured it out with that useless bitch, Zoe." He laughed. "I guess she was finally good for something after all. About damn time."

Claire's dam of professionalism broke. Her trembling and sobbing gave way to a white-hot rage that burned her throat. Claire stumbled to her feet and lurched toward the anti-magic field. Vengeance must have seen whatever darkness now glared out of her eyes, because he drew back and suddenly fell silent. Her hands shook, and her chest was a black hole sucking everything in, devouring her. Claire didn't know what she was doing. She couldn't think. The world was spinning, and she couldn't breathe and couldn't stop shaking and couldn't swallow the lump restricting her throat and couldn't suppress the rage devouring her whole and coloring the world blood-red.

She reached out toward the anti-magic field with an oddly steady hand and saw real terror in Vengeance's eyes. "What-what are you?" he stammered. "Who are you?"

Claire couldn't speak, couldn't see anything other than him. Everything around him swirled, and her vision grew dim and red, like the room was lit only by a red light bulb. Her fingers had gone numb, and her palms tingled, like they had fallen asleep and were just now waking up. There was a roaring in her ears, blocking out all other sounds. She realized that it was coming from her and that she was screaming. Vengeance stumbled backward onto his ass and cowered in his prison. She saw his lips move, but she couldn't hear him anymore.

The pressure on Claire's chest became more and more intense, the numbness traveled up her arms, and the roaring became louder. Her own lips moved: "About damn time." And then, everything went black.

Chapter 15

When Claire came to, she was back in the air vent leading into the command center of The Elite Five's secret base, disoriented, shaking terribly, and with a splitting headache.

"...and I will *not* be deterred by two errant Superheroes!" Vengeance roared.

"One of whom is a ghost."

Claire's head shot up at that, and she looked out of the grate. Everything was back to the way it had been barely fifteen minutes before. Had it really only been that long? Claire felt like she'd lived an entire lifetime since she last looked out on this scene. Vengeance was still stalking around angrily, Zoe was alive, and Thick Glasses Girl and Anime Hoodie Guy were still awake and saying things they really shouldn't if they valued their lives.

Claire had already heard this entire exchange. *Was it a dream?* she wondered. *Did I have a vision of the future?*

Vengeance once again appeared right in front of Anime Hoodie Guy's face. "What did you say?" he demanded. At the sound of his voice, revulsion twisted in Claire's chest. She clenched her fists in an attempt to still their violent trembling and inhaled slowly through her nose to keep her vision from going red with rage and anger and pain.

"The Shadow—she's been dead for decades, right? It has to be a ghost," the man responded nervously.

"And it couldn't *possibly* be someone in The Shadow's old costume," Vengeance shot back in the same sarcastic voice he'd used before.

"But have you seen the old newsreels?" Thick Glasses Girl asked. "If it's someone in a costume, she moves *exactly* like The Shadow."

It was all repeating, playing out exactly as it had before. *Did I somehow jump through time? Is that even possible?*

Right on cue, Zoe said, "Whoever she is, she's clearly more powerful than we expected. And she and Silver Fist seem like a pretty formidable pair. Maybe we should retreat and reconsider our plan."

As before, Vengeance raced over to the woman, lifted her from her chair by her hair, and threw her to the ground. She cried out in pain, and even more so than before, Claire saw the sheer terror in her eyes. All of Vengeance's lackeys were afraid of him. Deathly afraid. And as Claire had seen, they had good reason. She would not stand for that any longer.

Jack crashing around on the second story once again interrupted the scene, and Claire's heart began racing faster than her body could keep up with. It felt like it was going to explode out of her chest, as though the black hole that had been devouring her was now spewing everything out like a pulsar powered by her own heart. *Not again,* she promised herself. *I won't let this happen again. I'll stop it before it's too late.*

Everyone moved through the same motions as before: Vengeance shouting for Jack to come out and talk, Jack appearing and immediately sending Thick Glasses Girl and Anime Hoodie Guy flying through the air with swift, powerful punches, and Jack taking Zoe hostage. "Okay, here I am. Let's talk," he said. Once again, Vengeance shot a bolt of lightning at Jack and Zoe.

This was it. This was where Claire had to change things.

Not again. Not if I have any say about it.

With still-trembling hands, she slowly raised the grate. Jack and Vengeance traded barbs. As before, Claire slithered down and made her way over to the threesome by the far wall. She was still shaking terribly, but she realized that the hand that wrapped around her gun was steady the moment she touched it. She did not reach for the magic-containment-field gun at all. She didn't try to get within five feet of the Supervillain. There was no time for that. All Claire needed was a clear shot.

As soon as she had it, she stood, training her gun—a regular pistol that fired bullets—on Vengeance from behind. Zoe's eyes jerked over to Claire, and suddenly, the dark-haired woman looked even more frightened than she had before. Jack looked at her, too, his eyes wide and frightened. *Don't be afraid, love. I'll set this all right.*

"Claire, what the—"

Vengeance spun toward her. She fired.

The Supervillain didn't even complete his spin, and he crashed to the ground unceremoniously. The other two stared back and forth between Claire and Vengeance's prone form. No one moved or said a word for a long moment.

Then, the spell was broken. Claire's knees gave out, and she tumbled to the floor. Whatever force had been propelling her forward had run out, and now, she was like a marionette with its strings cut.

"Claire!" Jack shouted, releasing his grip on Zoe and rushing toward Claire. He was there in time to catch her upper body as she hit the hard, cold ground. "What did you do? What is all this stuff? What happened to—"

"You're alive," Claire breathed, tears springing into her eyes. His face was worried and frightened and so very *alive* that it cancelled out those other two emotions in her mind. She repeated it again and again, "You're alive, you're alive." Everything was becoming hazy again, and she was dizzy. Her heart still exploded within her, and all the energy it released was threatening to overwhelm her senses. She raised her hand to caress his cheek, and dark, wispy smoke trailed behind it.

Jack cradled Claire, confusion in his eyes. "Of course I'm alive. Are you okay? What happened?"

"I saw him... He killed you..." she whispered, staring intently at the dark smoke that poured from her shaking fingertips pressed against his skin. He didn't flinch from it. She had to be hallucinating. That was the only logical explanation. Zoe appeared in Claire's field of vision above Jack, and Claire added, "He killed both of you. I had to stop him. Had—"

"Shhh, it's okay now," Jack whispered, rocking her gently.

"What *are* you?" Zoe asked, her eyes wide as she stared at the tendrils of smoke spreading out across the floor from Claire's left hand, which lay palm-up on the cement floor.

Claire didn't have an answer for her before her world went black again.

Chapter 16

Claire awoke in a bed in a dimly lit hospital room, wrapped in blankets, and comfortably warm. She was no longer shaking, and her heart beat in its normal, steady rhythm. Tubes hooked to an IV ran under the blankets to her arm, and when she tried to move it, she felt the tug of the line going into her arm.

"Try to keep still," a light, airy female voice said.

Claire turned toward it and was shocked to see notorious socialite and tabloid-fodder heiress Giada England sitting in the chair beside her bed. Giada's stiletto-booted feet were propped up on the table beside her bed, in danger of knocking over several bouquets of flowers that rested there. Her bleach-blonde hair was pulled up in a messy bun that looked too perfect to have actually been thrown together without thought, and her long, lithe body was wrapped in dark-colored designer apparel that Claire couldn't even afford to look at. Claire's medical chart sat in Giada's lap, and she was reading it with interest.

"It says here that you're severely dehydrated and in shock, so you need to rest and let the fluids do their work," Giada said helpfully, pointing a pink-lacquered fingernail at her chart.

I must be dreaming, Claire thought, blinking a few times to clear her vision. *Why else would I be seeing Giada England, of all people, here?* She licked her dry, cracked lips and hoarsely whispered, "Where's Jack?" Her throat hurt just from that.

Giada smiled at that and put Claire's chart down. "He's just fine," she assured Claire. "He's next door getting checked out by the doctor. He didn't want to leave your side, but I threatened to use him for target practice with my new guidance system if he didn't see a doctor himself. He just stepped out a few minutes ago."

Claire nodded and sighed, settling back into the pillows more at ease. Her eyelids drifted shut. As long as Jack was okay—and not dead—all would be well. *Though that still doesn't explain why this woman is sitting by my bedside.*

"*So...*" Giada said it like a question, and Claire opened her eyes again. Giada sat up, swinging her long legs down to the floor. Her smile was still bright, but there was a probing intelligence in her gaze that didn't quite match the dumb-blonde heiress persona that she was known for. Claire felt a bit like a bug being examined under a microscope. "So," Giada repeated, "you're the famous Claire Green. I've heard so much about you. I suppose I ought to thank you for saving me eight years ago."

Claire's mind raced. *What is she talking about? Was Giada England in the crowd that day eight years ago when I first met Vengeance? Surely, I would have heard about that, though. The tabloids would have fallen all over themselves to cover her "dramatic story."* She blinked a few times and squinted at the blonde woman before her, trying to make sense of this whole exchange. "I'm sorry," Claire said hoarsely. "What is going on here?"

At that, Giada's smile widened and became genuine. Her expression lost its calculating shrewdness. "Oh, of course. I'm sorry. I just assumed you knew who I am. I'm Giada England, also known as The Electric Defender." She held out a perfectly manicured hand, and Claire numbly reached out to shake it.

Everything clicked into place and yet made no sense at all. *Giada England is The Electric Defender? What's next—Paris Hilton is also secretly Agent Elemental?*

And then, another memory floated to the surface: Jack talking about his friend Giada giving him a hard time about being single and offering to introduce him to her friends. *Jack's friend Giada is* the *Giada England?* It made sense; they had been working together at the time of his debut, after all, and they had tackled a number of cases together since then. They weren't exactly a team, but The Electric Defender and Silver Fist were commonly referred to as "allies" by Superhero bloggers and fans.

For a moment, Claire's jealousy swam to the surface again. Even if Jack claimed that Giada was just a friend, her glamorous beauty and model-perfect figure were just too much for Claire to compete with. She was short and covered with freckles and had a temper that she'd never learned to control and–

Claire slammed a door on that train of thought. *You and Jack are nothing, remember, Green?* The memory of that particular fact sobered Claire.

Giada apparently didn't notice Claire's somber mood. When their handshake ended, Giada remained close. "You know, I've never seen Jack like this," she said conspiratorially. "When the two of you came in, he refused to leave your side. Wouldn't even let go of your hand. If I didn't know better, I'd say he was... smitten." That probing, questioning, intelligent gaze was back. Giada studied her, and Claire realized with a jolt that there was far more to this woman than met the eye.

"What nonsense are you filling her head with, Giada?" Jack asked from the doorway.

Claire's heart burst with joy at seeing him standing there, looking whole and healthy and *alive*. There was a bandage on one side of his face, but other than that, he looked fine.

"Nonsense?" Giada echoed, sitting back in her seat. She shrugged one shoulder and rolled her eyes, the walls falling back into place over her expression. She was once again the vapid heiress seen all over social media. "How can you be so cruel, Jackie? I was keeping an eye on your lady love for you."

Claire's eyebrows rose despite herself, but Jack didn't take the bait. He entered the room and crossed to stand beside Claire's bed, glaring at the interloper. "Out. Now."

Giada sighed dramatically and hauled herself to her feet. "Fine. I'll leave you two love birds alone." She picked up a large black leather designer bag and headed toward the door, her heels quietly *clip-clopping* along the way.

At the threshold, Giada looked back at Jack and Claire. Her smile became soft. "You two really are cute. It's almost enough to make a girl believe in true love…" Her voice trailed off and became so low, Claire wasn't sure she heard her next words correctly. "Maybe one day, I'll find a love like that…"

Then, Giada shook her head, as if wiping away the thought like erasing a picture on an old Etch-A-Sketch toy. "Anyway, welcome aboard, Claire. I look forward to working with you." And with that, she was gone.

Jack stepped into the space Giada had just vacated, replacing that strange woman's wild energy with his calm presence. Dressed in dark jeans, a blue sweater that matched his eyes, and a white collared shirt underneath it, he looked like a piece of Iowa normalcy in what already felt like the third-strangest day in Claire Green's life. His gaze was anxious as he drifted to Claire's bedside. "How do you feel?" he asked.

"My throat hurts," Claire managed. "And I think I'm hallucinating. Did Giada England just reveal that she's a Superhero?"

Jack chuckled, leaned in, and placed a kiss on her forehead. His lips burned and seared her flesh like a branding iron. "Yes, she did. Sorry about that. Giada can be a bit much, but she means well. She's a good friend."

Jack took Giada's empty seat, and Claire tried to sit up. Jack's firm hand on her chest held her in place. She looked up at him with a questioning gaze.

"Whatever you did, it put enormous strain on your body. We couldn't even get you to stop trembling until the doctors got you warm and started pumping you full of fluids."

"Where am I?" she asked, looking around. It looked like a regular hospital room, yet the casual way Giada had mentioned her Superhero identity seemed odd for such a public setting.

"This is a private medical facility run by the International Association of Superheroes that specializes in treating Supers. They'll take good care of you." He reached up and brushed away a strand of hair from her forehead. His fingers felt wonderfully warm against her skin. "The first few times you manifest Superpowers, it takes a toll, though I've never seen a reaction as extreme as this," he said softly, his eyes not meeting hers.

Claire shook her head slightly. "What?" She couldn't fully process whatever he was trying to say.

Jack sighed, as if preparing himself say something important. "When you popped out of the air vent, you were... on fire, I guess. It looked like black flames were leaping from you, and white smoke was pouring off you. And your eyes... Claire, it's like they were buried deep in a well at the back of your head, and I was looking down a deep pit into them."

Claire swallowed hard and thought back to when she had come to in the air vent after having watched Jack die. Everything about that was blurry and fuzzy, but she somehow *knew* it wasn't a dream or a vision. It had been real; it had happened. And then, she had sort of... collapsed in on herself. It was the only way she could think of it. It had felt like there was a black hole in her chest, and it had sucked her in, shredded her, and then put her back together again in a slightly different form.

Just like in my apartment earlier, when Sucker-Punch had me pinned, and I fell into the gouge in the wood, she realized with a jolt. *I felt weak and unbalanced after that, too.*

Jack stared at her, his gaze desperate, pleading. "Claire, what *happened?*"

She shook her head slightly, trying to deny the memory that was forcing its way back to the forefront of her mind. Tears sprang to her eyes. "You died," she whispered despite herself. "I saw it all. Vengeance figured out how to kill with just a thought, and he killed Zoe." Claire opened her eyes and stared at him. His own blue eyes were wide with shock. "Our plan fell apart. You improvised, but I was too late. You were—" Her whisper died, and she had to swallow the lump that was suddenly choking her. "I was so angry, and everything got... weird," she finished uselessly. "And then, I was back in the air vent, where I had been when it all started, but you were alive. I had to stop it."

Jack lunged forward suddenly and crushed Claire in a hug. She yelped in surprise, which hurt her sandpaper-like throat. He just held her in place for a moment, and she relaxed into his embrace. She brought her arms up to wrap about his back in return, but the IV tubes in one hand restricted her movement, so she settled for resting her palms on his sides. His breath was warm and intimate against her neck. Her eyes fluttered closed, and she greedily drank in this moment. Even if she never saw him again after today, she had this moment, right here and now, in which he was warm and alive and in her arms.

Eventually, Jack drew back. He kissed her forehead, and the gesture made Claire want to cry. When he straightened up, his eyes were suspiciously moist. "I'm so sorry, babe," he said. "I'm so sorry you had to experience that. But... do you realize what this means?" Claire shook her head, and he continued, "I could be wrong, but I think—*I think*—you have some kind of time manipulation powers."

Claire stared at him blankly, not really comprehending his words. "You mean like time travel?"

"Kinda. Maybe. Perhaps. We'll have to do a lot more tests and training to see what you're actually capable of."

Claire's gaze turned inward. *It can't be... I gave up hope years ago... Does this mean...* "Are you saying I have Superpowers?"

Jack nodded, his eyes brimming with tears. A proud smile stretched his face.

Claire exhaled hard, staring up at the ceiling. It didn't seem real. After all these years of dreaming of becoming a Superhero, training to become a Superhero, and finally accepting that she would never be a Superhero and should probably just get on with her life, here she was, a Superhero. Her eyes filled with tears as well.

"Are you gonna be okay?" Jack asked.

Claire nodded, afraid to trust her voice. Her tears spilled over, and Jack leaned forward again, pulling her into a warm, comforting hug. She lay her head on his shoulder and allowed a grin to spread across her face, even as tears continued to fall. A whole new future spiraled out before her, like a map of some unknown country. New possibilities danced before her eyes.

For a moment, she recalled Great-aunt Lillian's reflection locking eyes with her in the ladies' dressing room of The Elite Five's HQ. Lillian's nod had been one of acknowledgement and recognition. *Maybe it wasn't a vision. Maybe I really did drift back in time for a moment, like a ghost in their world. Maybe Lillian recognized me not just as a relation but as a fellow Superhero.* The thought set Claire's heart alight with happiness.

Jack turned his head and kissed Claire's cheek, drawing her back to the present moment. Before she could explore any kind of dazzling new future, she had to address the past.

Claire placed both palms on Jack's chest and pushed him away so she could look into his eyes. He looked confused and hurt. Before he could say anything, Claire blurted out, "I'm sorry."

Jack opened and closed his mouth for a moment, as if trying to find the words to express his thoughts. He looked like a fish.

Claire forged ahead before her courage left her. "I'm sorry for breaking up with you back in high school and for the way I did it. It was wrong of me, and I regretted it before I even got into my car. I'm sorry for blurting out your name in the bank when Vengeance pulled off your mask. I was so surprised, it just popped out. I'm sorry for leaving up that old profile picture of us from all those years ago. I'm sorry I posted stuff online that attracted Vengeance's attention. I'm sorry that I put you and your family and my family in danger. I'm sorry that I basically blew your entire secret identity wide open."

Claire was rambling now. Her throat ached with the effort of so much talking, but she found that she couldn't stop. "I've been nothing but bad luck and a liability to you this whole time. You have so many reasons to hate me or at least want to stay as far away from me as possible, but you're still right here," she said, tears coming to her eyes again. "You're *right here*, and you're sweet and kind, and I don't know *why*. I've ruined your life twice now, so why are you still here, beside me?" she asked. Tears ran down her cheeks, and her chest shuddered with barely contained emotion.

Jack had listened to her entire speech in silence, his expression giving away nothing. When she was done, he leaned forward and wiped away her tears with a gentle finger. "Point one: apology accepted. And I forgive you."

Claire opened her mouth to protest, but Jack placed a silencing finger against her lips. She could taste her own salty tears on his finger.

"Point two," he continued, "you have *not* been bad luck or a liability. You managed to escape from Vengeance's goons three times, if I'm counting right. You rescued me from a Supervillain and then went back to help me defeat that same Supervillain. All without knowing you had Superpowers, I might add. And then, you literally reversed time and saved my life. I'd say that makes you more of a good-luck charm than anything.

"And point three..." Jack removed his finger from her lips and leaned in closer, lowering his voice slightly. "I'm still here, Claire Green, because I love you."

Claire's pounding heart thudded to a stop. She looked up at Jack with wide, wet eyes, not daring to believe that she'd heard him correctly. She blinked at him stupidly, then surged forward and pressed her lips to his.

Jack's hands were around her in an instant, one cupping the back of her head to support her, the other, her shoulder. He tasted of coffee and sunlight and something else. Something comfortable and familiar, yet dazzlingly new, like sparklers on a summer evening. Claire's hands gripped the front of his sweater, and she laughed dizzily into his mouth.

"Is this real?" she whispered breathily, her lips moving against his.

"You tell me," he whispered back, his lips tickling her own. "You're the one who created this new timeline."

Claire playfully bit his lip and drew back slightly, just enough to meet his eyes. Jack lowered her head and shoulder back to the bed, but let his hand drift around to cup her cheek. His eyes glittered and danced with mirth and mischief.

"But aren't you even the tiniest bit angry with me?" Claire asked, her fingers mindlessly rolling the folds of his soft sweater. "It's my fault that your secret identity has been compromised."

"Yes, and I can't thank you enough for that," he said, placing a kiss on her nose.

"What?" she asked, pulling back against her pillow to get a better look at him. *He doesn't look like he's gone mad*, she thought. "What are you talking about?"

"I've been doing a lot of thinking about something you said. You know, about 'going through the motions' and doing things because they're expected of you, not because you want to do them?"

Claire nodded, wondering where he was going with this.

"I realized that's what I've been doing for so long. I joined the army because I didn't know what else to do and because people expected me to do something physical, due to my height. I joined the IAS and became a Superhero because I didn't know what else to do after the army and because everyone expected me to use my Super-strength."

Jack's thumb began to caress her non-injured cheek, and Claire wanted to purr at the sensation.

"But when you talked about how much you love your work and what it means to you, I realized that I didn't feel the same way. I don't *enjoy* being a Superhero. I just do it because it's expected of me. I have Super-strength, so that must mean I *have* to use it, right? But I have other skills, too. Skills I would much rather use. Skills I enjoy using."

"Jack," Claire breathed. One hand released his sweater and came up to cup his cheek, mirroring his own position.

"Do you know what I felt when Vengeance revealed that he knew my full, real identity?"

Claire shook her head no, tears gathering in her eyes again.

"Relief. It's like a part of me said, 'It's finally over.' I could finally let go of all those expectations and figure out what I want to do and who I want to be," Jack said. "So I've decided. Once Professor Optimo is up and about again, I'm going to have a talk with him. And I'm going to resign as Silver Fist. Maybe he can get me into some kind of planning or logistics or communications position here at IAS. Maybe I'll go to college. Maybe I'll find a civilian job elsewhere. But the point, my dear teary-eyed, Super-powered love, is that I'm not going to be a Superhero anymore. And I'm so grateful to you for showing me the way and making that possible."

"You're insane," Claire said through her sniffles before pulling Jack in to kiss him again. "You're... completely... mad." She punctuated each word with a kiss.

The knowledge that Jack would be out of harm's way soothed something in her soul that she didn't know was raw and bleeding. Claire was sure she would be haunted by the sight of Jack's limp, motionless body for some time. Possibly forever. She hoped the memory of that other timeline—if that was indeed what it was—would eventually fade, but she doubted it would.

Claire had seen Jack die. She had pressed her lips to his quickly cooling lips. She had tried to pump his still heart with her hands. And she never wanted to face such a future again.

But with this news, the fear of such an outcome that unwittingly gripped her heart lessened. Jack would be safe. He would be doing what he wanted to do, and he would be safe.

Well, safer, a voice in her head pointed out. *He'll still be at risk. If I'm going to be a Superhero, that just means he's trading being a Superhero for being a Superhero's boyfrie—*

Claire cut that thought off. She wasn't quite ready to go there. Yet.

There's risk in everything, she told herself. *There's risk walking across the street. I was in danger countless times as an EMT. The point of life is not to avoid all risk. The point is to make a difference in the world and do something you love.*

She pressed one last, lingering kiss to Jack's lips and then drew back to look at him. "Jack Elliott, I love you. I loved you as a teenager, and I love you as a Superhero, and I will love you as whatever you chose to be."

He smiled down at her, his eyes dancing with mischief. "Well then, I guess there's just one thing left for me to say."

"What's that?"

"Would you like to go out and get a coffee with me some time?"

Claire threw her head back and laughed, sending bolts of pain through her head, face, and throat. "Oh, Jack, I wouldn't miss it for the world," she said, lowering her volume. "In this or any other timeline."

One year later...

Epilogue

Jack Elliott, formerly the Superhero known as Silver Fist, strode through the light-filled corridors of the New York headquarters of the International Association of Superheroes. There was a bounce in his step, and it wasn't just due to the still-hot Moonbucks coffee cup he clutched in his right hand. Claire's Superhero debut had been that morning while he was in class, and while he'd already watched the full news coverage on his phone while in line at Moonbucks, he couldn't wait to hear all about it from Claire herself.

Jack followed the twists and turns of the maze-like building and eventually pushed open the white swinging door marked 'Research.' Taped below that sign was another written on torn white lined notebook paper. It read, "Mathematicians not allowed," in black Sharpie. A yellow Post-It note was affixed to *that* sign, proclaiming, "Piss off, Greg!"

The inside of the IAS's Research Department was probably as vast as The Elite Five's base. Jack knew he had not yet visited each sub-department on all the various floors. It was a warren of cubicles, conference rooms, libraries, storage facilities, and probably much, much more. The first time he'd brought Claire in to show her his office, she had squealed at the merest glimpse she'd gotten of the 'Historical Superhero Artifacts' storage area.

"You know, you *are* a Superhero now," he'd pointed out, "not a fangirl with a blog. You can see stuff like this every single day."

"I know," she'd said, her eyes still fixed in wide amazement on the glass case housing Captain Trident's trident. "But this is different. Did you know that in 1963, Captain Trident used this very staff to drive off a horde of demonic, undead rats controlled by The Undead Maniac?"

Jack chuckled at the memory as he turned into his division, 'Digital Information Retrieval,' or, as they were affectionally known, 'The Hackers.'

The Hackers' main office looked more like a party room in an arcade that a workplace. A large, long table dominated the space, and projector screens could roll down from the ceiling all the way around the table, wrapping meeting-goers in a 360-degree bubble. But outside that circle of potential productivity, the room's walls were lined with classic arcade games and couches set up in front of televisions, each with a different video game system. Their boss, Andrea, maintained that in order to work hard, one had to play hard as well, which was why office-wide video game tournaments and impromptu arcade game face-offs were common.

As Jack burst through the main door, two of his colleagues looked up from their positions at the table. Amy and Indira often lingered after lunch, and today was no exception. Matching bento boxes sat before them, both empty, and they both clutched steaming cups of tea.

"I saw Claire on the news," Amy said with a grin. "She did great!"

Indira added, "Tell her congratulations from us."

Jack smiled, acknowledging their words of support. "I will. Thanks!" He desperately wanted to stop to chat and drink in the other women's praise of his fiancée, but he had work to do. And since he was only a part-time Hacker, spending the rest of his day as a cybersecurity major at CUNY, that meant he had to make the best of his time in the office. He waved to the two women and hurried down the hall to his private office.

His office wasn't large, but it was all his, which meant he could do what he wanted with it. A large desk with three monitors and his large, comfy blue-and-silver gaming chair dominated the space.

Claire had purchased the chair herself, laughing at his annoyed expression when he saw the color scheme. "You might not be Silver Fist anymore," she'd said, barely getting her words out around her belly laughs, "but you can still *smash* that keyboard."

It wasn't that funny, but he'd ended up doubled over with laugher as well, tears running down his cheeks, mostly due to how infectious Claire's laughter was.

Jack slid into that very chair now, appreciating for the millionth time just how comfortable it was. For a woman who had worked on her feet for the past nine years, he was amazed that Claire had such a talent for selecting seats. *Of course, maybe that's exactly why she's so good at it.*

He flicked on his small, soft desk lamp, which he greatly preferred over the harsh overhead light. As he booted up his system, Jack took a sip of his coffee and looked at the two framed photos on his desk. They shared a single frame but were taken fourteen years apart.

The first photo was of Jack and Claire at their junior prom—the very same photo that Vengeance had used to identify Jack, in fact. In it, seventeen-year-old Jack struck a ridiculous Superhero pose in his classic black tux, with his chest puffed out, jaw raised, and gaze fixed heroically on the horizon. Claire stood before him in her black sequined dress, facing the camera. She leaned back against him, looking up at him, one hand dramatically pressed to her forehead as if she were overcome by his manly charms. One tantalizingly pale thigh popped out of the slit that came dangerously high on her petite figure. Behind them, a city skyline that was clearly supposed to be New York's was painted on a canvas drop cloth. They both looked impossibly young to Jack's thirty-one-year-old eyes now.

The second photo was taken just a few weeks earlier, on Halloween, at a costume party thrown by Claire's former roommate, Ramona. Jack had talked Claire into going as a 1920s gangster and flapper and had even offered to put their costumes together himself, since he knew she was in the final phases of her Superhero training. The black tux and black sequined dress he'd found didn't exactly match what they'd worn to prom so long ago, but it was close enough for his purposes. He let Ramona in on his plan, only so she could take a photo of the moment he got down on one knee and asked Claire to be his wife. The results were perfect. In the photo, Claire's eyes were wide with shock, her hands pressed to her mouth. Ramona had somehow managed to capture the glint of tears already rising in Claire's eyes. The real New York City skyline glittered behind them.

His computer *beep*ed, letting Jack know that all his systems were up and running. He tore his eyes away from the photos and the happy memories they represented. For now, he had work to do.

Jack's current research project came directly from Professor Optimo himself. The objective: uncover who Vengeance really was and what had driven him to do what he did. The man was dead now, but his hatred of Superheroes was deeply concerning. Plus, for Jack, it was personal. According to Claire, the Supervillain had killed him in another timeline, a fact that never failed to send shivers down his spine.

Jack occasionally thought about what Claire had seen and experienced in that other timeline. He couldn't imagine watching her die like that: alive and vibrant one moment, and just gone the next, in the literal blink of an eye. From her point of view, when she had leapt out of the air vent, pointed a gun at Vengeance, and fired, she had just seen Jack die right in front of her mere minutes before. She had been through something Jack only experienced in nightmares.

If he were being honest with himself, in that moment, the sight of her had chilled him to his bones. She had looked possessed. She had looked wild. She had looked inhuman. But then, she'd collapsed into his arms, murmuring, "You're alive, you're alive," over and over again, and she was Claire again.

Even with Claire's new Superpowers and all the training she'd undergone to control and wield them, Jack still worried about her. He knew better than most just how dangerous that job was. He knew that one day, he might get the call letting him know that his Superhero fiancée—and eventually, someday, his Superhero wife—wouldn't be coming home. If or when that happened, he would know intimately the darkness Claire had faced in that other timeline.

But he also knew that she was Claire Green, and she could do anything. She would face any horrors, fight any Supervillain, defeat any monster to come home to him. He had faith in her, and he loved watching the rosy glow of pleasure on her face as she described what she was learning and doing in her Superhero training. She was made for this, and he wouldn't dream of holding her back. He let her go each morning, knowing that she would come back to him every single night.

Jack reviewed his current file on Vengeance before he dove into his work for the day. Vengeance had been extraordinarily tight-lipped while he was in prison and flat-out refused to reveal his true identity. Through a lot of backdoor work, Jack had managed to discover that the Supervillain known as Vengeance's real name was Albert Maurice Oakley. He was born in New York City to working-class parents and was an only child. Everything about his childhood appeared to be normal—up until he was five years old. That's when Albert and his parents were caught in the crossfire between a major battle between Superheroes and Supervillains at Coney Island.

The records were unclear about what exactly happened. All that was know was that Albert's parents were both killed in the conflict. Collateral damage. Little Albert was shuffled off to a distant relation's home. From there, he entered the historical record mostly through the juvenile detention system and with the label "juvenile delinquent."

Jack was still working on determining when, where, and how Albert Oakley, aka Vengeance, gained his Superpowers, but his motivation and choice of Supervillain names were painfully clear. Whether his parents had been killed by Superheroes directly or Superheroes had simply been unable to save them, Albert's vendetta against Superheroes began with his parents' deaths. From there, it was just a slow-moving tragedy, unfolding over time.

When Jack had told Claire this story, she'd spent the entire night in an agony of questions, pacing their small apartment. What if she could go back in time and change things? What if she could save little Albert's parents? What if he never grew up to be Vengeance?

Ultimately, she'd had to let the whole train of thought go on without her. She didn't have that kind of power. Her time-manipulation abilities were small-scale, generally working within a timeframe of one or two minutes. Going back in time fifteen minutes to save Jack's life had almost killed her; there was no way she could go back more than sixty years. But Claire could isolate tiny pockets of time, using them to heal wounds, rewinding the individual cells and tissues back to a point before they were damaged. And she could reverse the course of an entire battle, setting it back just a few seconds and making critical changes.

Claire's abilities had inspired her new name: Time Warp.

As for her Superhero costume, that was derived from her great-aunt Lillian's The Shadow costume and her old job as an EMT. Jack was a big fan of Time Warp's slinky black bodysuit, though he thought the reflective white symbol on her back was a bit much. It was the six-pointed Star of Life that served as the universal symbol of emergency medical services, though minus the Rod of Asclepius, the ancient symbol of medicine. Claire wanted to honor her past career and colleagues, while calling attention to her role as a healer—not with medicine, but with time. Jack wasn't fond of the idea of painting such an obvious bullseye on her back, but all of her Superhero trainers liked the design's elegance and meaning.

Jack was so lost in his thoughts that he didn't hear his door open behind him. It wasn't until it softly clicked closed that he realized he wasn't alone. He spun his chair around to face the door, and something warm, black, and firm landed in his lap.

"Hello, love," Claire purred, straddling him. "I had the *best* first day of work!" She pressed a kiss to his lips, and Jack squeezed her buttocks, grateful that she hadn't changed out of her Time Warp costume yet. This outfit did amazing things for her ass.

When Claire broke the kiss and pulled back, Jack realized that she had probably *just* come from work. Her hair was still in its tight bun that she wore to contain it under her hood, but stray red whisps stuck out every which way. She was sweaty and flushed, and based on the way her hands were suggestively caressing his chest, her blood was still pumping. She wriggled in his lap, and Jack moaned at the friction she was creating.

He'd be lying to himself if he claimed he hadn't thought about this exact scenario, but they were in the office. He didn't really want one of his colleagues to walk by and get an eyeful. So, he did the honorable thing, put his hands on her shoulders, and pressed her back a few inches. "Let's revisit this position tonight at home," he said, pitching his voice low and seductive. "But for now, tell me all about your day."

"I can't," she said, her eyes full of regret. "I still have to go back for my debriefing."

"You haven't debriefed yet?" he shot back, shocked and horrified that Claire had run off to leap in his lap and make out with him before she'd even fully reported in.

"I'm headed there now. I only got to detour and stop in to give you a message from Giada."

"Good old Giada," Jack chuckled, "the best wingman ever. I still can't believe you asked her to be a bridesmaid, though."

"What? She's been a good friend to you for nine years, and she's become a great mentor to me as well," Claire said, her respect for the senior Superhero clear in her tone.

"Okay, fair enough," he said. "So, what's the message?"

Claire's teasing manner fled, and she was all-business again, even though she was still perched on his lap. "She's lost Zoe's trail. It went cold somewhere in Russia."

"Damn," Jack sighed, leaning his head back against his headrest and closing his eyes in frustration. "And the Binding Amulet?"

"All evidence suggests that Zoe still has it."

"Well, I'm sure this will come back to bite us in the ass eventually," Jack muttered.

When the IAS team had eventually swarmed The Elite Five's base, both Zoe and the amulet that Vengeance had used to bind and control Jack disappeared in the chaos. At the time, both were fairly low priorities, given that Claire was going into shock after manifesting Superpowers for the first time and the Supervillain Vengeance was dead. But in the last few months, there were reports of a raven-haired female mercenary offering her magical services to various Supervillains and criminals around the world. She was said to have a pendant that matched the one in Claire's and Jack's descriptions.

The couple sat together in silent contemplation for a moment. But then, Claire brightened and leaned in to kiss the tip of his nose. "Don't worry, love," she said. "We'll find Zoe eventually. It's all a matter of... time." At the last word, she waved her hand dramatically in front of her face like a magician.

Jack groaned. "I'm really never going to hear the end of time-based jokes and puns, am I?"

"It depends. Can we have pizza for dinner tonight?""On your first day of work as an actual, card-carrying Superhero? Umm, yes! Of course!" Jack laughed, resting his hands comfortably on her hips.

"Then I will grant you a temporary amnesty from all time-related jokes for twenty-four hours," Claire said. She leaned in once more, gave him a quick peck on the lips, and slid off his lap. "I have to get going," she said, backing toward the door.

"Okay," he said regretfully. "I'll see you tonight."

Claire waved to him and dashed out the door. Jack leaned forward and stuck his head out into the hallway to watch the sway of her hips as she walked away.

Perhaps dating a Superhero isn't so bad, he thought.

Also by Lisabel Chretien

Superpowered Hearts Series:

Inside the Suit (Summer 2024)

Anthologies:

Rock My Heart (April 2024)
Protect My Heart (July 2024)
Love on the Clock (August 2024)
Tea with Austen (August 2024)

For updates on Lisabel Chretien's latest books, follow her on Amazon and Facebook.

Acknowledgements

First of all, I'd like to thank you, the readers. Thank you for spending time with me in this world of Superheroes, action, adventure, and romance. If you enjoyed this book (and even if you didn't), I encourage you to leave a review on Amazon or Goodreads to help other interested readers find and connect with this book.

Under the Mask began life in the spring of 2019 in Jeanne De Vita's fantastic romance writing course in the UCLA Extension Writing Program. I learned a great deal and grew as a writer both in the UCLA program and in Jeanne's class. But then, life and my day job interfered, and I put this novel away in a metaphorical desk drawer for four years and didn't touch it again during that time.

Then, in the summer of 2023, I discovered Maria Secoy, All Write Well, and the Writer-to-Author Program. Maria, this community, and this program gave me the confidence to pull this half-finished manuscript out again and finally complete it. Maria's excellent developmental edits helped push it across the finish line to become the book you just read.

I'd also like to thank my parents for inspiring my love of books and reading from a very young age. They read to me throughout my childhood, took me to the public library regularly, and definitely spent more money on books than they probably should have. When my love of reading began to morph into a love of writing, they were supportive of that, too. In many ways, this is all their fault.

Finally, I want to thank my husband, Jon. He has been unfailingly supportive and encouraging throughout my writing journey (and really, throughout my entire professional and academic career). He is an unparalleled sounding board for ideas, an excellent plot-bunny herder, and always excited to talk about both superheroes and character arcs. This book literally wouldn't have happened without him. I'm so glad he's my partner in crime through all of time and space.

About the Author

Lisabel Chretien wrote her first story—which was about vampires, witches, and a haunted house—in purple marker when she was eight. Since then, she has been a ballet dancer; a dance teacher; a choreographed stage-combat performer at Renaissance festivals; a writer, director, and actor in murder mystery dinner theater shows; the stage manager for a burlesque troupe; and a violin player in a nautical-themed folk-rock band. By day, her secret identity is as a mild-mannered nonfiction developmental book editor. When Lisabel isn't writing, editing, or on stage, she loves playing *Dungeons and Dragons* and video games with her husband, reading, hiking, cuddling with her dog and cat, and traveling.